THE NEW GULLIVER

THE
NEW GULLIVER

or
The Adventures of Lemuel Gulliver, Jr.
in
Capovolta

A novel by
Esmé Dodderidge

TAPLINGER PUBLISHING COMPANY
New York

First published in the United States in 1979 by
TAPLINGER PUBLISHING CO., INC.
New York, New York

Library of Congress Catalog Number 79-65728
ISBN 0-8008-5506-X

for
Morris

FOREWORD

This MS, originally written in a rather crabbed hand, was by some mysterious chance delivered to me in the winter of 1976–77. My first thought was to get in touch with Mr. Gulliver's wife and family, but in this I have been entirely unsuccessful. There is no Gulliver listed in the London telephone directory, nor in any other which I have consulted. Other researches have proved equally fruitless. It is clear from the MS that Mr. Gulliver desired as much publicity as possible for his strange story, so in compliance with what I take to have been his wish, I have submitted it for publication. I hope his readers will give his "case" the courtesy of a fair hearing, and not allow themselves to be prejudiced by his sometimes pedantic manner. He may strike them as a somewhat opinionated young man who takes himself and his troubles a deal too seriously, but I hope they will reflect on the provocation he received in Capovolta and forgive him.

Esmé Dodderidge

CHAPTER

1

Following the excellent example set by my illustrious forebear whose namesake I am, I am resolved to set down as true an account as is possible of life in this strange land, where circumstance has placed me. Of the manner of my arrival here, I shall say little, for extraordinary though that was, it is of less interest; and moreover, as the origins of my journey were then secret in my native country, I know not whether I am now at liberty to reveal them. Suffice it to say that with a group of companions, I was launched secretly in a new and experimental kind of airship in order to map the currents of the upper air and to take certain soundings there in zones which so far had, for reasons which you may conjecture, remained *terra*—or rather *aera*—*incognita* in my own country. We were progressing briskly and in apparent good order toward our goal when I was suddenly assailed by the most strange sensations, as though indeed my senses were deserting me and my body dissolving and becoming insubstantial. Upon opening my mouth to convey the alarm I felt to my companions, I found no voice issued from my throat. I tried to struggle forward to draw their attention by touch, and at that the whole cosmos seemed to whirl about me for a few seconds, and then I knew no more until I found myself, who knows how many minutes, hours, weeks or months later, lying upon what appeared to be some kind of bed or sofa. My whole being was in such a state of weakness and languor that at first I simply lay there, content to be safe and comfortable, but then memory returned and with it a sharpening anxiety. Where was I? What had become of my companions? Was I still aboard the airship?

I tried to sit up in order to look about me, but found myself too weak even for that. The movement, however, seemed to occasion a low murmur somewhere near me, as of soft voices talking. I turned my eyes about, but they fastened upon nothing, for I seemed to be enveloped in a dim, subaqueous kind of glow, which prevented the penetration of my vision. However, in a few moments I felt a gentle touch upon my wrists, feeling it would seem for my pulse. I turned my head in that direction and discerned a pair of eyes regarding me steadily from close quarters. The eyes vanished, and the low murmurs began again, but sounding more excited now. There were noises as of the gentle opening and closing of doors, and now out of the dimness several pale blurs emerged, which, as my eyes became more accustomed to this strange light, formed themselves into faces. I found that I was being surveyed by a group of persons all garbed in long, loose robes of white, from which I deduced that I must be in the operating theater of a hospital. In fact, I learned later that this was the common nightwear of both sexes in this country. But now the effect upon me was strangely soothing: something was clearly amiss with me, but I was in good hands. One of the persons laid a vessel with a long tube to my lips, and Nature told me that I was expected to suck. I did so, and in this way drank my fill of some cool, refreshing cordial. The languor I now felt was irresistible and I fell again into oblivion.

I will not weary the reader with a detailed account of my slow recovery, nor of my realization that I was in a land whose tongue was utterly unknown to me and whose inhabitants had no knowledge of mine; nor will I dwell on the difficulties and distresses I suffered both as a consequence of this and because there seemed to be no way of establishing communication with my own country and the loved ones I had left behind, or of finding out what had happened to my companions. Necessity is like to make an apt pupil, however, and my previous travels having given me a certain facility in the learning of languages, it was not long before I had conquered enough of this new tongue, strange and different though it was from any I had encountered before, to make my wants known and to converse on simple matters.

I had soon discovered that I was not in a hospital, but in a private house whose owner had given me refuge when I had been found upon a wild and desolate part of the shore of that land, cast up apparently by the sea. I can only conjecture that whatever accident or events took place aboard our airship that fatal day, the result had been to fling me down unconscious but alive into some unknown ocean, to my great good fortune, for had I been thrown upon land it is doubtful whether I could have survived. As we had a careful drill against such eventualities, totally unexpected as this one actually was, I think I must at the time of the disaster, for such I suppose it was, have been strapped into my parachute harness, though this I do not remember. It appears that I was borne up by some strange apparatus made of a lightweight fabric previously unknown to my rescuers when they found me, a plaything of the tides as the waves cast me up upon the shore, only to suck me back into the surf again as they receded.

The period of my illness was a long one. It was caused certainly by exhaustion and long exposure, but also perhaps by the penetration of harmful cosmic rays into the cabin of the airship, for my hosts when eventually I could make them understand roughly what had happened, thought that this might well have been the cause of the accident and of my condition, which took so long to ameliorate. They no longer made such explorations as I had been engaged upon, for their scientists had early discovered the harmful effects of these rays upon materials and men exposed to them; and for these and other more complex reasons of a moral or philosophical nature, they had abjured these ventures, which, in fact, they had begun earlier than we ourselves. However, to return to the period of my illness. The person who attended me for the most part was an elderly man. He was scrupulous in his care of me, but he seemed to maintain a rather frigid reserve, which I began to interpret as perhaps the resentment of a servant over the menial tasks he had to perform for me. Two other people, both women, visited me frequently, also, and as my health improved one or the other would occasionally bring in

my tray of food, or some device for my amusement, but they in no
way shared the real task of looking after me. These two women
made a great impression on me, for they were both extremely
handsome in a foreign way, with skins so dark that they might have
been of some inferior race had not both possessed an air of
assurance and command rare among women. As far as I could tell
they were graceful and comely of shape as well, especially the
younger one, but their dress seemed designed to conceal rather than
as with our women to reveal their elegance of form. They wore a
garment that I can only describe as a kind of tube of cloth: a long,
straight robe or dress which encased them from throat to ankle, with
a deep inset pleat on each side from just where the knee would be to
the hem. These garments were so designed that they avoided
shaping the outline of the bosom or buttocks, and it was only by the
angle which the cloth made between throat and chest before falling
straight and unindented to the floor that I could judge of the
undoubted feminine shape concealed therein. The stuff of which the
robes were made seemed of excellent quality but was always somber
in tone, as I later found out was the universal practice of this land
which I afterward came to know by its name of Capovolta. The
elderly servant on the other hand wore tight knee-length breeches of
a fine, silk-like cloth in rather startling multicolored patterns. This
struck me as somewhat ludicrous, not to say unbecoming in so
elderly a man. Had I at that time been able to comment upon it in
their language, I should have said something adverse and critical to
the younger of the two women, whom I found a most delightful
companion when she could spare the time to be with me. It was she
who embarked upon the formidable task of teaching me the
Capovoltan tongue. However, in that early time it was fortunate
indeed that I was unable to express the thoughts in my mind, for
imagine my dismay when the young woman eventually made me
understand that the elderly man was her father and not a servant at
all!

I had for some time been surprised that the head of the household
had paid me no visit, but concluded that the older woman, whom I
had taken to be the mother of the younger because of the strong

resemblance in their features, must be a widow. I had been courteous always to the best of my ability toward the supposed "servant," but in the light of this new information I could see that I had perhaps assumed a kind of superiority which was quite unjustified toward one who was, in fact, my host. This might account for the slight coolness of manner which I thought I discerned in his behavior toward me. I was much exercised as to how to remedy the matter, and had I been able to speak the language fluently, I think I should have tried to explain as inoffensively as I could that it was his performance of all the menial tasks about the household, and the fact that he waited on the women instead of the other way about, which had led me into my mistake. The two women were away from the house for the greater part of the day so that all the normal duties of the household fell upon this man. Once I understood this position, I felt it to be a most unnatural situation and would have often liked to defend the old gentleman from the presumptions of his wife and daughter, who would return home in the evening and accept his ministrations as though they were totally unaware that he had been working hard at quite heavy tasks all the day. Indeed, I began to feel indignant for him and would have liked to remonstrate with them. As this was not yet possible because of my insufficient knowledge of the Capovoltan language, as soon as I was fit I tried instead to shame them into a more decent kind of behavior by jumping up to give my aid to the old man, hoping they would feel rebuked by this and do what was right themselves. Imagine my surprise, if not dismay, when instead they remained themselves seated but gave me smiles and glances of approval. I began to feel that I was only doing what in fact they had expected of me. This was a novel and uncomfortable sensation, I can assure you, for I had had no intention of sharing in these lowly tasks on any permanent basis, only acting, as I have said, to shame them. However, I could not but observe that the old man was somewhat mollified by my action and seemed grateful for the help, so that I felt obliged to continue it.

Now that my condition was so much improved, my kindly rescuers began to take me about with them, and to invite in people who I imagine were friends or neighbors, or maybe relations.

Clearly these people were greatly intrigued by my appearance and the facts of my case, for I understood from the attention given and the tones of voice, even before I understood their actual speech, that the conversation was more frequently centered on me than not. Yet the strange thing was that it was always the women who took the lead in these conversations. I do not mean that the men did not join in; they did so from time to time, but usually it seemed to me that what they said was treated by the women with a kind of indulgence, as though their opinions were considered to be of less worth.

By the time my kind instructress had brought me to the point at which I could embark upon some conversation in her language, I must confess that I was beginning to be more than a little in love with her. However, I felt it my duty to try to tackle her on behalf of her father and to suggest that the behavior toward him of herself and her mother was no way to treat the head of the household. It was a very strange and difficult conversation, for at first she pretended, so I thought, a complete amazement, as though she could not begin to understand my meaning. However, in the end I made her understand that I considered the tasks which she and her mother piled upon this poor old gentleman were too many and too heavy, and that I could not comprehend why a young, strong female such as she was, who by now should be well versed in the household arts, did not relieve him of much of it so as to liberate him to pursue whatever profession he had been wont to practice before the present state of things had come about. At first she seemed to think that I was jesting; then when she took my true seriousness of purpose, she became angry and offended, and for the first time turned upon me a truly imperious and ireful countenance before sweeping angrily from the room.

Naturally I was much upset at this, for to the best of my ability I had tried to make my rebuke as gentle as possible. Now I felt most wretched, for clearly I had deeply offended my most charming teacher, whose approval was at that moment the thing most dear to me in the world. While I sat there in distress wondering what I should do, her mother came in to me and began to question me. I had the greatest confidence in this lady, apart from her cavalier treatment of her husband, for I could see that she was a person of great wisdom and understanding. I will give you the gist of the conversation we then had.

"Were you, child, a married man in your own country?" asked she. I was loath to admit the truth here, for I felt it might tell against me in her daughter's eyes, yet I could not bring myself to lie and so be disloyal to my wife.

"Yes, Madam, I was. I had been married a bare three years when I was dispatched upon the expedition which ended so fatefully for me."

She nodded her head thoughtfully and then said, "What profession does your wife pursue?"

"Originally she was a geometer and mathematician as am I, but now that we have a young family. . . ."

She broke in here, saying in some surprise, "*You* are a geometer and mathematician, you say? Do you still practice this profession, then?"

"Of course. As I have explained, that is why I was a member of the expedition."

"And yet you say you have children. Surely, young man, however modern you are in your outlook, you cannot really believe that it is right to neglect your home and children in that way?"

"But, Madam, what makes you think I neglect my home and children? I am devoted to them and to my wife and spend almost all my free time with them."

"But I cannot see how you can discharge your obligations to your family adequately and yet continue to work outside the home. Some of our young men do the same, but I find it difficult to approve of this. How do you find time to cook proper meals for them, or keep the house properly clean, for example?"

"Why, of course, my wife does all that," I replied in amazement. She looked at me most severely although with interest and said, "I had begun to wonder if there were not some such strange explanation of this affair. How can you possibly justify expecting such labor of a woman?"

"But, Madam, these are the normal female tasks, as everyone

knows—at least in our country. Indeed, it has been a matter of amazement and some distress to me to find your husband treated so strangely in your household, and not accorded his proper position as head of it. Here he performs tasks which are the natural work of women, and always have been."

"Do I understand that in your country it is customary for the child minding and the heavy work of the household to be done by the women?"

"Why, yes, of course. Is it not the normal case here?"

"Indeed, no, and I cannot see how such a situation can be justified. Are your women larger and physically stronger than your men, perhaps?"

"Oh, no—on the contrary, they are on the whole considerably inferior in physical strength. Why?"

"In that case, how can you expect them to perform these physically demanding labors? I find this quite extraordinary. It is perfectly clear from their physique that men were biologically designed for their functions as laborers and performers of heavy work. Surely this you cannot deny?"

"Exacting and arduous physical work is performed also in our country by men, Madam," I said with some spirit, "but the tasks connected with the running of a household are not by us considered to be beyond the strength of a normal woman. They are, in fact, particularly suited to their capacities."

"Yet," said this shrewd lady, "you have just suggested that the tasks my husband—a man of considerable physical vigor, I assure you—performs here are too much for him. Is that not strange? Perhaps it is that in your country your mechanical means for performing heavy labors are not as far developed as they are here and that consequently all your men are needed for the heavy laboring work, which here is largely performed by machinery."

"Indeed, Madam," I replied somewhat indignantly, "our country is very advanced in these matters, and the majority of men are certainly not engaged in heavy primary labor."

"In that case, it seems to me very wrong that women, with their inferior physique, should be engaged in work which you look upon as too heavy for my husband here."

I was truly nonplussed at this argument, and could think of no reply except that it seemed unsuitable. Of course, I meant unsuitable to the dignity of a man and to the proper position he should occupy, but I felt unable to say this to her face. And as I thought about it, it certainly seemed increasingly difficult to imagine this clever and commanding lady performing the tasks which her husband did. But although I did not express it, I felt her implicit assumption of superiority to be extremely riling. Whatever was said about male strength of physique, his position was that of an inferior: he ran about serving these two women as though he were a paid body servant, and it offended me. It offended me to be obviously considered as belonging to this same category of person; however kind and indulgent they were, it was, I felt, *de haut en bas*. It offended me, I confess, even more to be treated in this way by women guests in the house; with my two kind protectresses I had, after all, bonds of gratitude and affection, but what possible reason had these strange and unknown women whom I had never seen before for assuming that I was their natural inferior whose duty it was to wait upon them and perform manual tasks for their benefit? You may say that as guests of the household they were owed this courtesy, but they were the women's guests, not mine. Why therefore did *they* not perform these offices? You may think that I was extremely foolish not to assert myself and claim my rightful place in this society, but I will tell you that it is much harder to defy the expectations of conformity by everyone around one than I had ever previously imagined. I was, after all, greatly indebted to my hosts' household, and I found that I could not bring myself to appear ungracious and pettish by firmly holding to the normal masculine role to which I had been accustomed in my own land.

However, to return to the conversation with my hostess. I now changed my ground a little and brought forward the quite irrefutable argument that women are most clearly designed by nature to bear and tend children, and that they must therefore perforce fulfill the role of nurse, cook, and housekeeper. I put forward this point very demurely, but within myself I felt I had really clinched the argument.

"Your thinking upon this point is not very logical, is it?" said my hostess gently. "Certainly a woman is biologically designed, as you put it, to bear children, but why should you assume that after this arduous physical strain has been suffered over the long period of pregnancy, the actual childbirth and the necessary months of lactation, the poor woman should continue to bear such strains? Clearly, she needs to be relieved of every other care and especially those involving heavy physical tasks in order to give her every possible chance to recuperate. Surely whatever strange customs your country may have developed, you cannot regard it as remotely just or equitable that in this joint enterprise of forming a family the whole burden should fall upon one partner? It is clear that since the most important and responsible part has perforce to be borne by women, whatever can conveniently be handed over to men should be undertaken by them. Thus the many extra tasks, such as the daily washing of the child's clothes, the business of carrying it forth to take the air, and later the preparation of special dishes for it and so on, are all duties which by natural justice must fall upon men.''

I was rendered speechless for a few moments after these extraordinary ideas had been put forward and could not think how to begin to argue against such distorted notions of what was just or logical. However, I then recovered my native wit enough to counter with what still seems to me an irrefutable argument.

"But pray, Madam," I said, "who then at this time is doing what in *my* country is considered the most important and responsible part in this joint enterprise, and that is earning a livelihood to keep the whole family?"

"Why the mother of the child, of course," said she, apparently in some surprise.

"Indeed, Madam," said I in triumph, "and pray how is she to continue her occupation when by your own showing she is engaged upon the strenuous business of carrying, bearing, and then feeding the child?"

"You asked who earned a livelihood for the family, and certainly it is the mother who does this. This extremely important function of motherhood is naturally one of the most highly rewarded roles in society. Of course, once the vital period is over and she resumes her previous profession, her earnings will drop back to that sum which she was earning before. However, the special payments made to the child itself as a new young citizen do something to offset this fall in the income of the household.''

My mind was awhirl at this. How was it that the whole country was not swarming with tiny new citizens if the role of motherhood commanded such reward? Who did the work, whatever it happened to be, normally done by the mother during her leave of absence? But while I was still trying to formulate my questions, hardly knowing where to begin, my hostess said, kindly but with a trace of impatience, "Come now, child, I have been very patient in answering all your queries, in spite of their triviality and the evidence they give of careless thinking on your part; naturally one excuses much considering that you are not only a stranger in our community, but also of that sex which we must without prejudice acknowledge to be rather emotional than logical in the expression of its opinions. I will go and explain to Vrailbran [which is the nearest I can approach in our alphabet to the name of the younger of the two ladies with whom as I have already confessed I was now much in love] the unfortunate misconceptions which were the true cause of your offensive remarks to her. She has a kind heart and will I am sure forgive you once she understands that you spoke out of ignorance and are now heartily sorry for it.''

With that she left the room. I have to confess that I was prey to the most conflicting emotions. Yes, I did want to make my peace with Vrailbran; her displeasure had upset me a great deal. But her mother had freshly aroused my resentment with her animadversions upon my opinions and my capability in argument, and had made assumptions about my changed state of mind which were not strictly true, and I was determined to return to the attack at the earliest opportunity. However, I swallowed my pride and allowed the reconciliation to take place since Vrailbran made it easy for me, embracing me warmly and kissing me upon the mouth with more than a hint of passion. I was surprised indeed, but pleasantly so, of course, that a woman should so take the initiative, for I had been debating within myself for some time whether I should declare my feelings for her. After all, I was a guest in her parents' house, and a married man; these facts caused me to feel a little uneasy about taking advantage of the tenderness which I was fairly sure she felt for me, in spite of the way in which she allowed me to carry out servile tasks in the household. It is true that from time to time she would perform some small service with great gentleness and charm, but always with an air of doing me a personal favor, when the task involved would not really be for my benefit at all, but one connected with the general running of the household.

Now, however, I felt myself free to respond to her in the warmest possible manner. After a most agreeable but far too brief interlude she put me gently but firmly to one side, though smiling at me most tenderly and saying, "Ah, my dear, I was not mistaken about your feelings for me. I am greatly relieved that my mother was able to resolve this misunderstanding between us. I had thought for a moment that you were one of those New Men, so much talked about now, who repudiate all their true responsibilities and keep on talking about equality, as though we did not already have equality in all that matters. I agree, of course, that things were unequal in times past and that even now there are perhaps a few reforms still needed, but in all essentials the sexes are indeed regarded as equal, except in those few instances where nature has decreed otherwise. Of course, these men *cannot* give birth. Therefore truly they can never perform the most important function in society and so can never receive the highest monetary rewards, but surely it betokens a very sad and mercenary spirit that they cannot accept this fact of nature."

Had my physical passions not been so thoroughly aroused by quite other facts of nature, we must surely have quarreled again after this extraordinary statement, but I was barely listening to what she said, so moving did I find her beauty of face and form, for I had had more chance to judge of that during our close embrace than I had ever had before. At that moment I would gladly have been bound forever to those hateful household tasks if my passion could have found its right, true end. As it was, I had to be content with a few more kisses and what of her marvelous form my seeking hands could guess of under the severe, disguising dress she wore.

CHAPTER
2

One evening when I had been with my Capovoltan hosts for some months and my knowledge of their language was still very imperfect (though improving rapidly), there was a large gathering at the house, the purpose of which I found difficult to determine. It was possible that it was simply a kind of soirée for a group of mutual friends, but I thought it must have some more important purpose because of the atmosphere of excitement and the enormous amount of hard work it entailed; moreover the impression had been growing upon me for some time that my hosts were people of consequence. I was not yet sufficiently in the confidence of the family to ask direct questions about it, but the lavish purchase of strange and unusual foods and the prolonged preparations made by my host, who for days before was dashing back and forth to their equivalent of food stores with enormous baskets of food, and then spending all day in the preparation of complicated dishes and finally cleaning the house and its appurtenances until everything was burnished and shining beyond the normal—all this convinced me that something very special was afoot. By now it had become accepted, to my chagrin, that I should help in all these chores, and rarely have I been more physically exhausted in my whole life. I will acknowledge that far more of the work was done by my host than by me, but a large share of the unskilled tasks seemed by common consent to be regarded as my duty—nay, at times, almost as my privilege, as though I were fortunate to have such a chance to prove myself capable. You will wonder how I could so meekly accept this demotion to such a humble position in the household, but my gratitude to my hosts for their kindness, indeed the very saving of my life, made it impossible for me to refuse such services as were in my power, however much I might resent their being expected of me.

At length, the evening of the gathering was upon us. The guests poured in, it seemed to me, almost endlessly, and I understood my host's preoccupation with the preparation of such monstrous quantities of food. I began to wonder anxiously myself whether there would be enough, though why I should have worried about it I do not know, since I really could not see that it was in any way my business or responsibility. I suppose I was in spite of myself developing more and more of a fellow feeling with my overworked host.

The largest room in the house had been cleared of most of its normal furnishings and had been set about with numbers of high, narrow, crescent-shaped benches or tables. At first I was not sure of their purpose, but soon it became obvious that they were meant not to sit upon, but to rest plates and elbows upon while eating. No one sat; all stood at these benches, which I now saw were excellently devised in shape to facilitate conversation, as every person was within speaking distance of everyone else at the same table. I was shy about joining myself to any of these groups, but my dear Vrailbran took me by the hand and led me to one where there were two spaces. Hardly had I begun to collect myself sufficiently to look about me when I saw Vrailbran's father signaling anxiously in our direction. To Vrailbran I said, "Look—your father is trying to attract your attention."

She looked up at him and then at me with some slight embarrassment, saying, "I am so sorry, but he needs you to help him. I'll try to keep this place for you until you can come back." And so it was that with constant jumping up to fetch this or carry that or take such a thing to one of the guests, I barely succeeded in eating any of the food I had helped to prepare. Eventually, however, the activity began to die down and I was able to take my place by Vrailbran with less likelihood of being immediately disturbed again. I was extremely tired and very glad to rest awhile and watch the proceedings rather than participate in them. This did not altogether please Vrailbran, for after a while she asked me why I was so silent, indicating that it was my duty to join in the conversation. This so annoyed me that I might have answered sharply had not our attention been distracted by an argument developing at the next table.

I had particularly noticed a couple among this group of people. The woman was imposing and in a way handsome, I suppose, but she was clearly already in middle age, while the man with her was very young and of remarkable and noticeable attractiveness. All the company appeared to greet them rather deferentially and to treat them with a special courtesy. I had decided in my mind that the young man must be a person of great consequence and the older woman must be his mother. Perhaps he was a great musician, I thought. He had very beautiful and well-kept hands. Or a great dancer or athlete, for all his movements were of extraordinary gracefulness. Perhaps, indeed, he was the guest of honor at this party. Now it seemed that these two were at the center of the argument. I could not at all follow what was going on for thrust and riposte were too rapid for my imperfect command of the language to comprehend. The attention of everyone in the whole room was soon centered on that table, although for form's sake people tried not to stare noticeably and pretended to carry on with their own conversations.

I saw that Vrailbran, though pretending to be concentrating on her conversation with me, was in fact listening hard, with some degree of amusement mixed with disapproval. Suddenly the young man got up angrily, addressed several loud and presumably offensive remarks to the middle-aged woman and went—had he not been a man I would have said flounced—out of the room. The woman looked very awkward and embarrassed, but finally made her way to where Vrailbran's father and mother were. I could see from her attitude that she was excusing herself—and, I supposed, making excuses for her son. She cast her eyes up with a half–amused, half–rueful expression and shrugged her shoulders as she spoke. She then made her way through the room in the wake of the beautiful young man.

People were obviously uncertain as to whether they should salute her or not—but Vrailbran's mother by a gesture indicated that all should remain at their places. So the guests began to chatter very hard to one another and to pretend they had noticed nothing.

I turned to Vrailbran and said, "Whoever that young man is it was very ill-bred of him to be so rude to his mother in public." Vrailbran nearly choked with laughter and exclaimed, "His mother indeed! He's the governor's *husband,* not her son."

"What on earth do you mean?" I said in bewilderment. "I was talking about the young man and the middle-aged woman who have just gone out."

"So am I, of course. Who else? The 'middle-aged woman,' as you so irreverently call Her Excellency, is one of our governors, and the young man is her husband."

Seeing that I was still somewhat mystified, she explained further. "Her Excellency Mordleng Phurhalt [or that is what is sounded like to me] is one of the Band. Surely my father must have told you that the party was in her honor?"

Of course he had not told me. I expect he thought that Vrailbran would have done so. "The Band" was the governing group of people, rather like our Cabinet, whose individual members bore the title which I have translated as "governor" because the same word seemed to be used to describe anyone in a high position of authority within any given group. Perhaps "head" might be a better translation. In this case I suppose we should say "minister," but I did not understand the importance of the term in its particular context at that time.

I was quite amazed at this information and was still trying to make sense of it—a woman in a position of such importance with a boy, for he was little more; as her husband, it hardly seemed credible—when Vrailbran added with a mischievous look, "Of course, you can see she's terribly ——, poor woman." The term she used was one I had never heard before, and I begged her to explain it to me.

Repeating the word thoughtfully, she said, "It is difficult to explain. Literally it means when the female fowl is bullied or pecked by the male. Here, of course, it means where the wife is criticized and bossed by her husband. Have you no phrase like it? 'To be cock-pecked,' perhaps?''

"Why, no," I said. "We do not say 'to be cock-pecked.' We have 'to be henpecked,' which means, of course, when the female fowl pecks the male, and we do use it as you have done of human beings, where the wife is unnaturally domineering over her husband. Have you the verb 'to henpeck' as well as 'to cock-peck'?''

"No, indeed," said she, a trifle tartly. "We do not have such a verb."

"Now I wonder why you have no verb 'to henpeck' and we have no verb 'to cock-peck.' That is really strange, isn't it?''

We both agreed that this was a little difficult to explain. My first explanation to myself for the lack of ''cock-peck'' in the vocabulary of my country was that only women practiced the disagreeable activity known as henpecking; men being a more tolerant and rational set of beings were not given to it. But if I then applied this as an explanation to the society in which I now was, it would appear that here only men were domineering. Since this was so obviously the reverse of the case, I was forced to think again and could only come to the conclusion that the terms described a reversal of normal roles—that is, that here women were dominant in a partnership, and when the unexpected happened and the husband asserted himself, it was regarded as a reversal of the natural order and a special word coined for it. This caused me to think hard about the situation in my own country encapsulated in the verb ''henpeck''—and I did not much like what I was forced to think.

Now Vrailbran said, laughing, ''Well, to change the —— [here a word I did not know, but the context made me conclude it meant what we should call 'metaphor']. That young man is a bit of a fox, I'm afraid.''

"Fox? You mean sly and cunning?''

"No, no." She laughed a great deal more, and then with a face of conspiratorial mischief said, ''Well, actually he's a dog, but that's a very vulgar word and you must remember not to use it in front of other people. But he really is—just that—an absolute dog.''

"Dashing? Lively? Too interested in other women?'' I suggested dubiously.

"Well, I daresay the latter is true, but it's not what I mean. By 'fox' and 'dog' we mean someone thoroughly ill-natured. You know, bad tempered, mean minded, malicious. We say of a remark or action, 'That was a thoroughly doggy thing to say or do' when we mean really nasty and spiteful—but, of course, we don't use it in polite speech.''

Of course, then I realized what I should have seen immediately—that these words had the implications that we give to "vixen" and "bitch,'' but applied to the male sex. Seeking to find equivalent metaphors in our own language, I was amazed that I could find none. Was then the type of conduct so described the prerogative of women only in our society? To be honest, I could not pretend it was, for I had seen enough of both the business and professional worlds in my own country to know that these qualities are most marked when there is business or professional rivalry among men. Again, I could only conclude that these qualities were considered acceptable and normal among men, but because they were far less usual and considered undesirable among women, these special expressions had been coined. In the language of Capovolta, on the other hand, there was no equivalent implication to the female nouns, any more than with us to the male ones.

For some time after that, one of my favorite pastimes was the collection of such metaphors and the comparison of them with those in my native tongue. I will not weary my reader with a list of them here, and, of course, often there was no straight comparison, but my findings compelled me to conclude that whereas such metaphors are nearly always derogatory to women in our language, and where the male equivalent exists, complimentary rather than otherwise to men (e.g., "bull" and "dog"), in Capovoltan the situation was reversed. This general rule seemed to apply to other areas of language, too: special terms or verbs of derogatory implication had been coined in Capovolta to describe behavior which was commonly disapproved of in men, although no equivalent term existed to describe such behavior in women. For example, there was a Capovoltan word meaning, as nearly as I could determine, what our word "termagant" means, but it was applied in Capovoltan only to men. I have searched my memory for an equivalent word in our tongue meaning "a noisy, quarrelsome man" (and that such men exist there is no doubt for I have seen many outside public houses of a Saturday night), but so far I have not found such a word. Similarly much later I found no equivalent in Capovoltan to our word "nymphomaniac." I regret to introduce such an indelicate subject, but quite certainly among the Capovoltan women there were some who would have qualified for such a term at home. Here, however, there seemed to be no condemnation of this trait among women, though for the male equivalent there was what amounted to moral censure and a derogatory term for which I can find no counterpart in English. When, however, the realities of the sex bias reflected in the Capovoltan language had been more deeply engraved upon my mind by bitter experience, I lost my zeal for this game of comparisons, and if truth be told, desired only to return to my native country, where I should no longer be outraged almost daily by the humiliations put upon my sex. But that was still in the future and I see that I have jumped ahead too quickly in my narrative.

CHAPTER

3

During this period of my history my relationship with Vrailbran was the cause of considerable tumult within me either one way or the other, for at one extreme I was fired with such a passion for her that I felt I could override all difficulties and make her triumphantly mine, while at the other extreme I felt the wretchedness of my position. Here I was a stranger in this community, with no means of support save the generosity of my hosts, a self–confessed married man and father with, indeed, much residual tenderness for my wife and family, but the memory of them became always dimmer and more faded as though they had existed in some particularly vivid dream long ago: How could I possibly justify an outright attack upon the virtue of my beautiful Vrailbran? Was I not in honor bound, under her parents' roof, to "bridle my passions," as our romantic novelists put it? I could not but wonder if anyone using such a phrase had ever experienced what I was now experiencing. Vrailbran would enchant me by some delightful and explicit demonstration of affection, so unmistakable and so inciting that my whole being was aflame for her and I would seize her passionately, forgetting all my self–admonishment about parents' roofs and such, determined only to penetrate the lovely citadel of her chastity. At first she would be all complaisance and delight, but then as the work grew serious, she would fend me off, most tenderly but firmly, and say with a sigh, "No, no, my darling, I must not let you prejudice yourself in this way. I will not be selfish enough to let you risk your good name, indeed your whole life for me like this."

The first time this occurred I was almost incoherent with my desire for her, but managed to assure her that the only good she could do me was to let me finish what I had so whole–heartedly begun. She only smiled and sighed and kissed me gently upon that spot where my desire for her was most clearly manifest, saying, "It would be wrong of me, my love. I must be wise for both of us. Only wait, and perhaps in the end all will come right." And then despite my entreaties and my urgency, she withdrew and forbade me to follow her.

I could not understand the logic of her utterance, but when passion had subsided a little, I would once again be torn by the same old conflicting thoughts and emotions. Of course, when opportunity occurred I renewed the assault and came often within sight of victory before she escaped me.

I had reached the point where I vowed to myself that this thing must come to an end one way or another; either these exciting but frustrating encounters must cease or the next time she initiated one of our delightful interludes I would not let her escape but would use my superior strength to consummate what clearly she desired as urgently as I, whatever her reasons for abjuring it so long. On the other hand, I would not be the initiator.

When two days had gone by and I had taken no advantage of the opportunities she had offered me to touch her person or to take her hand and put it where she might feel the disturbance her presence caused me, she began to regard me with a doubtful and troubled air. I feigned not to notice, difficult though it was not to yield to my own desires and take her in my arms.

Finally she came to me and said gravely and rather sadly, "Klemo," (for that was how she said my name, there being no initial "l" used in the Capovoltan language), "Klemo, I think that perhaps you do not love me anymore. It is better to be truthful and honest about it now, for I was just about to take a very important and fateful step, which would be madness if indeed your love for me had already vanished."

How could I hold aloof after that? Of course, I cast my reserve aside and embraced her, babbling of my love—and gratitude, for naturally I thought the "fateful step" she mentioned meant that she had determined to yield herself to me. Her face broke into such a wonderful smile of relief and happiness as she returned my embrace that I thought the moment of my long–postponed felicity had arrived. Imagine therefore my surprise, indeed one might say dismay, when instead she broke away saying, "Ah, my darling, how happy you have made me. Wait a moment while I call my mother!"

It was with a very bad conscience and a most uncomfortable air that I went to greet Vrailbran's mother as she came into the room. She gazed at me long and penetratingly, so that I felt she looked into my very soul, and I was not at all happy at what she might think she perceived there. However eventually she said, though still holding my eyes with that keen gaze, "Well, my son, I understand that you and Vrailbran wish to marry."

You can understand my utter consternation. I thought I had made my position clear, and was glad later to have done so though unwilling at the time, but now it seemed they had misunderstood me. Perhaps they thought I was a widower?

"Madam," I stammered, "Vrailbran does me too much honor. If only I were free to marry her, I should have asked her long ago. I love your daughter dearly, but honor forces me to remind you that I am married already."

"It was hardly for you to ask Vrailbran to marry you, in any case," said my hostess a little sternly, "but, of course, we are aware of your status in your own country. That, however, hardly affects the issue here. You have only to sign a declaration that you are not married according to the laws of *our* country, and that frees you from any contractual obligation elsewhere."

Gradually the happy implications of this penetrated my brain. Of course, if I could so simply put aside my previous marriage here, no doubt this one would be equally null and void in my country since there I would be resuming an old marriage and not contracting a new one. It was a wonderful moment, to realize that I could, without dishonor or any illegal or unpleasant consequences, have the dearest wish of my heart.

I started forward eagerly and kissed the good lady's hand, saying, "Ah, Madam, you have made me the happiest man in the world."

She smiled, but somewhat rebukingly, it seemed to me, as she said, "Yes, Vrailbran has told me something of your overimpetuous nature. I think you must learn to put a certain curb upon yourself or you may get into serious trouble one day, my child. Not all women are as honorable as Vrailbran."

I was completely at a loss as to how to reply to this and was silent a moment trying to probe her meaning when she resumed with great kindness, "But do not let us dwell on such possibilities now. I will tell you that Vrailbran's father and I have been somewhat exercised about the development of her feelings for you. You are a stranger among us and in many ways different from our own men. You have a spirit and independence of thought unusual here, and often indeed sadly misled, I'm afraid; but both of us have found you honest and willing to correct your faults when once you see them. You have charm and intelligence as well as adaptability, and I think much affection for Vrailbran and much good will toward the family as a whole. These excellent qualities weigh much in your favor, and seeing how deeply Vrailbran's affections are engaged, we shall not only raise no objection to your marriage, but as Vrailbran wishes, we shall do our best to get it accepted as a family marriage."

"A family marriage?" This term was unknown to me but somehow sounded rather serious.

"Yes—a marriage where both partners are accepted as the right kind of people to become parents."

This seemed to me an extraordinary idea—indeed altogether a monstrous one when I thought through the implication, that is to say that some people were not thought fit to become parents, not that I was at all sure that I personally wished to raise a second family here, but then if Vrailbran wished it. . . .

"But how can you possibly stop people from having children if they wish to?" I said rather hotly. "It does seem to me to be a purely personal thing and no business of anyone else's."

"Of course, you can't stop people from having children if they want to, but you can do something to prevent them from wanting to."

I was horrified. Could this old nightmare of a whole population being drugged without—or even with—its own knowledge really be true?

"What do you mean? Some drug or other? That seems to me a really terrible and uncivilized thing to do." I was almost stammering with emotion.

"Drug? What drug? What on earth are you talking about, my poor child? If a thing is generally disapproved of socially, on the whole people will usually try not to do it. So it is that here couples who have not earned public recognition of their fitness to act as parents will normally avoid having children."

"How—I mean, what—well—do they . . .?" I could not find a delicate way to frame my question. However, Vrailbran's mother understood me immediately and said, "Well, of course, means of birth control are available universally here, and it is only really irresponsible men who father children unintentionally."

Why men? I thought. Again, this raised so many questions I wanted to ask that I hardly knew where to begin, but I wanted to get to the bottom of this "family marriage" business first, so I returned to my previous point.

"But suppose a couple who are not approved—or whatever you call it—strongly desire children? It seems to me very wrong that fulfilling this natural instinct should be regarded as a delinquency. Why should they not have children just as much as anyone else? As I said, it's a purely personal thing and no business of anyone else's."

"If they genuinely want children, they have only to apply to the Guardians for recognition and then behave in such a manner that they earn it. But as for it being a purely personal thing and no concern of anyone else's—I don't know how things are in your country, of course, and they may well be different, but here, many years ago, before we reached this present responsible attitude to parenthood, we had shameful examples of parental neglect and cruelty. The fate of helpless children is surely the concern of the whole community: you cannot wash your hands of that and say it is the parents' business and no one else's. Of course, we have not found the complete answer even yet, but the improvement over the years has been documented and the result is very impressive. It takes a long time, though, for a reform in social attitudes to come about. You cannot legislate about something like this. You can only encourage the attitude you want and discourage the others."

I still did not like this whole thing with its emphasis on prying into people's lives to decide if they could be given society's approval for bearing children, but at least a certain kind of freedom was still preserved. After all, I suppose a great many standards of conduct have social acceptability as their main sanction, though I realized I had not thought about it very much before.

It was much later before I discovered the significance of that "only really irresponsible *men* will father children unintentionally," but I will explain it here to save returning to this rather tendentious subject. In Capovolta, the whole responsibility for avoiding unwanted parenthood rests upon the male partner. It is he who afterward comes in for disapproval and for such social sanctions as there are. His position is a most precarious and unenviable one, for on him rests the sole responsibility for the care and upbringing of the child if the mother chooses to repudiate him—except that she must make some financial contribution to its upkeep. This seemed to me most unfair. The grounds upon which this attitude is based is that of the two partners, only the man demonstrably has been the active and willing one: there is no proof of the active cooperation of the woman. The consequence is that men will take great precautions to prevent such a relationship terminating in pregnancy. Indeed, it was in the light of these strange and unjust customs that I later understood also my future mother-in-law's strictures on my "overimpetuous nature." Women of a lustful nature, of whom there are a considerable number in Capovolta I would say from my own observations, may take several lovers at a time: this practice, though frowned on, does not bear the same stigma as in our society; even at times, I regret to say, it seemed to me that respectable women found the idea amusing rather than disgraceful. However that may be, if such a woman finds herself pregnant, she will probably name as the father the one of her lovers whom she least cares for, whether he is responsible or not, so that her more favored lovers are not inconvenienced. Her word is taken against his, so he has no redress. It thus behooves a man to be very vigilant in the company of such women and to avoid giving the slightest grounds for suspicion as to his relationship with them, which could afterward be interpreted unjustly against him. This was my mother-in-law's fear for me: I had by Capovoltan standards shown myself to be too impressionable and not guarded enough in my conduct toward Vrailbran and might therefore be expected to err similarly with other, less scrupulous women. I assure you it was a very strange position for a man to find himself in—that his future mother-in-law should warn him, however delicately, of the possible consequences of casting his eyes upon other women than his wife! But, of course, at the time I did not understand her meaning.

These remarks on family marriage by Vrailbran's mother certainly gave the whole affair a seriousness which, I must confess, had not been my conscious intention before. I now felt some uneasiness at the prospect before me instead of the unalloyed joy of the previous moment. Events were carrying me forward too precipitately now, and I should have liked time to think over the implications of my proposed new status. One point, however, occurred to me immediately, and that was my lack of means. From time to time I had suggested to my kind hosts that I should be grateful for their help in finding some kind of employment, however humble, to enable me to become independent. Naturally I hoped eventually to find suitable employment on the peripheries of my own special field once my knowledge of the Capovoltan language and methods of computation was perfected, but for the moment I was prepared to work in any capacity for which I was considered fit. At first my suggestion had been met by kindly insistence that my health was not fully restored after my ordeal, and as this was palpably true for a far longer period than I expected, I accepted gratefully their renewed hospitality. Gradually, however, I began to feel myself so much restored to health that I was filled with an abounding vitality and a great desire to be more suitably and worthily occupied than in helping Vrailbran's father in his household duties. But all my efforts to be taken seriously in this were blocked, kindly but no less firmly, by all three at one time or another, on the grounds that suitable employment for me would be extremely difficult, if not impossible to find *yet*. But all three had also seemed to hint of future possibilities, Vrailbran especially, who would smile at me tenderly and say that much thought was being given to it. Now surely this whole question could be put off no longer, and I must confess that I felt that it could serve me well as a delaying tactic while I considered more deeply the position in which I so unexpectedly found myself as Vrailbran's prospective husband.

"Madam," I said, "such a prospect of happiness as you now hold out to me makes it all the more urgent for me to find suitable employment. As you well know, at present I have no means of supporting myself, let alone Vrailbran and the family she hopes to have. In my own country I was considered a man of no mean ability; I hope you will forgive me for speaking in praise of myself in this way, but I have had no opportunity here of exhibiting such gifts as I know myself to possess, so that I can only trust that you will take my word for it. I had before me a promising career, which in the opinion of my superiors was likely to lead me to a position of considerable importance and authority. Here, on the contrary, I must begin again at the bottom, with the additional disadvantage of having to master not only a new language, but a completely different system of computation and indeed a whole new culture. It will take time for me to reach a position anything like the one I held in my own country, so with your help I should like to begin immediately the studies which will enable me eventually to use my specialized knowledge profitably, and in the meantime I must find some ordinary unskilled work by which I can at least support myself."

Vrailbran's father had joined us quietly in the middle of the previous discussion, so that courtesy forbade me to add that I had become inexpressibly bored by the predictable trivia of my daily life. All three of them had listened quite attentively to what I had said, but there was a certain expression of indulgent amusement on their faces which upset me, for I felt that they were once again refusing to face the gravity of my situation.

Now Vrailbran's father spoke in the discussion for the first time. "We do not doubt your word, dear child, that you are a gifted young man, but our attitude to your union with Vrailbran does not depend on that. We have watched you carefully and have come to see that you have those much more important qualities which make for a happy marriage. I will confess to you that I remained highly doubtful for a long time, for at first I found you thoughtless and, if you will forgive me for saying it, a little too selfish and self-regarding, but gradually I have been convinced that I was mistaken and that you have a good, kind nature after all, as well as being a very personable young man. I cannot be sorry, however, to have insisted upon a much longer period of testing you out than Vrailbran wished, for she is our only child and her happiness is to us of the utmost importance.''

This speech, though clearly kindly meant and welcoming, was slightly disconcerting, as you can imagine, and moreover seemed to be carefully sidestepping the issue of how I was to earn a living yet again. I was determined now to get a straight answer and so pressed on, after thanking the old gentleman for his great kindness to me while under their roof and for his good opinion, to repeat my request that they would give me advice and help in this matter of finding employment.

Again it was the old gentleman who spoke and I felt that the other two were waiting for him to do so; there seemed to be an interchange of significant glances between them. ''If your marriage to Vrailbran is brought forward and takes place as soon as possible, then this issue need no longer arise. It does you great credit that you should be concerned about it, however. It would be different, of course, if you were not to get recognition for family marriage, but I think there is little doubt that our recommendation will carry enough weight with the governors.''

It says little for my quickness of apprehension or my understanding of the true facts of my situation that I was perplexed by this reply and could only think that perhaps the old gentleman was hinting at some family connection that would secure me an opening in business, where I should have a chance to prove myself. Looking back, I find it strange that I was so slow to grasp what now seems obvious, but you must remember that my knowledge of the Capovoltan language was still far from perfect and that I have taken considerable freedom in translating these conversations into my own tongue, since the perpetual simplification, explanation and recapitulation necessary at that time would be tedious indeed for any other eye or ear. Moreover my penetration into Capovoltan life was also very superficial as yet. I met young men and women from time to time, of course, but our discourse was very limited; mostly people were intrigued by my coloring, so different from theirs, and wished to question me about the physical characteristics of my own people or to make simple comparisons about the nature of our food and theirs, the appurtenances of our houses and other such matters. I wonder how many people could recall a truly serious discussion carried on in a foreign country in a tongue other than their own on some social occasion. I observed men and women working together as in our own country, or so I thought; when Vrailbran had taken me to her place of work on one occasion, for example, there were a great number of people of both sexes at work there. The cast of thought habitual to me in my own country made me translate what I saw in the terms of my own culture, so that I viewed the prospect of marriage with Vrailbran exactly as I would have done at home. My experience as a married man, of course, made me more wary in the light of my lack of prospects, for already before I had embarked on that fateful expedition, my wife and I had learned that it is certainly not as cheap to keep four as it is to keep two.

For that moment, however, I had no chance to pursue the matter further, for Vrailbran with a face of great happiness ran to kiss her father, exclaiming, "I knew you would see it in my way in the end, when you understood what a good, honorable man he is." She kissed her mother and me in turn, looking even more brilliantly beautiful than before, and said, "Now let us see how soon it can be arranged."

So it was that I found myself being propelled into marriage with Vrailbran more rapidly than I could possibly have envisaged. How could I now hang back and beg for more time to consider this step, when clearly all of them thought that this had been my intention all along?

There was now a great deal of swift discourse between Vrailbran and her parents that I found difficult to follow exactly, but I understood that the date proposed was only a month away! My mind was awhirl indeed, for so many problems and speculations presented themselves at the same time that I found it impossible to order my thoughts and marshal them into coherent speech to Vrailbran's parents, but the moment I was alone with her I began to express my misgivings.

"Vrailbran," I said, as she turned to embrace me, enquiring tenderly if I was happy, "my dear one, of course, I am the happiest man alive, but there are so many purely practical things to be considered that I am a little overwhelmed. For one thing, where are we going to live? How are we going to find and equip somewhere within a month?"

I chose this one of all the dilemmas that presented themselves partly because I wished to make it clear that I had no intentions of continuing to live in her parents' house once we were married.

She laughed delightedly. "You remember that outing we had on the mid–rail?" By "mid–rail," which is the nearest translation I can give, she meant the moving roadway that they used for mid–distance travel. There was an excellent linkage of these moving roadways throughout the city and the surrounding countryside. The "slow–rail" was a perpetually moving band along almost all the main streets of the city center onto which one could step and be carried along at a reasonable walking pace; the mid–rail existed on all the main arteries of the city, but had recognized starting and stopping places since it moved too rapidly for one to step on and off while it was moving; for long-distance travel there were cars, something like our railway compartments, on the "quick–rail," which moved at a great pace, but very smoothly and noiselessly.

Certainly I remembered the expedition on the mid–rail, for it was the first time I had been outside the city's confines. Vrailbran had taken me out for what at home we should have called "a day in the country." The doctors who had attended me during that long period of my convalescence had previously refused permission for me to undertake anything in the least strenuous.

Did I remember, Vrailbran asked me, the charming little house which I had said was more like the houses, both in building and setting, of my own country than anything I had seen up to then?

Again, of course, I remembered it. It was a pretty house, rather like an old–world English cottage, set in its own garden, with its solar-heating and its water-recycling units so beautifully landscaped into it that I could almost have believed myself back at home; in fact, it had made me feel more homesick than anything else in that country. For the most part I thought Capovoltan architecture most unaesthetic, for in the city the skyline was dominated by the solar and water installations.

Now Vrailbran said, "That is where we are going to live, my darling—and as for equipping it, I have gradually been doing it for some time. On every occasion that you have expressed particular approval of something either here or in friends' houses or in a store, I bought it, or the nearest copy of it I could find, so that our house should be entirely to your taste."

I stared at her for a moment, aghast. I found this assurance quite alarming. "But, Vrailbran, how could you be so sure? I mean— suppose we had not been able to marry?"

"Of course, I am glad to have won my parents' consent, and I'm particularly happy that they will help us to get recognition from the Guardians, but, my darling, I should have married you and taken you off to live with me in that dear little house even if they had not agreed. After all, you must admit that you did not give me much cause to doubt your willingness!" She gave me a mischievous smile.

Here we had a short interlude in confirmation of this remark, and of that no description is necessary; it is, I think, much the same in any land. However, not even by this was I to be deterred from pursuing the disquieting thoughts by which I was assailed, and finally I came back to the subject of my greatest preoccupation.

"Vrailbran, my love, forgive me for returning to purely practical affairs again, but though what you have just told me is wonderful news, I cannot but think that a great deal of expense has been involved and there will be much more. How are we going to be able to afford to live in the house since I still have no work? However simply we live, we have to eat and there must be some cost involved in keeping the solar-heat and water-recycling installations in running order. Please try to be practical for a few minutes and discuss with me how best I may earn a living."

Of course, I hoped she would respond by suggestions such as I thought her father had hinted at previously. Instead she said, "I do assure you that there is no need for you to trouble your head about that. Had I not been well able to afford to take a husband, I should not have asked you to marry me. Although we have not talked much about my work, you probably realize that I have a position of some responsibility in the City Magistracy (that is as near as I can come to a translation: our institutions not being exactly parallel, there is no word that I know of which expresses exactly the area of responsibility indicated by their term), and then, of course, if we get recognition for a family marriage, once we start our family I shall be even more highly remunerated during that period. So you see, Klemo, you are quite unnecessarily worried about this."

"No—no—Vrailbran, my dear," I said emphatically. "I cannot agree to that. I could not possibly accept such a proposition. I could not bring myself to live on a woman's earnings. I do assure you it is quite impossible. It is a most unseemly situation for a man to be in."

"Klemo, please do not be so absurd. There is nothing unseemly about it. Why should there be? At least half of the married men, and probably more, are entirely dependent on their wives in this way. I really cannot understand you."

"Please, please, Vrailbran, help me to find some work. I do not care what it is. I will turn my hand to anything. I cannot live this idle kind of life anymore. I must do something useful, however humble."

"But, Klemo, what do you mean? What could be more useful than running our house and bringing up our family? Surely it is one of the most important things anyone could do. And as for an 'idle' life, have you not been perpetually suggesting that my father's duties are too arduous?"

By now I was quite desperate and as near to losing my temper with Vrailbran as I had ever been. But I took hold of myself and said, "Please think, Bran," for this was my "small name" for her, as they say. "Try to imagine how miserably bored and lonely I should be, by myself all day, without you and your family, without anyone I know nearby, a stranger in a strange country. Surely you cannot want me to be unhappy?''

She saw now how very much in earnest I was, and for the first time seemed to understand something of my point of view, for she said more gently and thoughtfully, "There is something in what you say, Klemo. And, of course, you *know* that I want nothing but your happiness." (Even at that moment it crossed my mind to wonder if any other phrase was ever so much misused as that one; it usually means, "I want you to be happy wanting what *I* want.") "Of course, there is no reason why you should not work for the time being. Plenty of young married men do. It will not be easy to find you suitable employment, though, for you have no qualifications for any skilled work and you are not physically robust enough for laboring work. However, I will make inquiries and see what can be done. I promise you.''

There was something irritating to my self-regard in being told so frankly that I, who in my own country had been used to being accorded considerable respect for my position and my abilities, was here of no consequence whatever. I could see that Vrailbran's remarks were justified, but that did not prevent some injury to my pride. But the relief that her capitulation on this point brought me was such that I was able to thank her sincerely and warmly. This melted her completely, and she took me in her arms smoothing away the lines of worry and uncertainty on my brow with little words of love. She was irresistible and I loved her. How could I continue my protesting inquisition on her plans for our future life? Now it was I who capitulated, glad to have won one point, closing my mind to all my other uneasinesses in the warmth of her embrace.

Things were now precipitately hurried on toward our marriage. This in Capovolta is a civil ceremony, as it is regarded as a purely civil contract, although of a very solemn and binding nature if it is a family marriage. Ordinary marriage is less earnestly regarded and may be dissolved without difficulty if both parties consent. I asked Vrailbran if marriage had for them no religious meaning, for so far I had not understood very much about their religious tenets. She said that it did to the extent that everyone was expected to put religious principles into practice in every undertaking embarked upon, and more especially so where such a serious step as a family marriage was concerned. This did not completely answer my query, but for the moment I pursued it no further.

As Vrailbran had so foresightedly already made provision for the needs of our married life, there was rather less of the practical detail to see to than I had expected, so that in fact a month was an adequate time for such further preparations as had to be made. Curiously enough, since the ceremony was not a religious one, it was nevertheless customary—or indeed it may have been obligatory, I am not sure which—to wear special ceremonial garments. These did not differ fundamentally from those of everyday life, except in color and in excellence of material and cut. Blue was the marriage color here; both partners wore clothes of the same material and the same shade: it had a symbolic meaning, that of a unity between the couple. I had, of course, no objection to this in principle, but it did occasion some argument between myself and Vrailbran, as you shall hear. However, all was accomplished in time, and in less than a month from that day when I found myself so suddenly obliged to have serious intentions, I became a married man for the second time in my life.

CHAPTER
4

To explain the quarrel which developed between Vrailbran and myself over my wedding garment, I must now give an account of something which for reasons of modesty I have hitherto been reluctant to do, and that is the strange costume affected by the Capovoltan men. I ask pardon in advance for any offense that may be occasioned to the more squeamish of my readers, but just as our men of medicine must set down truthfully in their records even the most unpleasing of their patients' symptoms, so must I as chronicler of the habits and customs of the land of Capovolta give a faithful description of all that I found there.

To those who have read my record so far with attention, it will be clear that I have found certain features of Capovoltan life to be astonishing and some to be downright displeasing. Of these, one is this matter of male attire. In my first perfunctory account of the dress of the inhabitants of this country, I mentioned that the women wore an unbecoming tubular garment which concealed completely those parts of the female form wherein my sex is wont to take most delight and to view with most pleasure. I mentioned, too, the gaudy breeches of the men, designed to set off a fine calf to advantage by their closeness of fit. What I then omitted to describe, to preserve my own modesty and for fear of giving offense, was the way in which these garments are designed below the navel. All that area where a decent man keeps his private parts in a kind of modest seclusion is here encased in a highly colored, tightly fitting three-pronged bag.

The effect of this is to draw the attention of all passersby to that part of the person, and I am filled with amazement that the women, instead of averting their eyes in *pudeur,* as our women would, gaze with interest upon each member so impudently displayed—and indeed even comment favorably or otherwise to one another upon the same. At first I could not look myself, for the shame and embarrassment which it caused me; as, however, I began to find that here it is taken as a matter of course, and that indeed even quite elderly persons continue to emphasize that part of the anatomy—I suppose to announce to the women that they are still potent—I began to allow my eyes to dwell upon this phenomenon. Some of these members seem so swollen and monstrous that either these men pad or enhance their size with artificial means, or indeed they are a better endowed race than we are. As I cannot believe the latter to be true, I must conclude that they wear bags specially constructed to make the member appear of greater size. When relations between myself and my wife had become sufficiently confidential, and being a little angered by the way in which, when walking with me in the street, she would openly scrutinize some of the more extreme and disgusting exhibitions, I suggested to her that there might not be only flesh inside the bag, but a good deal of padding, too. She smiled at that, patted me gently in that area and said I must not be jealous of these other splendid endowments, for although small I was excellently energetic in that field and she had no complaints! I was so angered with this that I spoke to her no more that day, and when she came to bed with me that night, sought to have none of her. But she, in her turn, would have none of that, for she has a passing large appetite for the fare I offer, and so cajoling me and laying siege to me in a way that in our land only, I must confess it, a whore would do, she had her way of me and was so complimentary about the service I gave her that what could I do but forgive her?

But I made a resolve that day that if my fate should ever again send me back to my own country and to the bosom of my wife and family, that I would be more circumspect in viewing the wenches in the street as I walked with my wife, and would be less eager to comment openly upon the luscious shapes they exposed.

The thoughtful reader will now be asking, What of myself? What dress did I affect? At first, of course, I wore those clothes in which I had been cast up almost dead upon that shore, but these occasioned so much mirth and drew so many strange looks that I was forced to allow my kind protectors to order some new clothes for me. At first I refused indignantly to countenance a garment which encased my members in that odious three-pronged bag, but when Vrailbran's father eventually made me understand that if I did not do so, all would take me for some strange neutered being with no manhood to me, my pride revolted against that and with much protest on my part and accommodation to my "whims" on the tailor's part, a garment was finally constructed which was passable by Capovoltan standards and not too offensive by my own. Of course, as time has gone on, I have become more tolerant, and now I do like to be seen in a garment with a really elegant cut. Not even to please my dear wife, however, will I wear the very latest fashion, which is to encase the middle member in a bag of a separate and most distinctive color, which is also designed to keep the member in an upright position at all times so that the women please themselves with the idea that it is their charms which have elevated him and that he would be ready at all times for some delightful play should opportunity present itself. It was this which occasioned the quarrel with Vrailbran over the design of my costume for the wedding.

She, wishing me, I suppose, to be as elegantly turned out as possible, instructed the tailor to fashion such a garment for me, the central portion to be, though still in the traditional blue color, of a stronger and more clamant shade. I had not understood this, and when I came to have a fitting for my wedding breeches, I was so furious and offended by this that I tore it out immediately in such a passion that I could neither make the tailor understand my displeasure, nor understand his protests. Eventually, when my choler had abated a little, he made me understand that it had been done to the express order of Vrailbran. Fortunately she had not accompanied me to this fitting, so I soon had the tailor refashioning the garment to *my* instructions this time, explaining that there had been a misunderstanding because of my lack of knowledge of the technical terms of tailoring in the Capovoltan language.

When Vrailbran understood what I had done she was at first much incensed, and in the ensuing discussion—our first real quarrel—we said some hard things one to the other. Vrailbran accused me of being stubborn and wanting my own way in everything, an accusation so utterly unjust and the exact opposite of the truth that I became almost incoherent as I tried to find the right words to refute it as vehemently as I wished. I in my turn accused her, with far more justice, of acting in a high-handed way and treating me as though I were her property, instead of a person in my own right. I do not know where all this would have ended had not Vrailbran's father, rather surprisingly, come to my rescue. He told Vrailbran gently that he respected my modesty: he himself also much disliked this new fashion, would never consent to wear it, and thought I had shown unusual sense and judgment for a young man in wishing to keep to the traditional dress, which, of course, should have been of absolutely uniform color. Fortunately for me, this argument convinced Vrailbran in the end, and so our first quarrel ended as such quarrels usually do, each slightly ashamed and sorry for the hard words said in anger and anxious to make amends; but uncomfortable, too, that a disagreement about something so slight could create such a rift, if only a temporary one.

The subject of dress brings me to comment on an even more odious custom, which, indeed, I should dearly like to avoid touching upon, but in the cause of honesty, clearly I cannot do so. This custom is that when a man appears alone, unescorted by a woman, in the street, and more especially in places of close concourse, there are women who regard it as their right to caress or pinch one's member with coarse expressions and gestures that leave no doubt of their meaning. And do not mock me, gentlemen; you may think, not having experienced it, that such adventures may be exciting, but pray imagine yourself confronted in this way by an elderly fishwife, in greasy overalls perhaps and weighing all of eighteen stone, and *then* reflect whether indeed you would want to be handled so intimately as though you were a vegetable exposed on a market stall. It is, I assure you, a most disagreeable experience. I have also been warned by my wife that such women may set upon lone men in gangs and drag them off to use for their pleasure. Men have been known to expire from the strain put upon them in this way, since the women have unmentionable means, it is said, for forcing the member to do its work repeatedly. Unfortunately the authorities do not take the matter as seriously as they should, for they are inclined to blame the man for provocation or for not taking greater precautions against being set upon in this way. But is it not altogether intolerable that a decent man may not simply go out for a walk on his own without risking such an outcome?

One day, indeed, I myself had a most unpleasant experience, of a different kind, but which clearly illustrated the existence of a very depraved set of people somewhere in the city. My "wife" had asked me to meet her at her place of work as we were to go out that evening to visit some friends of hers. I was still shy of the stares that my foreign appearance and accent provoked, so rather than go into the building and bear the curious glances of those within, I preferred to wait a little more inconspicuously at the bottom of the steps outside.

After I had been so stationed for only a few minutes, I noticed strolling along the pavement a very large and burly fellow, probably of about my own age, dressed in the height of fashion and with the most monstrous appendage I had ever seen. A moment or so later he walked back the other way, and then swung round and so back again. I looked at him with some interest because I began to think that he, too, must be waiting for his wife to emerge from the building.

After a few minutes he began to cast disapproving glances in my direction. I wondered if my behavior, inoffensive as it seemed to me, was in some way not quite of the standard expected of a colleague's husband. Should I, too, strut back and forth in front of the steps? I had not the courage, however, to draw such attention to myself.

Eventually the fellow, after a quick look in each direction and seeing that there was no one coming, advanced upon me menacingly and, seizing hold of my member and cruelly squeezing it, said the equivalent of "Bugger off, big brother, or I'll cut him off, see? This is *my* pitch, and don't you come here a-queering of it."

I almost screamed with the pain of it, but managed instead to gasp out, "What harm am I doing you? I'm just waiting for my wife."

"Oh, you are, are you, you little————" (an expletive I did not know). "Well, go and wait somewhere else, or I'll do you in."

I fled up the steps, almost whimpering with pain, and stood trembling inside the door until my wife came. One of the most distressing aspects of this affair for me, apart from the shock, was to understand that the fellow had indeed taken me for one of his own kind. Vrailbran was quite clearly amused as well as concerned for me when I recounted this little adventure to her, as she was when I first brought myself to confide in her about the maulings of my person which I had endured on the few occasions when I had been out alone. She explained that such behavior was quite common among women of the coarser kind, and that some young men appeared to enjoy it, as a kind of tribute to their obvious virility. This I greeted with some incredulity: agreeable as such exchanges are with a partner of one's own choosing, it is an entirely different matter to be treated and handled as an object or a piece of common property by any comer, as though one had no right to the privacy and possession of one's own body.

I grew so indignant about this that Vrailbran tried to calm me by explaining that I drew more attention upon myself probably because of my foreign appearance and deportment. This could hardly be expected to reconcile me to this offensive custom, but it is true that my appearance was the cause of much interest and comment everywhere. My great good fortune was that I am of a somewhat dark complexion with hair of a middling brown, for there exists among the Capovoltans a deep distrust and suspicion of fair-skinned people; but, as is not unusual among our race, I have eyes which are noticeable for the vivid blue of their color. This feature attracted much curiosity wherever I went, for if such a combination exists in Capovolta, it is very rare and I have never met any example of it myself.

The Capovoltans themselves have a most unusual and to my taste singularly beautiful type of coloring: the complexion is dark, but as though a thin, almost transparent film of bluish color had been applied to the top layer of skin and one could yet discern a paler skin below. The nearest thing to it which I have encountered elsewhere is the complexion sometimes found among people of Maori origin. The hair, which is abundant and quite straight, and the eyes are uniformly dark, usually of a deep blue-black. To my mind, they are a remarkably handsome race, for the most part, though naturally there are exceptions. They are tall and well proportioned, the average height being, I should think, at least a couple of inches more than among us; I myself am well above average height at home, but here found myself just about at the median.

Although I could not but admire the splendid physiques of both sexes, I found it something distasteful to have the qualities of my own sex so frequently judged only on our physical attributes. I regret to say that the women of Capovolta seemed to have less regard to character, intelligence and the finer qualities generally in men than for their physical strength and the handsomeness of their persons, and often they seemed to me gravely lacking in judgment in their choice of marriage partner. Finding these characteristics the most praised and appreciated, naturally the men themselves also attach more importance to them. While no one is more appreciative than I of a pleasing appearance in man or woman, though especially, of course, in the latter, it seems to me a denigration of the true qualities of manhood that such superficialities should be used as criteria. What is a man to make of himself if his learning, his wisdom, his humanity, his benevolence, his abilities of command and all other such true criteria, count as nothing against an accident of nature which has saddled with him unusual smallness of stature or an unaesthetic cast of countenance?

I myself was clearly the subject of some diversity of opinion on this matter. In my own country, though not of any unusual or outstanding handsomeness, I was, I may say without boasting, considered a rather personable young man, being above average height and well proportioned with it, with the rather noticeable blue eyes I mentioned combined with an agreeably tanned-looking complexion and darkish curling hair. Here in Capovolta this was in startling contrast with the prevailing racial type, and at first provoked glances wherever I went. For some I appeared to have the attraction of the unusual and exotic, while from others my different and paler coloring attracted odium. I shall never forget one of my early experiences when walking one day with Vrailbran in a part of the city new to me. This was the first time we had ventured so far during my period of convalescence. Suddenly a rowdy group of teenaged youths attached themselves to us, some walking behind, some prancing backward in front, and all yelling and jeering. The words I did not understand, but the taunting tone was unmistakable, and when one of those behind actually put his hand upon me and gave me a shove which almost sent me sprawling, I whipped about and in spite of my weakened state advanced upon him with upraised fist. There is no doubt that had I been alone I should have been involved in a street brawl, which would certainly have gone badly for me, given my feeble condition and the number of my tormentors. But Vrailbran held my arm, stood calmly looking upon them with a kind of cold anger which found vent in words cracked out like a whiplash, though she spoke so fast I could not follow, and to my amazement the fellows dropped back, looking sheepish and foolish, then slouched away.

I was so upset by this that we returned home immediately, and it took me several days to recover from the shock of the encounter.

At first Vrailbran evaded my questions and would not tell me exactly what they had said, explaining only that they were of the ruffianly sort that perpetually caused trouble one way or another if not held in check, and that when they realized that she was in the city magistracy, they feared the consequences of their ill–behavior. Eventually, however, she told me that it was the comparative lightness of my complexion at which they had been jeering so unpleasantly, and that they would indeed have attacked me solely for that and my general foreignness of appearance. It was then that she explained that the expression they had used most constantly, which literally translated would be "pink–skinned brute," I suppose, was used as a term of abuse or odium for a person of a thoroughly bad and treacherous nature. At first I thought that this was simply an extension of the emphasis put on physical appearance; that is, that such coloring was considered displeasing and had therefore acquired the prejudicial connotation. It seemed a sadly intolerant state of things, and I did not envy the lot of any fair–haired or fair–skinned Capovoltan. However, as time went by and I never encountered anyone with more than a minimal variation from the general skin tone, I began to speculate about this and to question Vrailbran and her parents further.

Although reluctant to give any further explanation for some time, at last to satisfy me Vrailbran began to recount something of the history of her people in order to show me that the prejudice I found so odious did have more basis in fact than many such prejudices have. Sometime in the not too distant past, their land, which is rich and well endowed by nature, had been visited by a group of people with reddish–pink skins. These strangers came with gifts of various sorts, nothing of great value, but showing, so the Capovoltans felt, a desire for friendly relations. They had with them as interpreter a young Capovoltan man who had vanished from his homeland some years before in very strange circumstances. His family had mourned him as dead, but here he now was, alive and well, having been received by the strangers and given some kind of hospitality. He was reluctant to account for his disappearance, but it was generally understood that as a teenaged youth he had been in trouble with the Guardians and had therefore determined to flee the country and seek sanctuary elsewhere. All Capovoltans knew perfectly well that there were other regions beyond their horizons, but their land offering all that man could desire, for the most part they had no wish to go beyond its confines. This young man, driven partly by guilt, partly by curiosity, partly by a sense of not having his true worth appreciated, had privately procured himself a boat and cast his lot upon the waves.

The visitors were well entertained and taken to see all the amenities of the land. They were much impressed by its richness and by the advanced state of its people, and left after a couple of weeks' stay, protesting great friendship. However, in a very short while they returned, but this time aboard a huge and well–armed warship, with another as escort. They demanded the surrender of the land and an acknowledgment of their sovereignty; if this was refused, they threatened to obliterate or take as slaves the whole population. What these invaders did not know was that the waters around Capovolta are under surveillance and control from underwater caves, with which the whole coastline is liberally endowed. The

Guardians courteously refused this capitulation, asking the warships to move out of Capovoltan waters immediately or take the consequences. These were made clear by the Guardians, who explained that the ships could be sunk within a matter of minutes. Of course, the invaders believed this to be a bluff and turned their huge armaments upon the city. No sooner had the first salvo been fired, carrying with it both loss of life and damage to property, than the underwater devices which protected the Capovoltan shores were exploded and the two battleships turned turtle and sank before they had any chance of launching the boats. A number of survivors, including the Capovoltan interpreter, had been rescued and brought ashore, and so it was learned what the Guardians had suspected: that the interpreter had been taken as a slave by the fair–skinned people and, eventually, in order to procure his freedom had told them of the richness of his country and offered to guide them thither. The first party had come in apparent friendship to see if his stories were true, and finding that the truth exceeded his account, their greed was aroused and they determined to conquer the country and exploit its riches.

Such abhorrence was felt for the treachery of these people that although allowed to live out the natural span of their lives and physically well treated, they were never forgiven and never allowed to mingle with the rest of the population—so the Capovoltan racial stock was never adulterated, as they regarded it, by any intermarriage. From that time forward, fair skin became synonymous for them with the idea of treachery and general villainy. After this recital, I could not but acknowledge that there was more to justify this intolerance than is usual with such prejudices.

CHAPTER

5

Now that Vrailbran and I were married, the most pressing consideration for me was that of some suitable occupation. Of course, the first few days or even weeks of our new life in our charming little house were sufficiently rapturous to make me willing to postpone introducing a possibly jarring note immediately. Once the charm of novelty had worn off, however, I began to be impatient that Vrailbran should do as she had promised and set matters in train. When I broached the subject, she was provokingly casual, and I began to fear that after all she had no intention of honoring what I regarded as the pact made between us on this subject just before our wedding.

One evening I felt I could stand the present situation no longer, and I said with as much restraint as I could muster on a subject which had become such a tender one for me, "Bran, my love, it is very nearly a month since our wedding day, and I see that you have been able to make no progress in the matter of finding employment for me. You have explained the difficulties to me more than once, and I understand that it is not easy to find anything that I can usefully do. I think, therefore, that I must take the onus of looking for work upon myself. Tomorrow I propose to."

"Tomorrow, my dear," she said, cutting me short and giving me a triumphant smile, "I have arranged for you to present yourself at the offices of the City Transport Company. They are prepared to give you a trial there as an————" (here a word I had never heard before and which probably has no exact counterpart in our language. In the light of my later experience of the job, it could be roughly translated as "invoicing or filing clerk"). For the moment, the word meant nothing to me, but I was transported with joy that at last I was to enter what for me was the real world—of occupation, of measuring one's skills against those of others, of contact with people of different types—and so to escape the comfortable but lonely and narrow world in which I had been living so far and which was beginning to stifle me.

I began to question Bran eagerly about the Transport Company and what she thought my work might entail. However, like most consumers, she knew little of the inside operation of the company. She warned me that the work would certainly not be very stimulating, but said that if I showed aptitude, I might possibly progress to something more responsible, as my knowledge of the language, and especially of the necessary technical terms, improved.

In spite of my strong desire to embark upon this long–delayed chance of proving myself in the world of affairs, it was with some trepidation that I presented myself at the company's offices the next morning. A pleasant and courteous young man showed me into a kind of waiting room, and said he would call me for interview with his superior in a few moments. He came back shortly and ushered me into an office where a kindly middle–aged woman was waiting.

She opened by addressing me under Vrailbran's family name, which was that of her mother. This so surprised me that I thought for a moment that there had been some mistake—but, then, with a shock I realized that my identity in this community was now that of Bran's husband. Of course, I had known this in a way, but no stranger had had occasion to address me since my marriage, and I was known to all our friends and acquaintances as Klemo, since none of them could manage anything nearer than that to Lemuel— and Gulliver was an even more unlikely sounding name from their point of view. This I had never minded, but now I felt quite resentful to be no longer officially Lemuel Gulliver, in however corrupt and complicated a version, but, to translate into our terms: "Klemo– Vrailbran–Zenhild's husband" (Zenhild is the best transcription I can give of Bran's mother's name). This was no time or place to protest, however, and I simply acknowledged that I was the person so described.

My interviewer, who was the supervisor of all the people engaged on the sort of work I was to do, explained what was required of me. Their method of correspondence is at once simpler and more complicated than ours. Anyone wishing to make a list, to send an order, or to communicate in any way with someone at a distance, simply spoke directly into a tiny device which was worn on a strap or chain around the neck. This device recorded what was said on a minute hollow cylinder of a substance which looked very like that of which spools of film are made in our own country. I suppose in a way it was something of the same principle as microfilm, for the length of message that could be recorded on one of these tiny cylinders was roughly that of a page of typescript at home, by my reckoning. The work of the filing clerks, or whatever one might call them, was to see to the dispatch of these cylinders to the correct recipient, and to receive and distribute incoming cylinders. Copies for filing had first to be made in a machine like a small camera: the imprinted cylinder was dropped into one compartment and a blank cylinder into the other, as it might be the full and the empty spool in a camera; the case was closed, a couple of buttons pressed, and—presto—there was a duplicate of the message. These were stored in a great room known as the "memory bank," strung on very thin steel rods about the girth of the finest knitting needle I have seen in our own country. Each one was coded as to position and content, and if anyone wanted a recapitulation of the content, it was only necessary to select the correct code, press the corresponding series of keys on a thing like a large typewriter keyboard, and the cylinder would drop into the tiny playback machine immediately under it and most uncannily the voice of the original recorder would be heard repeating the message or list or whatever it was. Incoming messages, after they had been received and played back by the recipient on the little recording machine which I have described worn round the neck, had also to be duplicated and correctly numbered and coded before being stored in another section of the "memory bank." This duplicating, coding and storing were to be my work. Of course, I was only one of a number of young men engaged on this particular process, and I was to spend my first day or two under the tutelage of one of the others. For the first day I was to follow him round and observe only; then I was to do the duplicating work under his surveillance and continue to observe and learn the correct method of coding and storing until I was sure of it, for mistakes in that vital operation could be costly of time and materials. It was not difficult work in any sense: it simply called for concentration and accuracy, but for me it was complicated by the comparative unfamiliarity of the coding symbols. So early are we imprinted with our own particular symbols and our method of calculating everything to the base of ten that they feel almost instinctive to us. It does not require any conscious thought to recognize that the symbols 1 and 9 put together indicate ten plus nine, or to recognize that f follows e and precedes g in our alphabet. Now I had to master the meaning and order of a completely new series of symbols to represent numbers and sounds. Moreover, the Capovoltan method of computation is with a base of twelve, not ten—so that if we used the same symbols, our 19 would be their 17 and our 12 would be their 10. Of course, I had already become to some extent familiar with the symbols and the use of base twelve, but not as with our own system, where I did not have to make a conscious effort of thought each time.

While on this subject of Capovoltan methods of computation and so on, it may be worth mentioning that the number twelve is for them the basis of almost all measurements and calculations. Certainly I myself found many advantages in the use of base twelve; it is after all divisible by two, by three, by four and by six. For duration of time, we ourselves use divisions of twelve for our day and night, and for our year. In Capovolta a day of twenty-four hours is divided into twelve equal parts, that is, lengths of time of two hours' duration as they would be according to our calculations. Each of these is divided into twelve equal periods once again, that is, periods equal to ten of our minutes, but in Capovolta the next unit was once again one–twelfth—and so on.

The Capovoltan month is a strictly lunar month; that is, the day of the new moon is the first of the month. This day is always a holiday, as is the day of the full moon. Between successive new moons, two work periods of twelve days each are fitted in, each period beginning on the day after the new–moon or full–moon holiday, so that at the end of each twelve–day period there is a holiday of from two to four days, according to the time between the phases of the moon. The main holiday periods of the year are around the summer and winter solstices, with shorter holidays at the spring and autumn equinoxes.

The unit of linear measurement is the span—that is, the span of a woman's hand, which by my estimation would be not far short of our own reckoning of nine inches to the span, for the women of Capovolta are on the average of larger physical build than our own. Weight likewise is calculated in units of twelve, as though the pound were made up of twelve ounces. Their liquid measure was correlated with weight, so that the volume of water which was equal to one of their "pounds" in weight was the basic unit, as it might be the pint with us.

The fact that I found this whole system more consistent and perhaps more sensible than our own did not help me, however, during that first day or two when to my chagrin I felt myself to be intolerably slow and awkward in carrying out what was required of me. At the end of the day I was exhausted with the effort of concentration which the work demanded of me, for I dared not relax for one moment in case my old habits of thought intruded and I perpetrated some disastrous stupidity. Vrailbran, though kind and considerate, could not altogether conceal an air of wishing to say, "I did warn you, but you would have it so." This steeled my resolution not to repine or complain in front of her, but within me a certain resentment began to grow that notwithstanding my new status as a wage earner, the same tedious household tasks were left to me to perform as before. I suppose I had assumed that now they would be equally shared. This did not seem to occur to Vrailbran, although it is true that she would rather more frequently than before perform the occasional small task or service, but always clearly with the conviction that it was really my duty and she was doing me a favor.

Also the fact that at the office I was the object of some amusement and some hostility depressed my spirits further. The amusement was at first more understandable than the hostility, for however much I tried to conform, my behavior could not seem other than strange and at times eccentric, and among the human race it is customary to laugh at what one does not understand. I was prepared to wait for acceptance until the novelty of my presence had worn off. The hostility, however, worried me more, because I could not understand its source. It was my great good fortune that the young man who had been placed in a superior capacity over me while I was learning the work was of a kindly and friendly disposition, so that gradually we gained confidence with one another and I became sure that I had at least one well–wisher among my fellow workers. It was from him that I eventually learned the reason for my hostile reception from some of my colleagues. It was that I had not begun my career there right at the bottom. The normal procedure was for a young man to be placed in the receiving and dispatching department to begin with and from there progress in time to the work, considered more responsible and in fact better remunerated, which I was doing. This had occasioned great jealousy, I suppose with some reason, for it was true that the post had been obtained for me by Bran's influence. The situation was one which no amount of goodwill on my part could altogether redress, but I did my best to be as pleasant and unassuming as I could, and redoubled my efforts to do my work efficiently, so that there could be no grounds for a further suspicion that I had been favored beyond my merit and capacity.

Although by now I had through personal experience become well acquainted with the inequalities so glaringly obvious to me in Capovoltan society, and should therefore have been prepared for further evidence of it in the structure of the office hierarchy, the complete dominance of women in all the higher ranks still came as something of a surprise and shock to me. It is true that most of the young men with whom I came into contact seemed to have little ambition and little interest in the work which they were doing, but when one realized how monotonous the work eventually became once it was thoroughly mastered, and, more important, how very little chance there was of any real promotion even for those who excelled at it, perhaps it was not so surprising. Among most of those young men, the chief topics of interest were first and foremost the personable young women in the office, and after that the latest fashions and the cultivation of the physical perfection of their bodies: although they did not seem to be destined ever to perform any very remarkable physical feats, they were endlessly interested in new exercises or new diets for muscle development and body building. Almost never did I hear any really serious subject being discussed among them. The one exception was my supervisor and friend, Tsano. He was of a most intelligent and thoughtful cast of mind, and there was no doubt that he was able beyond the average. He was slightly older than most of the others and ranked as chief of the filing clerks. I was curious to know what he thought of his prospects of promotion, partly for his sake and partly because I thought it might cast some light upon my own, so when an opportunity presented itself I questioned him about this.

"How long is it, Tsano," I said, "since you became a filing clerk?" for I knew that he had begun as was usual in the receiving and dispatching department.

He thought for a moment and then said, "About five years, on and off, I suppose."

"Five years!" I was unutterably dismayed by this information and indignant on his behalf, for I knew that there were several younger women in positions of greater responsibility. "That is really absurd. You should have been promoted long ago. You are clearly much more capable than ——, for instance." Here I named one of these young women, our immediate superior in charge of the memory bank, whom we both knew to be slow and unreliable, though she herself seemed unaware of it and was extremely self-satisfied. On many occasions I had seen Tsano quietly remedy some inefficiency of hers before it came to light.

Tsano shrugged and laughed. "Well, of course, that's one reason why I am where I am. She's known not to be very good, so she gets a seasoned trouper [the nearest I can come to the idiomatic expression he used] like me to keep an eye on her."

"That's monstrously unfair!" I said indignantly. "Why don't you protest about it?"

"Klemo, my dear fellow, where do you think such a protest would get me? All it would do would be to give me a bad name, and then next time they might not take me back."

"What do you mean, next time?" I said, remembering as I did so his odd expression—that he had been a filing clerk for five years "on and off."

"The job is very important to me," he said. "You see, my wife is not of a strong constitution, so her career has been rather frequently interrupted and she's had rather bad luck. My earnings form an important part of our resources, therefore. Because I am well thought of here, each time I have had to give up my job to nurse my wife, they have been willing to hold the post open and take me back. Of course, if it were to happen again, I should lose this particular position of chief filing clerk, but I think they'd take me back into the department. That's very rare, you know. Mostly if a man has to give up for family reasons, he has no chance of getting back."

"But I understood that here the rules of employment are very enlightened. Vrailbran says that when a woman has maternity leave it does not affect her career: she is even more highly paid during that period and returns afterward to the position she held before."

"That is true, but of course it's different for men. Marriage and family obligations disrupt things so much more for us. Ours is in fact a recognized family marriage, but we really dare not have children unless my wife's health improves—not only for her sake, but because I should have to give up work to look after the child and I don't think we could manage without my earnings."

"Would it not be more sensible, then, for your wife to look after the children and you to earn the livelihood for the household?"

"Why, Klemo, no. Then we should be much worse off, because of course my wife earns much more than I could ever hope to. Anyway, what you suggest is practically unheard–of here. The very idea of it would upset my wife very much. No, no, it is quite unthinkable."

I did not pursue the subject further at that point, for I could see that this dwelling on the difficulties of his life was only serving to upset him rather than to help. Certainly what I had learned did not augur well for my own chances, either. I had been overoptimistic in imagining that it would only be necessary to be efficient and conscientious to qualify for promotion. There were, it is true, a few, but a very few, older men among the upper echelons, but for the most part the men were young and employed in certain well-defined areas of work where accuracy and speed were important but where there was little responsibility and certainly no decision–making. Discussing this on another occasion with Tsano, I asked why there was such a preponderance of *young* men in employment here.

Tsano looked surprised that I should ask this, and almost as he spoke in reply I understood what I should have deduced for myself before: most men gave up working outside the home when they married, or at the latest when they began to establish a family. I knew better now than to argue about this, but I had another query. I was curious to know the basis of this unfair practice which daily aroused my indignation. Why was such a clear discrimination made between men and women in the type of work on which they were generally engaged? That done by men was of a less responsible kind and less highly paid. Why? Surely no one in their senses could argue that all men were less able or responsible than all women?

Tsano hesitated before replying. "It does seem a rather sweeping generalization, I agree," he said slowly, "but I suppose it is because we are later in maturing than women, aren't we? We are slower in learning to control aggression, too, so they say, and are by nature less patient and more impulsive. The general conclusion is that we are less suited to jobs in which those qualities—maturity, control, patience and so on—are required."

I was outraged by this. "The whole proposition strikes me as questionable, but it is idiotic to suggest that *all* women are more mature, more controlled, more patient than *all* men," I fumed. "I've never heard such utter rubbish."

"I'm inclined to agree with you, really," said Tsano, "but I suppose it's the average that counts."

"Why on earth must it be the average that counts? Why can't each person be judged on individual merit?"

"I suppose that would undermine the whole structure of our

society, wouldn't it? I mean some men would be doing women's work and some women doing men's."

This made me explode. "Really, Tsano. *Who* is this authority that decides what is 'women's work' and what is 'men's work'? Why can't we all do whatever it is we are most suited to do and share it all out more fairly?"

"Klemo, please," he said unhappily, "don't sound so *angry. I* can't do anything about it, and *you* can't do anything about it. It's just the way the world is."

"But it isn't, Tsano," I said. "You're quite wrong. It *isn't* the way the world is. I've told you things are almost exactly the opposite way round where I come from. I might just as well say that *that* is the way the world is. It is clear that the world can be in many different ways, and in all fairness things need thinking out much more clearly both in your society and mine. I will agree that until I came here I never questioned the correctness or the fairness of the assumptions upon which our society is based, but now I see that *both* are based on the same set of propositions, but that each of us draws exactly opposite conclusions from them."

Our discussion was interrupted at this point by a summons for me to report to the personnel supervisor, as I suppose we should call her. This was the pleasant, kindly middle–aged woman who had interviewed me on my first day. She had continued to take an interest in my welfare, as was presumably her duty, but she had been particularly concerned for me, as a foreigner, that I should settle down well in the office. She never said so, but I rather thought she might have been the friend of Bran's mother who had been instrumental in procuring this position for me.

"Well, Klemo, my dear," she said with her usual kindly smile, but with a more intimate tone than usual, "how are you getting on these days? Do you feel happily settled among us now?"

Of course, I was always diplomatic in my replies to her kindly meant inquiries, and now responded that I was beginning to feel much more at home than formerly.

"Good," she said. "I have been getting excellent reports on your work, too. I am delighted with your progress. It is not so often that a good–looking young man like you is endowed with intelligence as well''—and she gave me an approving, maternal sort of smile. Although this seemed a slightly unorthodox way of congratulating me on overcoming my initial difficulties, naturally I was pleased at her approval and murmured my thanks.

"I like to get to know all my young men really well," she continued, "and especially those in whom I take an interest because I feel they have a future, as we say. It is not easy always to find the time for an informal chat in the office. I was wondering if perhaps we might spend our break together one day?"

The break, or whatever we should call it, is shorter than the lunchtime to which we are accustomed at home, but that is not unreasonable since the working day in Capovolta is shorter. It is a pause of about half an hour in the middle of the working day, in the course of which one is free to have a snack at one's desk if one chooses, or to eat the rather indifferent fare provided by the office canteen; the time is too short to go elsewhere.

I suppose I looked my surprise at this invitation, and maybe showed some slight uncertainty, too, for I could not quite see what I was supposed to do. Should I take her to the office refreshment room, or provide food from home to be eaten–well–where? In the filing clerks' restroom, perhaps? After the slightest pause while I was trying to frame a reply, she added, "I'll have something sent up here for us both, if that's all right?"

With that difficulty out of the way, I accepted with alacrity, and the next day was fixed for us to have our talk. I went off in a certain excitement, because unlikely though it seemed after my conversation with Tsano, I could not help but think that she might perhaps be considering some form of promotion for me, and that she wished to test out my abilities and capacities in a more formal atmosphere than a work–time interview would afford.

I would have told Tsano of this immediately had he not already left for home before I got back. I went home myself full of my news, anxious to discuss it with Bran and see what she thought it might portend. However, I thought better of this and decided not to say anything until afterward. If my hopes had been raised without reason then I need not confess to Bran that I had ever contemplated such an outcome; if on the other hand I was correct in my conjectures, then it would be delightful to surprise her with the fait accompli. For the same reason I did not the next morning wish to discuss the thing with Tsano, after all, so I only mentioned it shortly before the break itself to explain why it was that I should not be spending it as I usually did with him. He looked a little startled, and seemed about to say something, but checked and contented himself with a nod and an odd little smile. Something about this made me feel uneasy: Could he possibly think that I was going to be promoted over his head in some way? Of course I wanted advancement but not at my friend's expense or with the loss of his friendship, which I greatly valued. So it was with some inquietude that I presented myself at the appointed time and place.

"Ah, Klemo, come in," she said in her usual welcoming way. "You are exactly on time. Our refreshments are here already."

"You are very kind, Madam," I said.

"Please don't be so formal, my dear boy," she said. "I should much prefer you to use my given name. You will do that, won't you, to please me?"

I found this request embarrassing; for while it was customary for our superiors to use our given names in addressing us, we always used the formal method of address to them. It was rather as though one's grandmother had suddenly asked one to call her by her pet name. What could I do but assent, however?

"Why, of course, Madam, if you wish me to."

"Now say, 'Why, of course, Avgard, if you wish me to,' " and she looked at me positively coyly. "Come on, now," she said in the indulgent tone of one coaxing a recalcitrant child, "say it after me, 'Why, of course, Avgard, if you wish me to.' "

I stared miserably at my feet and muttered, "Why, of course, Avgard, if you wish me to."

"There, now, it wasn't as difficult as all that, was it? Come and sit down."

I obeyed and she sat beside me saying, "I did say an informal chat, you know. How can we be informal if you address me as though we were having an ordinary office interview? Now isn't it much nicer to use given names like this?"

By now I felt that I had been ridiculously ungracious, and was determined to make amends, so in reply I said, with a little emphasis on the name this time, "Why, of course, *Avgard*—you are quite right," and smiled down at her.

She took a quick intake of breath, then let it out slowly, and patting my cheek very lightly with her hand as my mother used to do, she said, "You're a very charming boy."

Again, this struck me as a strange compliment in an office context, but not wishing to be churlish I said, perhaps rather too impetuously, "You remind me of my mother; she used to pat my cheek just like that."

She dropped her hand and her smile vanished, too. "Is that so?" she said in a rather cold and offended tone.

Fool, I thought to myself, what an idiotic thing to say to a woman who may not in fact be old enough to be your mother even if she looks it.

"Although," I added as smoothly as I could, "I suppose you can't be more than half her age."

She seemed to relax a little. "Well, you shouldn't be too shy of me if I remind you of your mother, I suppose."

"She was a wonderful person," I said with probably more enthusiasm than I had spoken of her before, true though the statement was.

Avgard seemed to approve of the sentiment, I was pleased to see, and then she began to question me about my old life. The time passed pleasantly enough, but no mention was made of the matter which had been uppermost in my mind all along, and I found no way of guiding the conversation round to it, although I had taken every opportunity offered by her questions to emphasize the position of responsiblity I had held in my own country.

When it was time for me to go she said, "This was very pleasant; we must do it again. I was quite right about you—you are a very unusual and intelligent boy as well as a very charming one." I was standing at the door ready to go. "Come here a moment, Klemo," she said.

I took a step toward her, and she put both her hands up to my face this time, pulled my head down to her, saying, "Is this how your mother bade you adieu, my dear boy?" and with that kissed me lingeringly and warmly upon the mouth.

As I stood almost paralyzed with confusion and greatly perplexed as to my right course of action, the blood rising into my cheeks in a tide of embarrassment for the first time since I was a youth, she released me with a calm and placid smile and a small gesture of dismissal. A moment later I was on my way back to the memory bank to resume my duties, much shaken and full of questionings and uncertainties. What was the true significance of Avgard's strange behavior? Could it be that she did indeed have for me something of a mother's affection? Had it not been for that last kiss, I might have managed to convince myself of this. On the other hand, the only other rational interpretation seemed quite monstrous, that this elderly woman, probably an acquaintance if not a friend of Bran's mother, in a position of considerable responsibility and authority, should be inviting amorous attention from me—hardly inviting it even, but bestowing it on me. It seemed a rank conceit, as well as a denigration of this lady's character, even to allow myself to think this. I was greatly exercised in my mind as to whether or not to confide in Tsano, but again, whatever Avgard's motives truly were, it seemed an ungallant as well as an embarrassing thing to reveal what had passed between us, even to Tsano; moreover, might it not strain his credence to the utmost and create some uncomfortableness between us? When, therefore, he asked me how the interview—for such I had made it out to be before I went—had gone, I did not give him a straight answer, but said that she had wanted to question me at length about my life before chance had brought me to Capovolta. This was at least part of the truth. He must have sensed something of my disquiet, however, for I caught him looking at me several times during the afternoon with a doubtful expression, as though he would have liked to speak, but could not bring himself to do so. Wishing to avoid any further questioning about, or discussion of my visit to Avgard's office, I found each time some other subject for the interchange of a few remarks.

I was much exercised in my mind also as to whether I should tell Bran of what had passed, but in effect my dilemma was the same with her as with Tsano, and I decided to hold my peace. I debated within myself as to how I should conduct myself if Avgard issued another invitation. Should I rehearse some excuses which would enable me to refuse without offense? This I could do once or twice, but if she persisted, what should I do then? It so happened that I had never encountered Avgard casually anywhere in the course of work, but only on those occasions when I had been summoned, for my work kept me mostly in the great underground storerooms and machinery rooms of the building to which there was a separate entrance, while supervisors and people of all the higher ranks worked higher up in the building, physically as well as metaphorically, and used various other entrances, none of them on the small alleyway which gave on to the underground areas. Consequently after all my cerebration about how I should respond to a further summons from Avgard should it occur, I was totally unprepared for my next meeting with her, which was when she came one day into the memory bank, where I was working with some of my colleagues. She was ushered in by a small retinue of clerks and my junior personnel, rather like an important surgeon in a hospital surrounded by respectful students and nurses. I knew not where to turn my gaze as in an agony of embarrassment I felt the color rising into my face again. Fortunately for me all my companions were too concerned with this unexpected and important visitor to spare a glance for me. Avgard's own glance swept quickly across the little group of faces in front of her, but without appearing to pause on any. She gave a general greeting to which we all chorused some kind of response. Among the entourage surrounding her was the young woman I have mentioned before who was our immediate supervisor. To her Avgard turned, asking a question which I did not hear, but the young woman looked around in a vague and helpless way and then said generally to the group of us, "Where is Tsano?"

Now I knew that she had summoned him to her office some short time before and he had not returned yet. While I hesitated to draw attention to myself to reply, one of the others volunteered this piece of information, reminding her in a slightly saucy way, I thought, of what clearly she ought to have known better than we did. Fortunately, at that moment Tsano came in with a trayful of recorded cylinders for duplicating and filing, which obviously she had sent him to get. The rest of us were told to get on with our work, which with some awkwardness we did under the gaze of the group of visitors. They moved round our work area, Avgard leading and questioning Tsano. Then Avgard came to each one of us in turn asking us about the particular job we were engaged in at that moment and following that up with one or two general questions about our working conditions, whether we found them satisfactory, whether we had any suggestions for improvement and so on. In each case she stood very close to the person she was questioning, leaning forward to see what he was engaged upon. I was in the middle of duplicating a set of cylinders, the simplest and most ordinary part of our work. However, she asked me to demonstrate to her exactly how it was done, leaning over me and pressing closely against me, as if by accident, as she peered down at the tiny duplicator. There was no noticeable difference in her voice as she spoke to me from the tone in which she conversed with the others, but I could not believe this pressure was accidental and was distracted from what I was doing by the fear that someone might notice. In my confusion I dropped one of the cylinders, and as I stooped to retrieve it, excusing myself to her as I scrabbled at the floor near her feet with my hand, she leant forward to pick the lamp up off my table to hold it so that it lit up that area of the floor, while to my startled horror, with her other hand she began urgently to caress my buttocks. It was, of course, only for a moment, as all the minions leapt forward to take the lamp for Madam, and when I stood up again, scarlet with embarrassment and stuttering further apologies—the retrieved cylinder in my hand—the look I received from my superior as she snapped out, "Really, Klemo, how clumsy you are!" boded me little good, I thought.

Avgard, however, with the same placid, almost motherly good

nature she seemed normally to show, intervened on my behalf, saying, "It really was my fault—I jogged his elbow," and turned away from me without a further glance. Shortly after, she left our department accompanied by her whole party as she had come in.

As soon as the door had closed, a babel of question and exclamation arose. What had caused this unheralded and unheard-of visit from on high? My relief was great that no one questioned me: all were asking Tsano what it portended. He, too, was puzzled, although he said that Avgard had explained that she was visiting all the departments under her control in turn, wishing to see at first hand the conditions in which we worked, and to have the nature of the work, which she knew only in theory, demonstrated practically. While to the others it seemed a matter of wonderment that she should have done this at all, to me it seemed strange that it should have been only the first time, for she was, as I have explained, in charge of all the staff engaged upon our particular type of work, and of the staff of several other departments as well. It never became quite clear as to what her whole list of duties entailed, but one of them certainly was to ensure the well-being of the employees, and how she could do this without frequent visits to their places of work, I could not see. However the others did not see it in this light at all: she was for them a person of far too great consequence to bother herself with such lowly creatures as ourselves.

Consequently for the rest of the day there was much excited speculation as to the true object of her visit. Some thought that she had begun to suspect the inefficiency of our immediate superior and had decided upon this sudden, unheralded personal investigation as a way of possibly catching her out. Others thought that she might have been considering Tsano for promotion, but he himself obviously placed no confidence in that interpretation. One or two of the younger and more frivolous ones also speculated as to whether she had "taken a fancy" to one of them; I do not think they meant this seriously but they sniggered together about it, accusing one another of being her new "favorite." Fortunately they did not include me, but Tsano gave me a long, questioning look which made me think that he suspected something. I determined that when opportunity offered itself I would take him into my confidence and ask him for advice, embarrassing though it might be to do so, for I had great faith in his judgment.

However, no occasion presented itself that day: it was as though everything had conspired against it, for whereas we usually had our break together and were often able to talk privately under cover of the noisy conversations and horseplay of the younger lads, on this particular day Tsano was sent on a mission to another group of offices, from which he had not returned by the break time. We were kept continuously busy during the second half of the day, and just as the time of release approached and I thought I should make an opportunity to stay behind with Tsano for a few minutes talk, I was summoned to our superior's office. Possibly she was afraid that Avgard's visit had been to check on her command of the department, as some of my colleagues had been suggesting; anyway, clearly she had heard of my visit to Avgard's office and wished to question me on its import. Possibly she thought I was Avgard's spy in the department, an illusion uncomfortable for me, and I did my best to dispel it. She was a foolish creature and could not bring herself to attack me outright about this, although I am fairly certain that this is what she wished to ascertain. She gave me a momentary shock by asking me whether Avgard had given me anything during our morning encounter. This query startled me considerably as I did not know whether the caress Avgard bestowed on my inner parts qualified for an affirmative reply. I repeated her question in such a surprised and bewildered way, being uncertain of its implication, that I think she must have been reassured, for she quickly said that of course she was only joking, but she wondered whether Avgard had jogged my elbow on purpose. I decided that half the truth was the best defense.

"I must confess, Madam," I said, "that it really was my fault. She hardly touched my elbow at all. It was just that I felt very nervous and afraid of making a fool of myself, and of course I did! You were quite right: I was stupid and clumsy, but I think the chief [my translation of Avgard's title] was kind enough to understand that her presence had upset me and to make an excuse for me."

"It's honest of you to confess that, Klemo. I understand that she had you up in her office the other day. Did she give you any reason then to feel particularly scared of her?"

"Not really, Madam, I suppose. But she questioned me very keenly about my old life before I came here, and I could not help wondering if there had been some adverse report about my suitability for the work. I have tried very hard and done my best, but I know that a foreigner is likely to be slower learning than someone brought up in the system. I am so happy working here that I should be very distressed if I were not considered good enough and had to leave."

This, of course, was a Machiavellian false modesty. I felt certain that this woman would feel less threatened by someone who appeared to be humble and to underestimate his own capabilities, and I was quite right, for she relaxed immediately and said quite kindly, "No, no, Klemo, I am sure you need not worry about that. Tsano reports very well on your work, and from what I myself have observed, I think you have the makings of a first–class filing clerk. I will certainly reassure the chief about that if she asks me about you again."

The "again" was interesting. So Avgard must already have made some inquiries about me. She had managed in this way to draw very unwelcome attention upon me, and I had to do my best to negate it. I drew a rather exaggerated breath of relief and said, "Ah, Madam, you have relieved my mind greatly. I have been so worried about the whole thing. Of course, during our conversation the chief seemed simply to be interested, as many of my acquaintances are, in whatever I could tell her of the strange habits and customs of my country, but naturally I could not help wondering whether there was some other reason behind it. I am so grateful that you should reassure me about this. Thank you so much."

The poor silly creature smiled quite pleasantly. "Not at all, my dear Klemo," she said. "I'm sure there's no need at all for you to worry. Another time just come straight to me if you have any difficulties, and I'll straighten them out for you."

"That is wonderfully kind of you, Madam," I said, giving her my most–sincere–decent–young–man look as I bowed my way out.

Of course, by now Tsano had gone. I should have no chance to talk to him privately until the next day, for it would have been impossible to go and see him at his home without an explanation to Vrailbran, and this was one of the things I wanted to consult him about: Would he, in similar circumstances, have told his own wife about it or not?

Slowly I picked up my apparatus and stowed my personal belongings in my locker, pondering the while whether or not I should tell Vrailbran of these latest developments—or, rather, how much of them I should divulge to her. Already I was later than usual and would feel obliged to give her some explanation unless she was also late. We normally had a rendezvous at a certain mid–rail stop convenient to us both, but if the other did not show up within twelve minutes of the usual time, then each proceeded on the homeward journey separately. It was far more usual for Vrailbran to be late than for me: her much more responsible job often occasioned her to be delayed, whereas my work normally finished precisely on the hour. If I had to explain my lateness, should I omit all mention of Avgard's amorous advances, or should I tell her something of the truth?

I saw that my duplicating machine had been left with its little red operating button flashing and with a cylinder ready in position. This normally indicated, "Important message. Please play back." Although I assumed that this was accidental and that in my momentary agitation at my summons to the supervisor's office I had left it so, I pressed the playback button almost automatically. I was quite startled when Tsano's voice came up with an eerie clarity in the empty room.

"Klemo, after you had gone up to see Madam, a message came for you to report to Block C at office 35. I sent a message back to explain that you were with Madam. Reply said you were to report at whatever time you came back down. Complete interchange and message follow. Good luck. Tsano."

There was a short pause and then came the first message in a voice I did not know at all: "Klemo–Vrailbran–Zenhild requested report immediately to Block C, office 35." Then came Tsano's voice in reply: "Regret Klemo–Vrailbran–Zenhild momentarily absent. Duty call to Block B, office 6" (that is, the supervisor's office). The tiny cylinder continued to rotate for a moment in silence and then the first voice replied: "Message received. Kindly inform Klemo–Vrailbran–Zenhild to report to Block C, office 35, immediately on return, no matter what time."

With a little whirring noise and a click the cylinder switched itself off, indicating that no further messages had been recorded on it. I sat back in some perplexity. I did know that Block C housed what we would call the "Top Secret" operations of the Transport Company. This probably sounds melodramatic, but I should perhaps now explain what I had only gradually begun to apprehend during the months of my employment at the memory bank.

CHAPTER
6

The City Transport, which, as I have already explained, consisted of the slow–rail, the mid–rail and the fast–rail, was in fact only a small section of a giant operation which controlled the generation of the power supply for the whole country. I have mentioned briefly the existence of the underwater caves around the whole coast of Capovolta, and the system of surveillance and control on Capovoltan waters which was excercised therefrom. What I gradually learned was that the energy which powered the country's transport, its water–recycling system and most of its industry was manufactured in these caves by devices which harnessed the power of the waves and the tides; in fact, these underwater caverns were like a series of giant generating plants. Of course, the defense system was also powered and operated from here as well, and although people were guarded in their talk, I had gathered that Block C was the operational center of this.

It was with some trepidation that I made my way to Block C. I presented myself at the desk in the reception vestibule after handing in my identification cylinder at the door. There was a long wait, far too long for them merely to have been playing back my cylinder, but then without further question I was admitted through the security doors. Here I was met by a group of three huge and stalwart young men. You can imagine that by now I was in some state of alarm. The young men, however, merely stood towering beside me, after nodding quite politely and murmuring a greeting. Almost immediately a young woman came out of an adjoining office, looked at me keenly and searchingly, then asked my name and an explanation of why I had come. This surprised me, for if they did not know, how could I possibly know?

I stammered that I had been sent for. Had I brought with me, she asked, the message I had received? Of course, I had not. It had never occurred to me to do so. She looked at me almost pityingly, I thought, and asked me where I had left it. Indeed I really was not sure by now, but I supposed I had left it in my recording machine as it had been set up by Tsano. In panic I thought of Tsano's "good luck" message at the end and could have kicked myself for not having expunged it. If I was in some trouble, there was no need to have involved him with it, dear, good fellow.

The young woman spoke briefly in an undertone to one of the large young men, and he went out through the great security doors which operated automatically, but at what commanding impulse I never discovered. She then gestured to me to sit down and wait, and returned herself to the office whence she had emerged. After a short interval the young man returned with my recording machine; the young woman emerged again and the machine was set in motion. You can imagine my embarrassment as the whole of Tsano's message was relayed. They all listened attentively, without a flicker of emotion at any point. Then once again the little machine clicked itself into silence, the young woman turned and walked ahead up a long corridor, telling the rest of us to follow. She knocked upon a door at the end of the corridor, was told to advance, and the whole party of us trooped in.

There, gathered at the far end of the room and seated in what looked like a high choir stall set on a dais, were five grave-looking middle–aged to elderly women, of whom Avgard was one. How I cursed the luck that had ever got me involved with that one! I did not know whether to acknowledge our previous acquaintanceship or not. However, she relieved me of this dilemma by greeting me as calmly and kindly as ever by my first name.

"Hello, Klemo," she said. "Now please don't be worried. These ladies are very interested in the report I gave them of my talk with you the other day, and they would like to ask you a few questions if you don't mind.''

The dire warnings I had heard about groups of sex–mad middle–aged women could not but force themselves into my wild and whirling thoughts. Perhaps my dismay was apparent in my face, for the oldest and most dignified of the five said gently, "Please do not be alarmed. There is no need for it, I assure you. All we want to do is to hear from you at first hand about your experiences. Now sit down and make yourself comfortable.''

My experience, I thought in a panic. In God's name what experiences have they in mind? However, I sat down as I was told, and the three stalwart young men and the young woman, whom by now I almost felt to be old and trusted friends, withdrew as commanded. How reluctant I was to see them go!

The dignified woman, who seemed to be the most important one of the group and who mostly acted as spokesman thereafter then said, "Recount to us, if you please, the circumstances of your coming to Capovolta.''

I was appalled by the sound of my own voice, low, frightened and obsequious, as obediently, though haltingly, I began to tell yet again the story of my fateful misadventure.

Soon, by the interjected questions I was asked, I realized that the story was in no way new to them. It was clear that they knew the outlines of it well, but they asked me particulars of the airship and the apparatus aboard it that were of a surprisingly informed and detailed kind. This put me in a very difficult position: it seemed absurd in my present circumstances to refuse to divulge what I knew, or to lie, but nevertheless I had, as had all the crew of the vessel, been sworn to the greatest secrecy before being accepted as an accredited member of the expedition. My courage and spirits had been much restored, however, by the nature of this interrogation, and I thought it best to cast myself upon their mercy by explaining my situation. This I did.

I do not quite know what response I had expected, but certainly not the one I got. Three of them burst into laughter; the other two, that is Avgard and my main questioner, looked at me in a kind of doubting disbelief. It was extraordinarily disconcerting, and I must confess, irritating. I could see nothing comic in what I had said. I surveyed them, perhaps a bit haughtily, in bewilderment and annoyance, saying: "Ladies, I cannot imagine what amuses you and surprises you so vastly in what I have just said."

One of the laughers rolled her eyes drolly and said in the Capovoltan equivalent of baby talk, "Oh, the little man was sworn to secrecy, was he? So he knew all the great big secrets, did he? Oh bless him."

The other two laughed more heartily than before, and even the lips of the chief interlocutor seemed to twitch with incipient laughter, which they tried to suppress. I did not understand this response, but the amused belittlement of me which was so clearly intended angered me intensely. I stood up, bowed stiffly and said, "You must excuse the underdeveloped sense of humor of my race, ladies, in that I find myself unable to share your mirth. With permission, I take my leave of you." With that I turned abruptly and stalked—I suppose that is the word for it—to the door. Of course, the anticlimax was that I was unable to open it. Fuming with anger and humiliation, I turned again with what dignity I could muster and said, "I should be much obliged if you would allow me to go."

My actions had at least taken them by surprise, for the laughter had stopped abruptly and they all looked slightly disconcerted. Avgard said soothingly, "Come, come, Klemo. Don't be so easily offended. Come and sit down again."

"I do not think there is anything to be gained by prolonging this interrogation," I said stubbornly and I suppose rather rudely, "since you are unable to take seriously what I say."

Avgard made no reply, but the older spokeswoman cut across her saying in a sharp, hard tone, "Klemo–Vrailbran–Zenhild, it is not for you to decide how long this interview lasts, nor the degree of seriousness which we are obliged to accord you. Sit down."

The authority in her voice was such that I nearly obeyed her: remember that I had been now for more than a year in a completely subordinate position. However, my old habit of command reasserted itself, and I stood my ground, though replying in a tone more moderate than before.

"Madam, I recognize that you are a person of command and

authority by your presence and by the deference paid to you by your companions. I have, however, no other means of knowing your worth. What means have you of knowing mine? Surely it is a mark of grave lack of judgment, of ignorant prejudice to laugh at what is unusual or ill–understood. There are those in my country who would do the same, but I should not expect to find them in positions of high authority. I am no tyro in the exercise of authority myself, although so much younger and therefore less experienced than all of you, but I should have been ashamed to see any of my peers indulge in ignorant laughter at the expense of a stranger among us. My estimate of your civilization is a high one in many ways, although critical in some, but certainly this I put heavily on the debit side.''

This spirited attack affected them all differently: naturally the laughter of the three scoffers turned to anger, but Avgard and the leader of the group accorded it a surprised respect.

The latter replied to me in much milder and more measured tones: ''Many would regard your attack upon us as an impertinence, Klemo–Vrailbran–Zenhild, and I consider that you have been unwarrantedly harsh in your strictures upon us.'' (I honored her for not dissociating herself and Avgard from the three younger women.) ''However, there is some truth in what you say. I do not know how we are to measure your worth, though, since as you so rightly point out there is no one to speak for you. I think you have perhaps misunderstood the nature of our doubts—and indeed of our amusement. I will tell you frankly that if one of our young men had been included in such an expedition as yours, an unlikely supposition in any case, he would have been there to perform duties necessitating a superior physique, but he would have had no knowledge of the really important or secret facets of the enterprise. For us it is almost as though the cabin boy or ship's cook had been claiming knowledge of a secret navigational device, or of the strategy of a battle.''

Here it was again, the offensive presupposition that I was of an inferior order. I restrained my anger, however, and said smoothly, ''I accept your explanation—or perhaps I should say apology?—for I have seen enough of the inequalities of your society to understand the source of your prejudice. However, if one of you ladies has any knowledge of aerodynamics, you could make some small test of my worth. This is not, of course, my specialization, but I understand well enough the principles on which our vessel was constructed to be able to convince you that I was not exactly a cabin boy on this expedition.''

I chose this field because it would divert them from my own specialism, which I did indeed still hold secret. Unless one of them was at the very spearhead of research in aerodynamics, there would be little danger in discussing the general principles of the vessel's construction. By now I had learned from Tsano and from mathematical works he had lent me enough of the Capovoltan system of mathematical symbols to be able to express the equations of dynamics fairly reasonably.

They were clearly surprised at this, but the leader of the group said in an indulgent tone, ''If you really wish, of course, we will ask our colleague here to test you out.'' She indicated one of the three scoffers, who with a disagreeable, sneering alacrity began to question me in the elementary principles of aerodynamics. I replied to all she asked with such ease and fluency that they were all impressed, and when she paused uncertainly I said, ''Come, come—this is no real test of knowledge or capability. Any intelligent schoolboy interested in the subject would know that.''

I thought, you see, that she was one of those persons who pretend to knowledge which they do not really possess, and I was determined to show her up. She was nettled by the slightly taunting note in my voice, as I had intended, but the result was different from that which I had envisaged. She now began to question me on highly technical and intricate details which only a true aircraft designer could have known. I was, I must confess it, amazed at this, for I had never seen any type of aircraft whatsoever during the whole of my stay in Capovolta and had therefore assumed that their researches were much behind in this field. Fortunately I had the knowledge of physics necessary to understand her questions, though not the direct technical experience, so with a little thought I was able to work out the answers. I think that this is what finally convinced her: she saw that I was having to work things out from first principles and

was not giving her parroted replies that I could perhaps have learned
without understanding their significance.

I apologized a little defensively for my slowness in reply, explaining that not only did I need to work it out, but as my ability to
work directly in Capovoltan symbols was limited, I had to work in
my own way and then transliterate, or transnumerate or whatever
you would call it. She examined my calculations, and I explained to
her as best I could our equivalents, explaining, too, how we worked
to a base of ten in everything instead of twelve. She was greatly
interested, and then suddenly looking up at the others, she said,
almost aggressively: "This young man is a genius. It is a most
extraordinary thing. I have never come across such potential in a
man before."

Now, of course, I was filled with confusion. It is one thing to feel
aggrieved because one is underrated, but quite another to be
acclaimed as a genius when one is quite aware that one's abilities are
certainly not in that category. Moreover, I understood that it was as
much because I was a man as because of my abilities that she was so
surprised. I could not but think of that celebrated remark of Dr.
Johnson's about a woman preaching: "Sir, a woman's preaching is
like a dog's walking on his hind legs. It is not done well, but you are
surprised to find it done at all"—and I found myself wondering that
no woman had smacked his self–satisfied face; at least my new
advocate had not voiced quite such a denigratory statement.

She now turned to me and said with great sincerity, "I do
apologize for my gross misjudgment of you and for my unmannerly
behavior. You had every right to feel aggrieved and to rebuke us as
you did. I hope, however, that you will forgive us."

What could I possibly reply to such a handsome retraction except
to say that I accepted her apology with all my heart and in turn asked
their pardon for my overreaction to their ridicule. And so we
finished that discussion with mutual goodwill.

They all now treated me with far greater respect and courtesy, but
still the catechism continued. I realized I had made a mistake in one
way by revealing my real abilities, for naturally they now understood that I did indeed know all about the true nature of the

expedition. At first they were pressing about the secret purpose of it, but when they saw my unhappy dilemma, they suddenly switched to asking me far more general things about it—and especially exactly what had happened at that fateful moment when I had lost my senses and somehow been cast into the sea. There was little I could tell them beyond what I have told here, but again as they talked I became aware that they knew a great deal more about me than I had supposed. It was clear that they knew of the doctors' reports on my condition and of the inordinate length of time it had taken me to recover my strength.

I cast about in my mind to try to understand how all this was of such interest to them, and finally curiosity getting the better of caution, I asked them outright. There was absolute silence for what seemed a long time, though it was probably no more than half a minute. They appeared quite nonplussed—as though they did not know how to reply, or did not wish to.

Eventually the group's spokesman said gravely, "Klemo, I should like to tell you, but just as you feel in honor bound to respect the secrecy to which you were sworn about your own mission, so we in our turn are bound by factors far beyond our control and cannot honorably tell you much. I can only say that these are not idle inquiries; they are concerned with the security of our land, and indirectly with your own well–being, too. I hope you will accept that as an adequate explanation just as we have accepted your limited and guarded disclosures. If at any time you feel that there is more you can tell us without dishonor, please come straight to me and tell me. I can assure you that nothing you have told us or may tell us will ever be bruited abroad in any way, although naturally we have to report it to the Guardians, since it concerns the security of the state. If in particular you should ever be able to reveal to us whether the purpose of your expedition was defensive or aggressive, we should be grateful."

Strangely, they had not asked me this directly during the whole of the interrogation, nor had I understood that this was where some of their questions were leading.

"That I can answer immediately," I said. "Its purpose was not directly either defensive or aggressive, though more the former than the latter. It was purely a research project, to arrive at knowledge and understanding of certain puzzling factors encountered in our upper–air investigations. The resulting information, had our mission succeeded, could probably have been made use of both for defense and for attack, but the principal reason for the expedition was defensive. That is, it was hoped that the information gained would have enabled us to improve our air defenses and to explain certain strange happenings which I do not wish to disclose.''

It was really quite extraordinary, but I got the impression that they were all much relieved and yet also in some way slightly uncomfortable. This impression was only momentary, for the elderly spokeswoman got up almost immediately, saying, ''Thank you very much, Klemo. You have helped us a great deal and we are grateful. We understand absolutely your reservations about revealing secret matters and respect you for it. I am sorry to have taken up so much of your time. Wait here for a moment and I will send the boys to escort you out.''

As she moved toward the door, the others following her, Avgard drew her aside and murmured something. The spokeswoman looked a bit surprised, but nodded acquiescence. At the door, which opened in front of her without my being able to observe how, she turned to me again and said, ''Your chief wants to have a word with you, so she will let you out afterward. Goodnight.'' With that she was gone and the three younger women with her. The door closed behind them of itself—and I was left alone with Avgard.

She smiled at me very kindly and approvingly. ''Klemo, my dear boy, I'm really very proud of you, and very pleased with you. It was splendid the way you fired up like that and put those three silly creatures out of countenance. It was admirable.''

''Thank you, Avgard. It is kind of you to say so. I'm afraid I was rather rude and must have sounded insufferably conceited, but there seemed to be no other way of getting you all to take me seriously.''

''Ah, Klemo, dear lad, *I* take you very seriously.'' And with that she moved up against me so unexpectedly and so rapidly for a woman of her bulk, that I found myself trapped between her and the choir–stall arrangement where my interlocutors had been sitting. "You look very handsome, you know, when you are angry. You are so delightfully masculine. I find you rather an exciting person."

Her eyes were bright and her cheeks flushed, and she certainly did look excited. I backed away as far as I could, but the choir–stall thing effectively cut off my retreat. She leaned heavily against me and began to fondle me in that area of my person which I have indicated seemed to be thought fair game for any pair of roving female hands in this extraordinary country.

"Avgard, no!" I exclaimed, pushing her hand away in real horror. It seemed not only undignified but almost disgusting to me that this elderly, respected woman should behave in this wanton way.

"There, my dear, don't be shy," she said, now pulling my head down toward hers and pressing her full, wet lips on mine in a way that filled me with aversion. She held me firmly to her and began as it were to rub her person against mine in a highly suggestive way. The whole thing was really horrible.

I felt as Joseph must have done when besieged by Potiphar's wife. Perhaps it will seem that I was unnecessarily nice in my appetites, but I must confess that whereas I could set to work with the best upon a dish of young lamb, especially if dressed with a piquant sauce, elderly, fat mutton has always turned my stomach. The feel of those great, plump, quivering haunches pressed against my person filled me only with repulsion.

I could not help recalling a story told to me by my wife—my real wife I mean in the old life that now seemed so remote that it might have been a dream and yet was still to me my *real* life—about an old professor whose interest in the young women studying under his guidance was centered in other portions of their persons than the minds he was supposed to be training. He began by demonstrating an apparently avuncular interest in the prettier of the young women, but progressed with lightning rapidity to lecherous old satyr, using his privileged position to foist his attentions upon them, making the more timid ones miserably afraid that their rejection of his loathsome advances would tell against them in their final examinations. I could not altogether prevent some sneaking sympathy with this old man at the time, and pointed out to my wife that there were she and her companions looking as delicious and inviting in their form–molding clothes as a tree of ripe peaches with a notice attached saying, "Pick me." She was extremely angry with me and recounted vividly the sensations of disgust which this man's mere physical presence inspired in her—the loose, overhanging belly, the sweaty hands, the pink jowls—and the resentment that she and her friends felt at his refusal to recognize their rights as individual persons to bestow or withhold favors where they chose. Then I had thought how hard these young women were upon this rather pathetic old man (who in fact when I met him on one occasion turned out to be a perfectly respectable man of middle age and not the doddering old satyr I had envisaged), but now I had a great deal more sympathy for and understanding of their point of view.

"Please, Avgard!" I said, trying once again to push her away, but without hurting her, of course. But now she began to mutter endearing words and to pluck at the front of my breeches in the most embarrassing way. How I wished that I had had a chance to talk to Tsano, for perhaps there was some recognized way of dealing with this kind of situation without being unutterably offensive.

In a very little time she would have had my breeches off me, so now I used some force to push her away. It was like trying to fend off a large and loving sea cow, but I managed to separate our bodies by an inch or two.

"Avgard," I said, gently but as firmly as I could, "I'm so sorry, but this is quite impossible. You have been very kind to me and I am grateful, but it is really out of the question that we should"—here I hesitated for somehow I could not find the right words for what was quite, quite out of the question, so I went off on a new tack. "I respect you far too much for any such thing," I ended a bit lamely.

"I could do a lot for you, you know," she said, seizing my hands and pressing them over her bosom. Despite her bulk, it was a surprisingly shapely one, concealed though it was under the tubular dress commonly worn, as I have said, by all Capovoltan women, and perhaps I might have responded more warmly to that in spite of myself if she had not spoken. But that remark really offended me. It was as though she thought my favors could be bought. What sort of person did she think I was?

"Avgard, I know you could—but if I loved you, I should not mind whether you were the humblest person on earth or the grandest. I am very sorry but I do not love you, and although I am grateful for what you have done for me, I cannot pretend that gratitude is love or ever could be."

I had spoken more severely than I meant to, perhaps, for she dropped my hands and said rather sadly and slowly, "I did not mean to try to buy you, Klemo. Please believe me. I only meant that if you really returned my feeling for you, I would marry you and give you everything your heart could desire. I understand you enough to know that an ordinary man's life here in Capovolta is not for you. I see your great potential, not only here," she said with a rueful little laugh, touching my person again, "but here," and she touched my head and ran her fingers gently through my hair. "I would set you upon a real career, and you would never need to break off to look after children because you must realize that I am past child–bearing age—and anyway have had enough children to satisfy any desire to perpetuate my own image, for I have two daughters and two sons by former husbands. I would be content to see your talents recognized by others, and my reward would be to see you one of our few true careermen. But if there is no feeling for me here," and again she touched me, "then it is of no use. But all the same there is a little feeling *here,* isn't there?" She was right, for the feel of her shapely, full breasts in my hands had done what none of her other caresses had—woken the interest of the alter ego whom I carry between my legs.

At that moment I almost loved her indeed. She had understood me as no one else in Capovolta did, and her kind, good–tempered acceptance of my rejection of her advances endeared her to me, but I knew that I could never feel for this woman one–tenth—or, to be Capovoltan—one–twelfth of the feeling I had for Vrailbran.

"Oh, Avgard," I said, "you dear, good woman. Yes, I do wish I could love you. I really do. But I am still quite besotted with my wife. I have only been married a few months, as you know, and she is still a kind of fever in my blood. I have only to *think* of her and my desire rises immediately. I hope you can understand that and not be hurt.''

"That was the nicest, kindest refusal that I have ever encountered, Klemo, my dear. If you should ever change your mind, just let me know. I really think that you will be my last love. It would take a very splendid and talented young man to oust you from your place in my affections. Now run along while I still have some sense and some control.''

Back in the memory bank collecting up the little satchel in which it was customary to carry one's possessions, I sat for a moment to think. I should have to explain my lateness to Vrailbran, who was probably already at home wondering whether some misadventure had occurred. I had never been as late as this before. But how much of all this should I tell her? I could not make up my mind what to do: there seemed to be no reason why I should not tell her of the summons to Block C; no one had asked me not to divulge what had happened there, but I did not want to tell her about Avgard. She had in her way been very kind to me, and it seemed poor repayment to hold her up to ridicule, which would be the effect of the story if I told it to Bran, I felt sure. Moreover the whole episode was closed unless I chose to reopen it. So by the time I reached the end of my journey home, I found myself quite decided: what had happened between Avgard and me should remain known only to Avgard and me.

7

Bran was much interested in my account of my interrogation in Block C and questioned me eagerly about it. We pondered together on the significance of it. There are countries in the world where such an interview would have been an ordeal indeed, and would have left me with a feeling of great unease or even of real menace. This I did not feel at all: their dealings with me had been straightforward and honest as far as was consistent with their duty of guarding the security of the state. The one thing that had puzzled me was the brief moment when I had sensed a mixed reaction to my reply about the purpose of our expedition, as though they were both relieved and yet also slightly uncomfortable.

As I talked to Bran, it became clear to us both that they had wondered if the expedition had had some hostile intent. We also realized that they had more knowledge of it than they could have gained from the accounts of my rescue which had been circulated at the time. The period of my illness and convalescence had been so long that I had ceased to be a nine days' wonder to the populace before I was aware of being so, but now Bran told me what a great public interest there had been for the first few weeks, until some new drama had succeeded mine. She also explained what I had never understood before, simply from not having known the language until the matter had long ceased to be of interest to her and her family, that the doctors who attended me had, in fact, been appointed by the government. Obviously the Guardians had had their fingers on the whole affair right from the beginning. What had suddenly rearoused their interest neither of us could understand. But now Bran suggested something that had not occurred to me, but which took on the aspect of truth the more I thought about it. She thought that by some extraordinary chance our airship must have intruded on Capovoltan airspace, and either in fear that it had some hostile intent or maybe even automatically, the defense system had caused it to disintegrate in the air. She then explained how the integrity of the country was preserved by a defense system which was very simple in conception though difficult, and needing a highly developed technology, to carry out. By some means akin to our radar warning system, they had advance knowledge of the approach, either by sea or air, of any vessel while it was still at a great distance. Since the whole country was united in its desire to remain unknown to the rest of the world as a consequence of the still vivid folk memory of the pink–skinned visitors whose treacherous behavior I have recounted already, their defense mechanism was immediately set in motion. This was the emission of a series of microwaves which distorted the readings of the vessel's instruments, causing it almost infallibly, without anyone on board being the wiser, to set a course which would take it well outside the area of sea and airspace which the Capovoltans deemed it necessary to keep inviolate. If in spite of this, anything managed to insinuate itself through the defense barrier, then it would be challenged and told to redirect its course, or that was the theory of it. If it refused it would be in some way destroyed, though Bran did not know enough about it to tell me how this was done. She said that in her lifetime as far as she knew nothing like this had ever happened, but my arrival on their coasts was such an unprecedented occurrence that she and her parents had speculated whether some such thing had happened but had been kept secret from the public.

I was sure that no kind of communication had been received on board our vessel, nor indeed should we have understood it had it been sent in the Capovoltan language. Bran said, however, that the Capovoltans were aware of international signaling systems, although how this was achieved again she did not know. Eventually we came to the conclusion that the special nature of our vessel and the altitude at which it was traveling had caused it both to enter Capovoltan airspace undetected and to fail to receive the transmission of the challenge. Consequently the security force would have concluded that its intention was hostile and would have destroyed it in the air. Now suddenly we both saw the reason for the mixed reaction to my announcement that the expedition had been a research project only: they were relieved at the reassurance that the outside world had no hostile intentions, at least known to me, but had been made uncomfortable by the realization that my companions had been killed quite unnecessarily. I do believe genuinely that this must have been the reason for their reaction, although most outside observers might think that rather too nice for people engaged in anything as vital as ensuring the security of the state; but however much I may criticize certain aspects of Capovoltan life, their true respect for human life and values is quite undeniable. They are a most humane and scrupulous people even if limited in their imaginative understanding.

One point continued to puzzle me. Why had they allowed me to live and move freely for so long in their community before my interrogation? Why had I not been imprisoned until this had been carried out? Bran, too, was uncertain about this, although she did know that her parents, being highly respected citizens, her mother especially, holding as she did a distinguished position in the government although not herself a Guardian—I imagine she was what we should describe as a very senior civil servant—had been entrusted with the responsibility of exercising a kind of loose surveillance over me. Clearly I was for a long time in no condition physically to cause anyone any worry; moreover even after my recovery I could move nowhere in the community without being immediately under surveillance by every pair of eyes that fell upon me or ears that heard me because of my foreign appearance and speech. Bran also confessed that she had been asked to try to teach me the language and at first had begun this as a duty, but soon found herself falling in love with me. One reason for the long period of probation, as it were, to which she had held me was because it had been necessary for permission to be granted from the very highest source. With great common sense, permission had been given, for indeed what is more likely to bind a man than a wife and home and, as they hoped, children? In this way I should have an acquired loyalty to the community through my family which, together with my isolation from any contact with my own country, would render me harmless.

It was Bran's parents who provided the last piece of the puzzle. We went to spend the new moon holiday with them that month, and the matter still exercising my mind somewhat, I recounted to them all that had passed and our suppositions concerning these happenings. In general they corroborated these as correct as far as their own knowledge went. I still found it a little strange, however, that so much liberty had been granted me—so much that I personally had never suspected that I was in any way under surveillance or had ever been an object of interest and concern to the security force. It was my father–in–law, whom I had come to like and respect as well as pity, who explained to me, very kindly and gently, that no one had ever seriously entertained the idea that I would have any real knowledge or information to impart: they all assumed that I had been one of the crew of the expedition vessel simply in a laboring capacity; that is, to carry out work too heavy or too menial for the more important members of the expedition, whom they assumed to have been women. Had I been a woman, the surveillance would have been a great deal more intense and the interrogation much more severe. Was ever a man placed in a more absurd position than to owe his liberty to such a fundamental and humiliating misconception of his position and his powers?

I kept to my resolution to say nothing of Avgard's part in my story as far as Bran and her family were concerned, but I did in the end take Tsano into my confidence. It fell about in this wise. For several days after my interrogation, Tsano had leave of absence because of his wife's illness; fortunately for him the period this time was not a long one, and his great efficiency in organizing his work meant that for that period the rest of us could between us manage the urgent matters. I was so anxious for him, knowing how important his work was to him, that I took on rather more than my fair share and got permission to stay late each evening for half an hour or so in order to keep things up to date for him. When he returned, our superior, now much more amiably disposed toward me since my interview with her, allowed us to spend an hour together after work that evening for me to explain to him exactly what I had done. I had kept a very strict record of it, but wished to check with him that I had done all correctly. In fact we finished the check very quickly. Tsano was greatly relieved and most grateful, fearing for the consequences if anything had gone wrong during his absence. He told me rather more of his own private concerns than ever before—and then remembered the message he had left for me that evening. Gradually as we talked I found myself revealing everything to his sympathetic ear. He did not make a coarse joke of it, as some men might have done, but listened very gravely and then said, "I thought that something of that nature was happening, but you have nothing to fear from the lady Avgard. She is a good person."

"How did you guess?" I asked. "Is this a well-known foible of hers, perhaps?"

"No, no, you wrong her. She is not at all like ————," and he named an elderly, acidulated–looking woman who ruled one of the upstairs departments with which we sometimes had dealings.

I expressed my astonishment, for I could not imagine this woman to have any sexual feelings at all.

"Ah," said Tsano with a sad little laugh. "You learn to expect it in the most unexpected places, I can tell you! After all, would you have expected it from the lady Avgard?"

"No, I wouldn't, that's true, and had I not experienced it I shouldn't have believed it, either. I am surprised, I suppose, that you did not question what I told you about her."

Tsano said nothing, but simply sat tracing some indefinable pattern on his table with his finger. A sudden illumination burst over me . . .

"Tsano!" I exclaimed, "did you—I mean—did Avgard—well did she—approach you, too?"

Tsano looked up then and said, "Klemo, please promise me you will never discuss this with anyone, not even with Bran."

"Of course, I won't tell anyone," I said. "You are the only person I've told about myself and Avgard. I promise."

He then told me how, when he had first come to the Transport Company, now about ten years ago, as a very young man in the dispatch and receipt section, one of his regular assignments was to deliver and collect from Avgard's own office, then that of the assistant personnel supervisor, and not the chief, as now. She was, of course, a younger and more attractive woman in those days. She was very pleasant to him always, as indeed she was to all her subordinates. She was one of those rare people who are automatically accorded respect but who do not seem to extort it from people. He began to realize that he looked forward very much to his visits to her office, and gradually he began to think that his feelings were reciprocated. But, of course, the unwritten code in this country is such that he could not make the first advances. One day, by chance, she happened to be quite alone in her office when he went to collect her cylinders for dispatch—or perhaps it was not by chance: it could be that she had arranged it. That he would never know. He stood beside her, almost touching her as he recorded his acknowledgment of the receipt of the cylinders, listing them into her recorder, as was the custom. The proximity of her then very comely person disturbed him greatly, and with some embarrassment he was aware that this disturbance was being made visible. She either sensed or saw the stir that she had created, and in a moment they were embracing. He was reticent and did not tell me the whole outcome of this business, but I think I would be correct in assuming that they became lovers for a while. But it was a wretched time, too, for Tsano, for she did not try to deceive him but told him frankly that she loved him and would have liked to marry him, but that she felt she owed a duty to her husband, who was, of course, caring for her children and her home. She acknowledged that she had been trying to resist her desire for Tsano for some time, and that she would perhaps not have succumbed to her passion had she not been fairly certain that she would not have any more children. Thus there was little danger to Tsano in the liaison. Perhaps she hoped that when her children were older she could free herself for Tsano, but the affair dragged on in an alternation of elation and misery for him, and he could see no end to it. That summer during the festival period, when everyone was on holiday and in holiday mood, poor Tsano was alone and wretched, since Avgard had gone off with her family, as was the normal practice. It was then that he met the young woman who eventually married him. She fell in love with him immediately and wooed him tempestuously. When Avgard returned, he told her about this girl. She asked him to tell her honestly which of them he loved and he had to confess that he loved them both, in different ways perhaps. Avgard he loved and was grateful to, for she was his first real love. I think he meant that he had never slept with a woman before and she had been a wonderful lover, but the secrecy and uncertainty had begun to turn it sour for him. With Aniad, his future wife, things were straightforward and in the open. He was hopelessly torn between the two of them. It was Avgard who in the end with great wisdom and some self-sacrifice had told him to marry Aniad, for she could see that it was the best thing for him. He said she had been wonderfully kind and understanding, and that had she not freed him, as it were, he could never have broken away from her.

I found this story very touching, but I could not quite see why Tsano was so sure that Avgard had not made a habit of such liaisons with other young men who took her fancy and were accommodating. I did not put it quite so crudely to Tsano, for I could see that in some strange way he was still very much bound to Avgard. He merely smiled and said that if I cared to listen carefully to the gossip among the young lads in our department, I would soon know why. It is true that I rarely listened with much attention, for as I say I never heard them discuss any serious subject at all, and moreover many of them spoke with a kind of slurring speech or dialect which I found difficult to follow, and often they used terms which I did not understand. If I asked Tsano or Vrailbran they would explain them, but usually insisted that the words were those of a jargon current today among the young, but which would tomorrow be replaced by some other coinage and that it was better for me *not* to learn these slang terms which I might use incorrectly or even offensively to other people. Of course, I was aware that the names of the women in the office and gossip about them were common interchange among these lads, but that was all. Now Tsano explained that any indiscretion or mark of favoritism was within minutes common gossip in the office. Avgard's name was never mentioned, while the woman he had named was known to them all. She expected as a right to bestow caresses where she wished and if refused could "turn very nasty indeed," as these young lads put it. Fortunately for me, the very young lads were her particular fixation, and part of the art of survival was to keep out of the way as far as possible and then to be accommodating if cornered, or otherwise one was likely to find one's services dispensed with. The young men at risk usually tried to go about in pairs if they were anywhere in her vicinity, but even this was not always proof against her appetites!

I was greatly incensed by this account and asked if there were no means of redress. I could see that individuals could do little against someone so powerful, but had they no organization something like our trade unions which could make representations on their behalf? Tsano was much amused at this suggestion. He explained that if the women were threatened by some sort of reprisal of this kind, a great number of these young men would never get themselves married. Very frequently liaisons begun in this slightly discreditable way did in fact end in the woman divorcing her by now more elderly husband and marrying one of the young men, who thus acquired a position and status impossible for him otherwise. Naturally this did little to reconcile me to the social organization and customs of Capovolta, and most especially to the position of men as second–class citizens whose position and status in society depended for the most part not on their own capabilities and qualities but upon those of their wives.

But Avgard was, Tsano thought, truly one of the few women who had a real understanding of and sympathy for the position of able or ambitious men in their society. She had been, maybe still was, a highly sexed woman for whom, however, there was more to the relationship than a simple sexual satisfaction. He knew that she sought a fulfilling relationship such as she had not found in her two fairly conventional marriages—a union of mind and spirit as well as of body—and in each of us she had found the kind of man with whom such a union might have been possible. Poor Avgard—old now and no longer physically attractive, a distinguished career behind her, home, husband, children, too, but not the one thing she had longed for—and now it was too late to hope for it. Tsano thought she was very unusual in being so perceptive, and in her ideas, for most women seemed perfectly content to marry one of the strong, handsome young men who appeared to abound in the country, and thereafter to devote themselves to their chosen career while the young men wilted into a depressed and early middle age as they dutifully tended the children and the home.

CHAPTER
8

Slowly the pattern of Capovoltan life and society was revealing itself to me, but there still remained a number of puzzling factors. For example, I worked for the City Transport Company, but there was really no visible "transport" in our meaning of the term—no buses, no cars or trucks for transporting people and goods from one point to another. Of course, I could see that the three types of moving roadways were part of the answer to this, but often I felt that it would be infinitely quicker and easier to have some private means of transport such as I had been used to at home instead of depending entirely on the public system, excellent though that was.

I had tended to assume that such inventions had not been thought of here, and I decided that I could probably do the community a service as well as make my own name and fortune by designing and building some type of conveyance of this kind. I had already begun on the drawings in private and for my own pleasure in design as much as anything, but I realized that before I went any further I should have to decide on the source of the power that was to drive my machine in order to incorporate a suitable unit in it. I had seen little evidence of the use of any combustible fuel as a source of energy, but that it existed somewhere in Capovolta I did not doubt. I questioned Bran about this, and she agreed that plenty of reserves of oil and a coal–like substance existed, for, she said, once upon a time their heating and cooking facilities had depended on these. I began to explain to her then what I had in mind, for I should need her help to get in touch with sources of supply.

Instead of being respectfully amazed at my inventiveness as I had expected, she replied quite sharply that such contrivances were forbidden by law and rightly so.

"Forbidden, Bran?" I said. "What do you mean? If they have never existed, how can they be forbidden?"

"Why do you imagine they never existed?" she asked. "If you go to the Folk Museum [I suppose that is the best equivalent of what she meant] you'll see it is full of such superannuated devices."

I could not really believe that she had understood me, and began again to try to explain my design. But she cut short my explanation with some impatience, saying she perfectly understood the principle, for although such machines were no longer allowed, care was taken in the course of a child's education to see that the basic technology was understood. There was a determination to pass on the knowledge of the advances made even when they were superseded. At first this seemed a strange proposition and an unlikely one to me, but then I thought of the way in which a whole mass of long dead matter is incorporated in our own educational system either because it is considered a valuable part of the history of our culture, or because no one has ever thought to challenge its usefulness. At the moment, however, I was less concerned with the philosophy of education than to understand why, if these machines had been invented, they were now forbidden.

"For a whole number of reasons," said Bran reflectively. She paused. "The most important one, I suppose, is the rate at which they use up nonrenewable resources. What is the true value of machines which are designed to exhaust the source of energy which powers them? If you think about it, you will see that really they have what could be called a negative value: a whole community changes its way of life and comes to depend on a thing which of its nature must cause its own demise. Of course, it is even more negative than that, because we found that they caused grave pollution of the environment as well. Perhaps that is the most important reason after all, for it is against our religious teaching."

I found that most strange and most interesting, for everyone had been so reticent about religion that I thought perhaps they had none, although Bran had said that they did. However, she had never wanted to discuss it. Now I seized the opportunity to ask exactly what religious tenets were broken by the use of the combustion engine. Of course, I suppose I could not quite keep a slight mocking note out of my voice, because you must agree that it seemed rather an absurd religious principle on which to take a stand.

Bran eyed me gravely and said, "Klemo, you are usually surprisingly perceptive and intelligent for a man. It is not like you to ridicule things you do not understand, and it does not become you."

I was immediately ashamed of myself although still rather skeptical within. I apologized and begged her to explain to me nevertheless, for I truly did not understand in what way such machines could offend religious principles.

"Our most important commandment is to honor the whole creation. All the rest of our religious principle and practice is based upon this. We do not know whence we come nor whither we go; all we know with any certainty is the creation as we perceive it. That it may be a very distorted and partial view we have is probably true, but all we can do is to try to understand more of it, in a spirit of true humility before its wonders, whether these seem to our partial gaze good or bad. Anything we do, which we need not do, which alters the environment so as to make it less hospitable toward our descendants seems to us wrong. For this reason we no longer use up nonrenewable resources if we can find any alternative. So, all our power—for transport, for heat, for light, for manufacture—comes from sources which occur naturally and either renew themselves, like the waves and winds and tides, or are gradually exhausting themselves of their own accord, like the sun or volcanic heat."

That there was a great deal of sense in this view of the universe I could not deny, but it seemed to me to lack the force of a religious precept, and I said so.

"What," asked Bran, "creates 'the force of a religious precept,' as you phrase it? We know enough of other people's religious beliefs to realize that the most dearly held tenets of one group can be anathema to another. There is no outside absolute of which we can have certain knowledge against which to measure our beliefs or from which we can derive an immutable authority. If one is to be honest about this, the religion of a people depends not at all on outside authority, but on the body of belief inculcated into the children in each generation."

"Do you then have no belief in a Person who rules the universe?" I asked, for I did not know the word for God. "It is true that in our land many people lament the decline of religion, but I suppose most people still accept the existence of such a Person, although they may now be in much more doubt as to His true nature."

Bran laughed and said, "I'm sorry, Klemo, but the very idea that you should conceive of the First Cause—for I think that is what you mean—as masculine—*His* nature, you said—is to us almost incredible. Of course, I agree that none of us can have any idea of the true nature of the First Cause, but if sex must be ascribed, clearly it should be feminine. Early on in our history, before the vast and complex nature of the universe was realized, our ancestors did worship such a personalized creator—the Great Mother—the Genetrix of everything. Now we understand that that was a very simple and partial view, but it is, I know, common to most of the old religions. It was intuitively understood that the feminine principle was the ruling power of the world."

What on earth was one to make of this? I could only feel what an incredibly biased view this civilization took of everything, even when it was trying to be broadminded. The old joke about the suffragette who admonished her fellow prisoners to "pray to God, ladies, and She will help you" occurred to me, but though I had found it funny when I first heard it, clearly Vrailbran would not think it so, and now even I wondered quite why it had seemed so delightfully ludicrous—no funnier really than "He will help you"—and from the Capovoltan point of view, infinitely more logical and likely.

Whatever one thought about that, my "invention" was abortive, and all my rosy dreams of future success and fame stillborn, for I could hardly set myself up as a one–man revolution against one of the sacred principles of the state religion, even if I was myself a skeptic. Of course, there were other reasons, too, Bran explained. If everyone were to own such a vehicle, the resultant density of traffic and of air pollution would be intolerable; if only a small section of the population were to be allowed to own them, then what was the criterion to be? It was feared that it would cause envy and social divisiveness between those who had vehicles and those who did not. It was regarded as a healthy thing that everyone, Guardians included, had to travel in the same way. Exceptions were made for invalids and disabled people, of whom in fact I saw few. These people were allowed a small wheeled carriage which could be put on to the moving roadways and anchored there. Public responsibility was very high about this, and such travelers always had precedence at mid-rail stops and so on.

I could see that there was something to be said for the social concern behind this strict regulation, although I should have elevated none of it to the level of religious principle, but it seemed a sad discouragement to inventiveness and to individual initiative. However, although I might regret this, I saw that I must also accept it.

As Vrailbran was in an expansive mood and readily answered my questions, I went on to try to satisfy my curiosity on a number of allied subjects. For instance, I had understood from previous conversations that boys and girls received substantially the same education here in Capovolta, yet the upper echelons in medicine and other professions, in industry and in public life generally were staffed almost exclusively by women. Why? It is true that there were a few men in positions of power, but the proportion was a very small one. The achievements of these men, however, were cited as proof that equality of opportunity existed, but also that the general intellectual caliber of men was inferior to that of women. Why in *our* society did a nondiscriminatory system of education produce almost exactly the opposite results?

One unusual fact of the Capovoltan system had interested me very much when I first heard of it. This was that at the age of about thirteen there was a compulsory break in the schooling system, and all children, girls as well as boys, academically able as well as less academically able, were distributed throughout the various practical trades and crafts on what might be loosely described as an apprenticeship basis for a period of about a year and a half. The reasons for this were manifold. To begin with, it was generally recognized that this is a difficult stage in the development of the human young: they are no longer undeveloped, totally dependent children, nor are they fully matured adults; they resent the old constraints and are often unwilling to apply themselves to learning or to accept discipline. Thrust into the adult world, which is where they desire to be at that time, they find themselves subjected to the different but more effective disciplines and pressures of physical work. In addition, they receive firsthand experience of the working world in at least three or possibly four practical areas during the eighteen moons, so that even the most remote academician or most elevated politician in the country has direct knowledge of the manual crafts and skills on which the country's economic stability depends, and of the working conditions of the largest section of the community. They keep a tenuous hold on the more academic side of their education during this period by regular courses for two days out of the twelve working days between each full– and new–moon holiday. At the end of the eighteen–moon period, they return to full–time schooling for at least one more year. The more able pupils stay on and continue their formal education; the less academically able, as with us, leave school and rejoin the working world.

There seemed to me to be a sound bottom of sense in this idea, and at first I could not see how it could be prejudicial to a boy's educational chances any more than to a girl's—and yet a far smaller proportion of boys continued in full–time education than of girls once the statutory time had been completed. I cross–examined Vrailbran about the methods of selection which decided who stayed on at school and who left, and here lay at least part of the trouble in my opinion. Ability and aptitude tests were carried out *before* the apprenticeship period; that is, when the children were about thirteen. Now it is true, I believe, that girls on the whole show greater promise than boys at that particular age since they mature more quickly, and so far more girls than boys reached the required standards. The factor of expectation also comes in here, for although in theory the children had a free choice of the trades where they would get their first experience of the working world, there was a tendency if they showed little academic promise to advise them to choose the areas where they were likely to end up during their adult working life. So to low achievement was added low expectation. A further factor, too, was that many parents considered prolonged education a waste for boys, who, whether able or not, would most likely marry and be absorbed by the care of their families. That this was an incredibly shortsighted view did not prevent it from being quite widely held, however, according to Vrailbran, and this disadvantaging of boys became a self–perpetuating system.

I was outraged by the unfairness of it, but Vrailbran could not be induced to see it my way.

"Look, Klemo," she said, "you must face the facts, however unpalatable you find them. The boys have equal opportunity, but far fewer are capable of using it. That's all there is to it. On the whole people do find their own level and enter the trades or professions for which their talents suit them. Of course, there will be exceptions to this, but I do assure you that they are few."

Again I tried to point out how the selection procedure told against the boys, but she would have none of it, simply saying, "But, my dear, you are giving your own case away. Yes, it is true that in general girls do better at selection time than the boys do; I'm afraid they simply are more able. We don't know quite why this is, for our geneticists assure us that the mechanism of inheritance is the same in both cases, only that girls have two X chromosomes where boys have an X and a Y, and though these primarily determine sex, they probably determine certain other characteristics, too. The Y chromosome is like a mutilated X chromosome, I understand, so we can only assume that boys are girls manquées!" (I translate freely into our own terms here).

"Girls manquées indeed! My dear, dear Bran, if you will study the anatomy of both sexes you will see who is manqué and who is not!" Of course, here I was thinking of Dr. Freud's ingenious theories about penis envy in women.

"Indeed?" she said coldly. "And where, my dear Klemo, have you the apparatus for housing and feeding a fetus for nine moons and then bringing forth a complete and fully formed human being? We find a great deal of mental instability here among men—the incidence is far higher than that among women—and our mind doctors believe that often it is due to a subconscious envy of the higher development of the female. Of course, I myself think this is a rather far–fetched explanation, but there may be something in it.''

I was greatly surprised to hear this, for of course in our society we have the reverse problem—a far greater degree of mental instability among women than among men. How could one reconcile two such diverse findings? As for the supposed womb envy among men, for this was what she meant, I have always regarded this as one of those absurd fancies that psychologists dig up to try to explain things they do not understand. I was, however, reminded of the tantrums of my small three–year–old nephew when he first realized that he would not be able to give birth although his baby sister would. He flung himself down in a passion of rage and grief, screaming, ''I want to have babies, too. Yes, I will, I will. I'm going to have babies, too!'' His mother explained that he could be a father, though not a mother. The tears stopped miraculously as he sat up, saying eagerly, ''Oh, can I have motorcars then instead of babies?''

To return from this digression. I wanted to get away from the discussion of genetics and back to what I could only regard as a kind of semiconscious social engineering. Boys may not have been deliberately educated and groomed for the humbler role they mostly played in society, but that is the effect that was produced. I had noticed, for example, during my long illness that there was certainly a preponderance of women in the medical profession, yet on inquiry I found that the actual nursing of patients was done by men. Now why was this? Vrailbran's answer was immediate: of course, nursing was basically a man's profession. It required more physical strength and stamina in the handling of heavy patients and so on than could possibly be expected of women. What was I to say to that? I could only fume impotently at the topsy–turvy logic of it all, and knowing that I should lose my temper if we continued this discussion, I changed the subject.

CHAPTER
9

It was drawing on toward the winter solstice and the associated holiday. I had still been convalescent at this time the previous year and had lived so quietly and in such seclusion at the house of Bran's parents that I had been unaware of all the bustle and excitement normal to that time of year. Now I felt it in full, for the young men in the office were almost beside themselves with excitement. They were forever exercising their bodies, rubbing nourishing oils into their muscles and generally behaving like athletes before some great contest.

I commented on this to Tsano, who said, "It is only natural. It's the one chance any of them get of some excitement, and perhaps of becoming famous."

"Why, Tsano? I don't understand. Are they really preparing for some athletic contest then?"

"Of course," said Tsano. "Didn't you know? It is the time of the Great Games, you see."

I did not see, and Tsano began to explain. During the long holiday round the winter solstice, almost the whole population adjourned to a huge natural arena on a plateau in the central mountains of the country. Here physical contests of every kind were arranged for both sexes, and naturally here it was, because of their superior physique, that the young men came into their own. There was fencing, wrestling, boxing, unarmed combat of every kind, foot-races, jumping, swimming, various games, both in teams and as individuals, water sports on the huge lake and the violent rivers that fed it, skiing and sledding on the snow–covered flanks of the surrounding volcanic mountains: the number and variety of events were endless. The outright winner of any of these contests was a feted national hero for a brief while, and the prizes were special privileges for the rest of their lives, such as the best seats at future Games, or an extra holiday at the expense of the rest of the community.

There were training facilities at points scattered over the country. The nearest one was reachable by our young men fairly easily by fast–rail, and this is where many of them exercised each evening after work. Indeed, it was rare to find a single one of the younger men still on the premises after the official end of the working day. I had understood, of course, that some communal activity went on somewhere, but had not realized its nature.

"But, Tsano, you never go on these things, do you? I never heard you mention them, at least."

"No, I haven't done anything like that since soon after I was married. Most of us have to give up when we marry. There really is no time if you continue to work as well as run the house, or if you have children. Some people manage it, if they are exceptionally good at something and neither work nor have children, but it is mostly the younger ones who can train regularly and who therefore win the contests. I haven't been up to the Winter Games at all now for several years."

"But surely it must be rather exciting just as a spectacle, even if you don't take part?"

"Yes, it is, but it is also very exhausting, and my wife's health has been such that she has to take things very quietly. There is a great deal of rowdyism up there, and almost no Games ever end without bloodshed one way or another."

"Bloodshed? That sounds rather melodramatic, Tsano. What do you mean?"

"Oh, well. Fights between rival teams or their supporters and so on. If you go, you will soon understand what I mean. The Guardians are rather worried, I believe, because this kind of thing has been getting worse of late years."

"I should dearly like to attend the Games, all the same. I wonder if Bran normally goes. She hasn't mentioned it at all."

"Then probably she doesn't usually go, either."

That evening I asked Bran about the Games and whether she normally attended them or not.

"I used to go very regularly, but last year you were here and I decided not to. And now that we are married, I think I find our life together satisfying enough. I'm not sure that I want any more excitement."

She looked at me with such a delicious, demure little smile that I fear our evening repast was unduly delayed that night and I thought no more of the Games until I was back at work and saw once again the great preparations our young men were making. I determined to tackle Bran about it that evening more soberly.

"Bran, darling," I said, "please let us talk sensibly about our plans for the winter holiday. Could we not go up to the Games for at least part of the time? I know that it will not be as new and as interesting an experience for you as for me, but I should dearly like to go, just to see what it's like."

She looked at me with a doubtful air. "I really am not very keen to take you there, my dear, to tell you the truth. All the rougher elements of the populace will be there, and often it erupts into physical violence. I do not want to expose you to the dangers."

"Bran, surely you can trust me to look after myself. You know that I'm no weakling, now that I've properly recovered my strength. And why should you think there is more danger for me than for you? Is it because I am a foreigner?"

"Partly that, and partly because naturally the troubles always break out among the men rather than among the women, though I will admit that they are not above criticism: there is a great deal of licentious conduct among them, though little violence. I should not like there to be any trouble between us, my darling, as a consequence."

"Bran!" I exclaimed. "You cannot mean that you fear I shall desert you for someone else! Surely you know how much I love you?"

"You do not quite understand things, Klemo. The atmosphere up there is very heady: there is a general feeling of license around, and behavior is tolerated at the Games that would be severely reprimanded anywhere else or at any other time. It is a special place and time, you see. It is difficult for anyone to be certain of how they will behave in those conditions, when the normal restraints do not operate. You must understand that all the strongest and most daring young men will be competing in the sports, and all the most handsome in face and figure will be taking part in the body competition. Of course, people do get rather swept away by it all."

"Body competition? What on earth do you mean, *body* competition? What an unpleasant–sounding term!"

"Do you think so? I don't know what else one could call it. The competition is to choose the handsomest and most attractive body in the land. That really is rather fun, you know. One cannot help enjoying looking at gorgeous men, after all, can one? Or wanting to touch them, either?" she added, beginning to caress me in the surprisingly immediate and intimate way she had.

I held her off, however, for I did not at all like the preceding remarks. "Are you trying to tell me that this is some kind of beauty competition for men?" I demanded.

"Ah—so you have it, too, in your country, do you? Yes, you could call it a beauty competition, I suppose. It is really to choose the most beautiful man, but we call it a body competition here."

"As I do not intend to compete in this nauseating display," I said stiffly, "I cannot see why you should imply that it constitutes some sort of threat to me."

"No?" she said in an enigmatic tone. "In that case, of course, there is nothing to worry about, is there?"

I sensed that she was mocking me in some obscure way, but I could not understand how or why. I was annoyed, and pride made me wish to pursue the matter and get to the bottom of it. Wisdom and experience dictated otherwise, however.

I took her into my arms instead and kissed her, saying, "I'm sorry, Bran. I did not mean to be critical. I suppose it is just that I had set my heart on going to the Games, and like a spoiled child I became bad tempered when thwarted. Forgive me, please? And, of course, if you are so against it, we won't go."

She saw through this immediately, but gave in laughingly. "Ah, you could wheedle anything out of me and you know it. All right, we will go to the Games, my dear, but if you do not altogether like the consequences, you cannot say that I have not warned you."

"Darling Bran, you are the kindest wife on earth, I do believe," I exclaimed, for the prospect of going elated me, perhaps beyond reason, but by now I had begun to miss so much the liberty of decision which I had enjoyed in my old life that any change from this perpetual subservience and dependence upon others seemed an enfranchisement indeed. I had never fully appreciated my freedom when I had it; perhaps up in the freer, exciting and excited atmosphere of the Games, I might feel my own man again.

There were still some weeks to go before the winter holiday, and never did time seem to move more slowly or the routine tasks of planning meals, buying food and supplies and looking after the house seem so relentlessly recurrent and boring. In the early days of our marriage my lack of familiarity with Capovoltan customs had perhaps been fortunate for me: my father–in–law and Bran, too, had understood that I had had little of the experience required to run a home efficiently in Capovolta. Consequently my father–in–law had helped me greatly with his advice on the planning of my work, on the best places to shop and on the preparation of food, while Bran had doubtless been more helpful and accommodating than many Capovoltan wives, although I have to confess that she gave a minimum of help and exacted the maximum of appreciation for it. If she made a bed, or helped to prepare a meal, or brought in some shopping, I knew that I was expected to express gratification and appreciation, whereas I performed these tasks regularly with no recognition of any kind. Privately I thought I worked as hard as Bran at my job in the Transport Company: it was considered less important and responsible, certainly, but it required a high degree of concentration and efficiency and usually kept me busy without any chance to relax for more than a few minutes during the whole of the day. Bran, after all, was much more mistress of her own time; no one questioned her if she took more than the regulation half–hour break, or fulfilled some private commitment during her working day, provided, of course, her work was not neglected. Why then was it considered normal that she should return home declaring herself quite exhausted, while I battled with the shopping crowds on my way home, prepared the meals and looked after the home generally in my so–called spare time? I loved her and gladly did things for her, but I wanted what I did to be recognized as such—not "my duty" any more than it was hers, but a service or a favor done with love and recognized as such, just as I gave recognition and appreciation for what she did. If, indeed, my superior strength and physique made it easier for me to combine the two jobs (one outside and one inside the home) than it would have been for her, I still wanted recognition that I was doing both. I sometimes castigated myself for this and felt almost guilty that I should not be able to accept the situation as equably as most Capovoltan men, including Tsano, appeared to do. I tried to analyze why I felt resentful as I knew I often did, although I might swallow it down and not show it. It seemed to me that the seat of my whole disquiet was the subtle implication that I was in some way an inferior, a kind of loved and licensed servant. It was less the doing than the assumption that I *should* do that irked me. The prospect of the winter holiday seemed to promise a release, albeit brief, from these tensions, and I looked forward to it with great expectation.

A week or so before the holiday was due to begin, Bran announced that she thought we should have some of our friends in for an evening. My feelings about this were mixed, for much as I enjoy parties, I knew with a horrible sinking of the heart that for this one, for the first time in my life, I should bear the main responsibility. Bran would expect me to plan and prepare in the way that her father did when they entertained at home, and the prospect filled me with dismay; already she was suggesting numbers that seemed astronomical to me.

"Bran, I'm so sorry, but I really don't think I can manage it alone. I just haven't enough experience in catering yet. Couldn't we get some help somehow?"

"But I'll help you, of course, Klemo. You know I will."

"Will you really, Bran? It would be a great help if we could plan it together; if you could tell me what food we ought to have, for instance."

"Oh—food—well, really, Klemo, that is your department, you know. I don't mind what we have. Whatever you think."

"But, Bran, you know I don't know nearly as much as you do about Capovoltan food—and especially the sort of food you have at parties. You must have been to plenty. You must know the kind of thing we ought to have."

"Oh, well, the usual sort of thing, you know. Bits of this and that."

"Yes, Bran, but *what?*"

"Those little round things filled with savory sauce, for instance. They are very good—not difficult to make, I shouldn't think."

"*What* little round things, and *what* savory sauce? And how exactly do you make them?"

"Really, Klemo, how should I know? You do seem very helpless. Get yourself some 'Hints on Party Catering.' There are plenty of them about."

"Bran, how would it be if *you* got them and *you* did the catering for this party? Then we should be certain to get it right. After all, I might make the most awful hash of it, being a foreigner. But I'll help you, of course."

She stared at me—between annoyance and bewilderment, not at all sure how to take this. Then she decided to take it at face value and said, "Nonsense, Klemo. You are getting very good at things. You'll do it beautifully, I'm sure."

"I can't do it, Bran. Really I can't, if you won't help me."

"But I *will* help you, Klemo. I've told you I will. But you must see that this cooking business really isn't my job."

"And what, pray, makes you think it is mine? You know that the people you wish to invite are mostly your friends; Tsano is the only real friend I have, and he and I do not need a party to cement our friendship."

"Tsano!" she exclaimed angrily. "I warn you, I won't have that woman in the house."

"What woman?"

"You know perfectly well—Tsano's wife, of course. I have never liked the creature and I'm certainly not going to start making a friend of her now. She is a conceited ass who thinks everyone has done her out of the job she ought to have. It's her own stupid fault for being so utterly wet." I render this extremely colloquial speech into the nearest equivalent I can find in English. I may say I had never heard Bran use such expressions before, but I was too angry at the time to think about it, and only later did I wonder at the vehemence of her utterance. Now I quite boiled over at the implication that I was not to be allowed to ask Tsano to this wretched party.

"In that case," I said, "you are at liberty to entertain your friends in your own way and by yourself"—and I left the room.

What a storm in a teacup, you will think. Indeed, it does seem a ridiculous and undignified quarrel, and I am not too pleased with my own behavior when I recall it. I record it, however, to demonstrate the irritations and frustrations of my life at that time, and Bran's total lack of comprehension of my difficulties or my feelings.

Yes, of course, we made it up, with me wretchedly and cravenly apologizing and saying I would do my best, and with Bran saying of course she did not want me to take on something I found too difficult. But in the end the idea of a big party was quietly shelved, and instead we had a few friends of Bran's in to the kind of simple meal that I was accustomed to prepare. So the question of Tsano's wife was not raised again; nor, at least for the moment, that of where the responsibility should rest.

The occasion did not pass off, though, without incident. Bran, as anxious to make amends as I was, assisted me more than usual that evening, carrying in dishes and helping me to wait on the rest of the party. After the supper, as I was serving the various little delicacies with which it was customary to finish a meal, while Bran was carrying out some of the empty dishes, one of the other men said to me, "What a marvelous girl Vrailbran is, doing so much to help you. You're a very lucky man, you know. Yram never helps me like that, do you darling? Never lifts a dish!"

What was I supposed to say to this? Why did no one think that Vrailbran was a very lucky *woman* to have all this done for her?

Yram, a pretty and very intelligent young woman who was making a name for herself in the law courts, threw back her head and laughed charmingly, "No, I'm afraid not. It's not my thing at all, you know. Don't know a kettle from a frying pan" (the nearest I can get to the idiom).

"It isn't really as difficult as all that, you know," I said. "I'm sure you could learn. I'm afraid it wasn't my thing either, as you put it, but it's surprising how quickly one can learn if one puts one's mind to it."

There was a slight pause, and then Yram gave another of her tinkling, charming laughs. "Ah, yes, I suppose I could learn, as you say, but my work takes all my energy, and, anyway, why should I bother since I have Drynco to do it for me?"

"Why, indeed," I said, "if Drynco is content to spoil you so outrageously. What an extraordinarily lucky woman you are—although, now I think of it, I am not quite so sure. Perhaps it isn't very complimentary of Drynco to treat you as though you were either infirm and incapable, or a half-wit."

I could almost hear the shudder that went through them all, and Bran said in a voice of ice, "Klemo!,", but before she could continue I took her hand and said in a teasing, indulgent tone, "Now you see *I* on the other hand prefer to have a full-witted woman who if driven to it can actually boil an egg. You see, she's nearly as good as a man, aren't you, darling? But how glad I am that you actually aren't one, though!" and I kissed her fondly.

None of them knew quite how to respond to this. Bran thought it best to laugh as at some absurd caprice of mine, and one of the other women said in an amused but slightly nettled tone, "What do you mean, *nearly* as good as a man, indeed?"

"I mean that most of us men can do an ordinary job to earn our living as well as looking after the house and so on. As far as my observations of Capovolta go, it is most unusual for women to do this—so clearly they are not as able as men, are they?"

"Come, Klemo," said Bran. "A joke is a joke, but this one has gone far enough."

"Oh, yes, if you think so, my dear. I could easily take it a lot further, but I will not do it if you prefer me not to."

Of course, it was foolish of me to take issue over it, for it embarrassed Bran and antagonized the other women, as they all knew that for all my lighthearted tone there was an edge to the banter.

CHAPTER
10

At last the great winter holiday had come. The last day before the office closed was quite extraordinary. Almost no work was done: everyone was in a highly excited, euphoric mood, and people wandered about from office to office, greeting and being greeted, wishing luck to other contestants at the Games and being wished luck. Tsano and I felt quite left out: I had not realized before how many of my colleagues were taking part in one or other of the various competitions. It really seemed as though everyone except ourselves was competing in some capacity or another. I began to wish that I had done some training and so might have entered for something, not with any idea of winning, of course, but simply to feel a part of this great jubilant throng of excited young men and women. There was a much greater camaraderie than formerly between the young men, who were underlings, and the young women, who already had a foot on the lower rungs of the promotion ladder. It was almost as though some of the boys were being accorded an unusual deference, even a kind of precedence.

I mentioned this impression to Tsano, who confirmed that it really was so. These were the young men who were regarded as favorites and were tipped to win in one of the events. I understood and sympathized with the zeal with which these young men cultivated their bodies since it earned them a status and a recognition which otherwise they would certainly never know.

Their excitement communicated itself afresh to me, and I longed to be away home and off to the mountains. I must here confess that Bran had done all the planning and made the necessary arrangements for our stay up at the Games. She had simply taken charge of it once the decision was made and gone ahead with a minimum of consultation with me; I was grateful for this, but felt that perhaps I had not taken a fair share in dealing with all the troublesome detail. I said something of this to Bran, and thanked her for doing it all. She was pleased, but only said, "There you are, you see—I do do my share after all." It would have been churlish to rejoin, "Why, yes, indeed, once a year, so you do"—so I said nothing, but of course she really had still not understood my point of view.

When I finally left the office that last day before the holiday, Tsano and I still did not know whether we should see one another again before the next work session opened a month later. It was late to find a place to stay for the Games, but he was still hoping that his wife might decide to come up. The idea of our being up there together pleased him: he had felt that it was so long since he had been that he would find himself out of things and at a loss, but the thought of having a friend there in similar circumstances made him wish to come. His wife, however, had not wanted to at first; now he thought she was beginning to change her mind. My feelings about this were very mixed, for whereas originally I had thought how much I should enjoy having him there as a companion to show me round and explain things, and had encouraged him to try to persuade his wife, after my quarrel with Vrailbran over the party I thought it might be difficult and embarrassing if the two wives were at loggerheads, as Bran had implied. I had no idea that they knew one another, of course. Bran had never mentioned her before although I had often spoken of Tsano, nor had Tsano himself ever indicated that either he or his wife knew Bran. I had cogitated about it a good deal and had hoped for some kind of opening in conversation with Tsano which might have enabled me to learn when and how the two women had had whatever contact with one another it was that had caused Bran to speak so critically. But I had found myself quite without opportunity of raising the matter with Tsano or with Bran. I had thought of asking her outright without waiting for a diplomatic opening, but I rather shrank from the mention of anything which might remind her of that absurd quarrel.

So it was that Tsano and I bade one another farewell without being certain whether we should meet again within the month or not. He looked so wistful when we parted that I felt quite sad for him. I understood that if they did not come up he would miss me a great deal, more than I should miss him, I fear, for fond though I was of him and much as I valued his friendship, the prospect of a month in the mountains with my beloved Bran amid all the excitement and released from all the irking chores filled me with an elation I could not conceal.

Bran had decided that we should spend the first few days of the holiday at home, since the quick–rail cars would be very crowded, as all the contestants, their trainers and supporters would be going up immediately. I was so impatient to be there that I would gladly have gone straight to the nearest quick–rail stop, but I acknowledged that Bran knew best and so we passed a very pleasant though quiet few days, partly alone at home and partly visiting Bran's parents. We took much pleasure, too, in walking through the deserted city streets at leisure now that there were time and space to enjoy them.

During these days we also assembled the clothes and equipment we would need. The climate of Capovolta as far as I had experienced it was very equable, so that I was quite amazed at the quantity of warm clothing that Bran insisted we should take, but the height of the plateau and even more of the surrounding mountains with their peaks perpetually above the snow line meant that it might be beautifully warm during the day, but piercingly cold once the sun had gone down. We took also things that resembled Canadian snowshoes and a pair each of a kind of short, wide ski.

At last came the day of our departure, and we set our baggage on a kind of wheeled handcart to take it to the depot. All our heavy luggage was taken charge of separately and moved to the end of the quick–rail by the great underground network that dealt with all freight. Then we boarded the quick–rail ourselves and were off. During the whole of my stay in this country I had never been on so long a journey, and it was my first glimpse of the more distant hinterland.

It became wilder and more exotic in its plant life the further we went. I was enchanted by the colors, by the rich profusion of the vegetation, by the sculpturing of the more distant landscape: I could not look enough. Then gradually this richness dropped away, the vegetation changed in character, began to thin out, and the air seemed to become even clearer and all outlines sharper, all surfaces more crystalline. Very gradually we were making height; it was so gradual that one was only aware of it from the changes I have described. Then suddenly ahead I began to discern huge snow–clad peaks, so high that they seemed to be hanging in the sky rather than to be based on earth. By now it was late in the day and the sun was on its way to setting; soon the shimmering white and pearly summits began to glow with an amazing deep–red light, reflected from the sky, so that they seemed to be topped with crystal fire. It was extraordinary and awesome.

Darkness fell as we drew into the quick–rail terminus on the flank of the great plateau, which had gradually obliterated the mountains from our view as we'd come in closer under its rim. Here we embarked on a kind of cable car, which took us up to the top of the plateau; this stretched away before us, endlessly it seemed as the twinkling lights of the encampments, or whatever they were, multiplied and replicated themselves on and on as far as the eye could see.

I was fortunate in having Bran, who was familiar with the place, to arrange for our baggage to be delivered and to find our way to the residential hall where we were to live while at the Games. Alone, I should have been completely at a loss, for the noise and confusion and the press of people were to me totally unexpected and confounding after the recent days of near solitude in the city and the quiet peace of the long journey through a countryside where we had scarcely had sight of human life. The Capovoltans were wont to comport themselves in a most orderly and civilized manner normally, but here the excitement which I had witnessed in the days before the holiday began had transmuted itself into a frenzy of activity and a babel of shouting and laughter which astonished me and assailed my ears quite painfully.

In a state of dazed and uncomprehending bewilderment, I followed Bran wherever she went, and it was with relief that I eventually climbed into another car something like those in which we had traveled on the quick–rail. Bran explained to me that these cars ceaselessly circumnavigated the plateau, carrying people between their halls of residence and the various points at which the different events were held. She had warned me that physical existence up here was lived at a more spartan level than in the cities on the plains below. I was, however, much impressed by the efficiency and by the degree of comfort which prevailed, and speculated with interest on how this holiday city (for such it really was) was serviced and provided for at such a remove from the normal life of the country and from its main source of power, the sea waves round its coast. Bran expressed a mild surprise that I was not already informed about this, since I worked for the City Transport Company, under whose control all these arrangements ultimately fell; but of course, such cylinders as I might well have recorded or banked dealing with this area of the company's responsibilities would have been unintelligible to me in my lowly capacity, since I did not know the basic facts which might have rendered them intelligible. Bran then explained that the whole of this area was rich in hot springs and that the mountains were volcanic; the energy used in this great City of Sport was all derived from the harnessed power and heat of the volcanoes and the hot springs.

Had I not been in a state of considerable fatigue as a result of the long journey and the sudden exposure to so many kaleidoscopic impressions, I wonder if I should have slept at all that night; for although the hour was extremely late before Bran and I (having arrived at our particular hall, settled into our rooms and eaten) were ready to compose ourselves for slumber, the restless babel as of a great crowd incessantly on the move had never ceased for one moment. I could hear it swell and subside, swell and subside in an almost mesmeric rhythm, which gradually receded as sleep overtook me.

We awoke next morning to a sun so splendid and an air so clear
and exhilarating that the whole landscape seemed to be sentient,
pulsating with an exultant, secret life of its own. We were fortunate
to be resident in a hall positioned right on the edge of the meadows
which sloped gently down to the central plain of the plateau; this was
shaped rather like a giant oval saucer, lying from southwest to
northeast, but bounded on the eastern rim by the towering range of
volcanic mountains I have mentioned. Without consciously considering the matter, I must have been expecting to find the whole
area under snow, and I exclaimed with surprise as I looked out upon
the verdant pastures below me. Once again Bran resolved the
mystery for me. The heavy snows did not normally fall until after the
winter holiday, while the customary light flurries rarely settled for
more than a matter of minutes because the warmth from the plentiful
hot springs and their underground sources was enough to melt them
almost immediately, although only a few hundred feet up the
mountains lay the mantle of permanent snow.

From our window I could see that the long meadow grass was
starred with a resplendent largesse of heliotrope flowers, their color
so lucent that they seemed to be themselves a source of light, rather
than to be merely revealed by it; they were, I suppose, some kind of
autumn crocus, but never before had I seen such a luminous
intensity of color. I found in the succeeding days that this was
characteristic of everything in that extraordinary place: the particular quality of every object seemed to have been developed to a
degree of intensity beyond the normal, as though some great surging
force of life were informing every mountain, every rock, every blade
of grass. My own feelings of well–being and exhilaration were such
that the very earth I walked on sent some current of life and energy
spurting up into my body through the soles of my feet, as though I
were some latter–day Antaeus.

The program of the Games was so extensive that it was as though
one were being offered a bill of fare with so many meats and rarefied
dishes as to inhibit choice; one turned greedily from one possibility
to the next, hovering over each in an agony of indecision, unwilling
to choose for fear of missing the pièce de résistance. Tsano had told

me that I should not on any account miss seeing the canoeing contest, the twelve–man sled team race and (since I had some slight skiing skill myself) the solo downhill races, which were performed on various kinds of ski and sled–like apparatus. He said that these were some of the most dangerous events, but also the most exciting. Bran, who had herself once competed in some of the swimming events in the lake, wished to see the long–distance swimming competition and the sailing events, but above all she wished to see the body competitions! This did not appeal to me at all, since it would mean missing several of the other events which attracted me—especially the team fighting, which sounded very exciting indeed since it involved teams of about fifty young men fighting and wrestling with one another, using no weapons but with otherwise few rules as far as I could understand. This contest continued for two hours, unless of course all members of both teams had been incapacitated before the time was up. If some of the contestants were still on their feet at the finish of the allotted time, then the team which had most men able to stand up was declared the winner. There were several rounds of these contests, according to the number of teams which had entered, and after some days' respite had been given so that the "survivors" had had time to recover, there would be a grand finale between a specified number from each of the two remaining teams, lasting until the final champions emerged. Bran had no desire to witness this: it was, she said, a disgusting and bloody sight and the whole thing such a mélée that one could never properly follow the fortunes of any single participant. Had I been competent to find my own way about, I should probably have suggested that the logical thing would be for us to split forces. As that was not practical for me at the moment, I accepted for the first day's program whatever Bran might decide upon, but reserved for myself the right to strike out on my own at a later stage when familiarity with the terrain should render me more independent.

However, fortune was with me that day, for the particular series of aquatic events which Bran had wished to see were postponed until the next day, when it was thought the weather would be less perfectly calm and still and would therefore render these events more exciting and a greater challenge to the skill of the contestants. Bran was therefore perfectly ready to acquiesce in making the canoeing contest our second choice. This event was held on one of the torrential rivers that poured off the mountains, fed and kept flowing even at this season by the hot springs that gushed forth on the lower slopes. It was a precipitous and terrifying course, for the torrent flung itself down toward the lake in the plain below in a series of great leaps from one level to another, so that the canoes had not only to steer a course which avoided the great rocks and boulders with which the stream bed was strewn, but were obliged to shoot three separate sets of rapids—one of them so fearful and narrow that it made one shudder to look at it, for the direction and force of the current would naturally hurl any object upon its surface toward the jagged rocks which lined the passage.

As if these hazards in themselves were not enough, by the rules of the contest the participants were obliged to follow one another at twelve-second intervals, launched remorselessly upon the course by the official starters without regard for the position or condition of the boat in front of them. It was an incredible spectacle to see this never–ending line of canoes hurtling down one after another, and of course inevitably colliding and becoming entangled if the occupants made the smallest error of judgment. The most difficult points were the churning pools below the rapids, where a kind of whirlpool effect was created by the violence and depth of the cascade and which therefore took precious seconds of time as well as skill and daring to negotiate without accident. The vessels themselves were of light and fragile construction, rather like that of a coracle, although they must have been less fragile than they seemed to survive the battering they perforce received. They bobbed about like so many corks on the boiling water below the falls, and only the immense skill and daring of the crews prevented them from turning turtle and foundering. Each was manned by a crew of three, two with paddles, the third with a long pole something like a punt pole with which he steered as much as was possible and with which he prevented collision with the rocks and boulders and fended off other competitors if they came within reach. The "steersman" had the most vulnerable and dangerous position in this most dangerous of sports, for he stood astride the bow of the craft, balancing himself on the gunwale, each foot held into a contraption rather like the safety binding on a ski. The paddlers had not only to paddle with all their force, but they had also to watch out for the maneuvers of the steersman, so that if in fending them off from some hazard he was obliged to alter his balance, they must shift their weight in turn to counterbalance it. I have rarely witnessed a sport demanding such a degree of coordination of intent and movement between three persons where the result of failure was so dangerous. The accidents were numerous, and often, I feared, near fatal, but in some remarkable way the contestants even when injured avoided being bashed to pieces either by the natural forces they fought with or, as often seemed even more imminent, by one another.

The spectators roared their support for their favorites or jeered at the misadventures of rival crews with the most bloodcurdling adjurations to maim or cripple. Cries of "Bash his head in," "Shove the————under," or, "Give him a swipe in the————" resounded on all sides. Of the crews who actually completed the course and survived intact, the winner would be the one who had achieved this feat in the shortest time, but the result, of course, would not be known until the timekeepers had correlated the start and finish times of each surviving crew at the end of the day.

I noted that each crew was distinguished by the colors of the exiguous costume it wore, but that several crews wore the same colors, though never two consecutive crews. I commented on this to Bran, who then explained to me a feature of the Games which up to then I had still not understood. The whole organization was territorial: that is, each crew, each team, each competitor in any sport was regarded as the representative of the district from which it came. The whole country, including the city of Capovolta itself, was divided up into districts and the districts into subdistricts; although these varied greatly in size, in terms of population they were more or less equal. The districts and subdistricts were administrative units, each preserving certain areas of self–government within the general framework, so that each of the numerically quite small subdistricts had certain matters within its own control. In the city, a subdistrict would consist of only a few streets, so that each citizen had a chance to make his voice heard on local matters, such as the opening hours of shops, how the funds allotted to local amenities should be spent and so on. This meant that behind each competitor or team there was certain to be intense local support. In the canoeing contest, for example, care was taken that two crews from the same district were never put next to each other in the starting order.

Although the canoeing contest was a riveting spectacle, after several hours of it, Bran and I were happy to go in search of other diversion, especially as the crews from our district had all finished the course before midday. I marveled to Bran that no fatal accident had taken place in this time, for often it had appeared to me that such an outcome could barely be averted. Bran agreed but added that there probably would be one before the day was over, as it was rare for that particular contest to finish without fatality. This remark, made in a calm and factual manner, had a sobering and chilling effect on me, for it is one thing to witness so many narrow escapes, marveling at the skill and courage which avert tragic outcome, but another to learn that in sober truth these qualities are not always enough.

"Could we perhaps go and watch a less violent sport for a while, Bran," I said tentatively.

"I warned you that you needed a strong stomach for some of the fare up here, did I not, my dear?" she responded with a smile. "Perhaps you begin to understand why I have no enthusiasm for the team fighting. But, of course, there are plenty of things which do not end in bloodshed, although truly many do. This afternoon we could watch the horse racing, or fencing—or the gymnastic competitions—whatever you prefer."

The mention of horse racing surprised me, for I had seen horses used for work in the fields on our occasional expeditions beyond the city confines, but I had never seen them ridden for pleasure nor had ever heard of horse racing as a possible pastime. Bran observed that although it might seem strange to me, I must understand that—as she had told me before—many normal restrictions and taboos were lifted during the period of the Games. Normally horse racing as I knew it in my own country would be against the ethos of Capovolta; it would be considered "an abuse of the Creation," as Bran sententiously expressed it, but an exception was made for this occasion. The horses were not bred and trained for racing, but were ordinary working horses chosen for their stamina rather than their speed, for the course was a long one involving several circuits of the arena where it was staged, part of which included a fairly steep uphill gradient with a corresponding downhill one on the other side. Of the choices mentioned by Bran, this was the one which most appealed to me, for I had always had a great love for horses and had been something of a horseman myself as a boy. So it was decided that we should make our way thither.

The racecourse was laid out against a section of the oval saucer or shallow bowl formation of the plateau, so that the greater part of the course lay on the flat center, but part carved a crescent–shaped curve across the rising ground on the side. The upper slopes of that part formed a huge natural grandstand from which the race might be viewed. The more fervent partisans, however, preferred to stand close against the track, either on the level ground around it or within the large enclosure round which it was laid. I could not quite understand this, for they could not have the complete, even if distant view of the course which our position at the top of the slope gave us. The horses and their jockeys, one contestant only from each district which decided to compete, ran in heats of about twenty, so that the whole event was staged over several days. I asked Bran how they compensated for the very unfavorable position on the outside from which some of them must start: with twenty contestants the disadvantage would be great. "Wait and see," was Bran's response.

Of the twenty–odd horses competing in the first heat, none was wearing the colors of our district, so that I was able to watch with some impartiality. I was soon relieved of the illusion that I had come to watch a less aggressive and violent sport, if such it could be termed, for rarely have I seen any so–called sporting event where so much overt foul play was allowed. The competitors on the outside simply made a straight charge across the paths of their rivals to gain an inside place, striking out indiscriminately with the short but savage–looking whips with which they were armed—for that indeed was the word for it. I had thought both horses and riders strangely caparisoned, more like medieval jousters than anything else, and now the reason was clear. Both were padded against the lashes bestowed alike on rider and horse by their rivals. The aim of the jockey was to remain seated himself but to unseat anyone else in his path, and to force his rivals to swerve and lose ground in any way he could. Again the excitement generated among the crowd was enormous. A great roar would go up as some particularly dangerous play was executed, or as some unfortunate was toppled. Any horse or rider that fell seemed likely to be trampled by the others, but the horses appeared to have more sense than their riders and of their own accord would swerve to avoid an unfortunate fellow creature on the ground. The thrown riders were mostly capable of scrambling to safety of their own volition, but when one was too injured to move quickly, course officials moved with lightning speed to haul him to safety. The horses for the most part continued their wild career, riderless, but keeping pace with those about them.

The spectators crowded about the rail that enclosed the track joined in this free–for–all whenever they could, and now I understood the reason for the way in which they had positioned themselves. If a horse from a rival district swerved near enough to the rail, they would explode a firecracker, beat a gong or ring a bell immediately under the poor creature's nose, or seek to trip him with a cane thrust between his legs from under the rail, in this way sometimes causing the animal to panic and blunder off in the wrong direction or to rear violently and unseat his rider. Thus it was that the warier riders kept their mounts well away not only from the outside barrier but from the inner one as well, making up for the distance lost by their immunity from interference.

By the time two circuits of the course had been completed, the contestants had thinned out to a mere handful, and only five in all survived to complete the course. The winning horse and jockey were greeted with roars of applause and cheers from their supporters and a fusillade of catcalls and booing from their opponents. I was shocked at the totally unsportsmanlike way in which the whole contest was conducted and could not help commenting adversely to Bran upon it. She made no reply, and I saw that her attention was engaged by the horses already being brought out for the second heat, for among them she fancied she had glimpsed the colors of our district. She stared intently down on the mêlée as the riders tried to bring the horses about and get them into line, her concentration yielding to an electric excitement as she began to jump up and down exclaiming, "There he is—look—look! I *thought* it was!" Then, joining in with the rest of the crowd, she began to shout advice and encouragement at our man. At first I could not identify him in the kaleidoscope of color as the throng of horses wheeled and shoved into one another, but eventually my eye singled out the heliotrope and silver colors that he bore. In a moment they were off, for the starters made only an approximation of the lineup procedure of a proper race. This was more like mounted combat than a race. Our man, who started from an unfavorable position near the outer barrier, immediately fell back a pace or two, amid agonized groans and exclamations of surprise from our camp, but I thought that he had deliberately held his horse in, for now he was able to choose his position in the field at the rear. He held his own there, not increasing or decreasing the distance between himself and the mêlée of striking jockeys and charging horses in front, but allowing himself enough room to take avoiding action when fallen horses or riders blocked his immediate path. Bran and the band of his more vocal supporters were screaming themselves hoarse, urging him to greater efforts, as though they thought he was already defeated. I found myself becoming violently partisan, too, but as much because this man seemed to me to be showing intelligence and acumen, given the way in which the event was conducted, as because he was our district champion. At the end of the first circuit he was still in the rear of those left in the race, and Bran was almost sobbing with agitation and disappointment. Now, however, he began to attack from the rear, overtaking the man immediately in front of him, and with a skillfully placed thwack at the legs of his mount, he sent him prancing toward the center enclosure, fouling another couple of riders as he did so. This considerably cleared the field in front of him, and caused Bran to grab hold of me and scream again, but this time with jubilation. I found myself running the race inside my head with this man, for I had known a second or so before he did it exactly what he was going to do, or rather I knew that was what he should do. Once again I felt certain that the correct strategy was for him to remain in his new position on the uphill stretch of that circuit and then sweep round outside the main contenders as they bunched together all thrusting and fighting to maintain a central position themselves and at the same time to oust their rivals, as they began on the downhill stretch; with luck, he would thus gain ground that the others would find hard to catch up. This is exactly what he did, and by this time I, too, was shouting and cheering and jumping up and down with the best of them. The third and last circuit began therefore with our man actually in the lead, but this, of course, was a vulnerable position, for now the others abandoned their mutual battle and made after him, urging their mounts on with spur and whip. I still think he would have done it had not one of the riderless horses, now about to be lapped by the oncoming riders, panicked at the thunder of the hooves behind him and, flinging his head up with a snort, galloped directly into the path of our champion, thus causing him to check and swerve toward the inner rail. One of the ruffianly crowd on the qui vive for a chance like this managed to catch his mount's foreleg a glancing blow with a long pole thrust out between the rails. The poor beast stumbled, but bravely recovered himself and carried on. He was badly lamed, however, and now stood no chance against the determined group of riders behind him.

Bran burst into tears, and I felt such a murderous impulse toward the author of the mischief that I truly think I should have throttled him with my bare hands had he come within reach. I was not alone in this, for in the enclosure when the foul blow had been launched, furious fighting broke out, and for a few moments the situation looked ugly indeed. However, the horses for the third heat were already being led out, and as soon as the starting signal was given, the rough–and–tumble in the enclosure stopped as the participants made a dash for the rail to regain their precious positions of vantage.

I asked Bran whether there were not serious injuries sometimes as a result of all this violence: she said that this was often the case, but usually at the end of the day when there were no more heats to engage attention. If the violence which flared up then continued too long or looked too dangerous, the course officials, who were all tough–looking older men, were given orders to pick out the worst spots with powerful searchlights and to turn hoses of cold water on the fighters. This was usually enough to quell the trouble.

As far as I had been able to observe, the fighting had mainly been with fists, and I wondered that no knives or other weapons had been used. Bran explained that weapons of any kind were banned by law; if people wished to fight, then they must do so only with the means with which nature had endowed them. As I had seen, people had smuggled canes and sticks into the enclosure as part of their dastardly attack on the horses; Bran said that the authorities tolerated this as long as they were not too liberally used in the ensuing fights. The penalties for being in possession of any other weapon, let alone for using it, were so severe as to discourage even the most aggressive and partisan people. Moreover, the use of weapons earned great social censure and was regarded as evidence of the greatest cowardice.

CHAPTER

11

That evening when we returned to our hall surfeited with the excitements of the day, I was delighted to find a recorded message from Tsano awaiting me. He and his wife had come up to the games after all. Should I, he said, find myself free, he would be delighted to accompany me to whatever event I wished to see. He would call in the morning to collect my reply. I noted that the dear fellow had made no suggestion that the four of us should meet, so I felt sure that he must know of whatever ill–will existed between his wife and Vrailbran, that had caused the latter to speak so sharply when Aniad was mentioned. Although my first impulse was to suggest to Bran that we invite Tsano to accompany us, I wisely held my peace and made no mention of this message for the moment, deciding to wait until we came to discuss our program for the next day. Here a cleavage of interest became apparent. Bran was determined to see the aquatic competitions, which, you will remember, had been postponed for a day, while I was little interested in them, but passionately desirous to see the downhill sledging and skiing races of which Tsano had told me and which were being held at the same time as the water sports. Bran also announced that in the later part of the day she wished to attend the body competitions. Although I found the title rather a crude one, I should, of course, have been pleased to go with her had the bodies of the fair sex been on display, for I could not but feel a little starved on the diet I was forced to keep to here since all women went about in public so swathed from head to foot that one could only guess at the hidden beauty beneath the clothes. Not that I had any criticism or complaint on the score of Vrailbran's beauty of form, but I would be wonderfully glad to feast my eyes once again on the profusion of breasts and buttocks veiled only with the scantiest of costumes which was common in my own country.

My tentative inquiry of Bran received a reply so vehement, however, that such a pleasant conceit had to be dismissed forever. "Klemo, don't be so absolutely disgusting!" she exclaimed. "I have never heard such an offensive suggestion."

"But, Bran, why isn't it considered disgusting for men, too?"

"Really, Klemo, I don't know whether you are just being silly or if you are trying to be insulting. You must see that it's an entirely different thing. It would be quite indecent as well as appallingly undignified for a woman to display herself in that way. Surely you can see that?"

"You must forgive me, Bran, but I don't really see it. It is the custom in my country."

"*Your* country! *Your* country! Look, Klemo, I am tired of hearing about how things are in your country. I do not at all like the things you have told me about it, in any case; it sounds a vulgar and degraded place to me, and you would do better to start thinking about Capovolta as *your* country now. As my husband, you have been honored by having Capovoltan nationality bestowed upon you, and the least you can do in return is to accept gratefully the superior way of life to which it entitles you."

"But, Bran," I protested, "you aren't being fair." At least, that is what I started to say, but she cut across me, saying sharply, as though, I felt, she were my mother or my schoolteacher, "Now that's enough, Klemo. I do not wish to discuss it further. Why will you always try to make an argument about everything. Let us hear no more about it."

Of course, I *did* wish to discuss it further, but I knew a real quarrel would develop if I did, and Bran's anger upset me greatly. I had begun to find myself frequently taking steps to avoid argument, so that her accusation of fomenting it struck me as particularly unjust. I relapsed into a resentful silence.

Being convinced that she had "won" the argument by this ploy of bulldozing me into silence, Bran was disposed to be placatory, and after a little while returned to the subject of our program for the next day, which she began to describe for me very amicably. I was greatly exercised as to how to respond. I wanted at all costs to avoid incurring her displeasure yet again, but on the other hand I did so dearly wish to view the snow sports.

Attributing my silence, not altogether incorrectly, to some residual soreness from what I am sure she regarded as my defeat in argument, she came up to me very sweetly and gently and kissed me, saying, "There, darling, I am sorry I was a bit sharp just now, but you must try to cure yourself of this habit you have of turning everything into an argument."

Naturally this did little to soothe me and might well have started the whole thing off again had I not wished to keep her present mood of goodwill. So instead of saying, "It takes two to make an argument," as I should haved liked to do, I simply said, "I am sorry, too. It makes me quite miserable when you are angry with me."

"Dear, dear Klemo, you *know* I am never angry with you. Of course, two people cannot be expected *never* to have a difference of opinion, but that is all it is. I love you too much to quarrel with you, and you know that in the end you always get your own way."

The enormity of this lie was difficult to swallow, but I managed it, and so our "difference of opinion" was healed, as it always was, by the close embrace of body and body.

Later on I said as casually as I could, "By the way, there was a message from Tsano this morning to say that he was up here. I forgot to mention it—but I suppose I ought to arrange to see him sometime, oughtn't I? It seems rather rude to ignore it, don't you think?"

"Oh, dear. What a bore! I don't really want to be involved in a get–together between you lads. I'm glad he's had the guts to leave that tiresome woman to her own devices for a while, though."

She had assumed, as I suppose I had meant her to, that he was up here alone. I did not correct this impression, but said tentatively, "How would it be if I offered to do something with him tomorrow on my own? I should have done my duty then, without involving you."

"Would you really not mind doing that, Klemo? That does seem a good solution. Tsano knows his way around so you'll be quite safe."

And so to my joy it was settled between us that I should wait for Tsano in the morning and spend the whole day with him, as Bran wished to be off very early to get a good place at the lakeside for the water sports. Moreover, as she had no idea when our district champions would be competing in the various sports, there seemed no point in trying to make arrangements for meeting up again before evening. She was so sweetly solicitous about all this in case I minded her desertion for the day that I felt ashamed of my duplicity, for, of course, I was delighted at being freed in this way and so being able to pursue my own interests with Tsano.

The good fellow was wonderfully pleased to see me, having not really thought I should be able to free myself to be with him. We were like a pair of schoolboys let out for an unexpected holiday. I had never seen Tsano look so young and so carefree as he beamed affectionately at me from the couch in our room while he waited for me to put on my warm clothes and snowboots and find the short, wide ski–type apparatus with which we had come equipped. We traveled by plateau car to the lower slopes of the mountains; from here we could have taken a cable car all the way up to the sledging course, but we were both in such high spirits and so intoxicated by our freedom and the exhilarating air, that we determined to take it only about halfway between the snow line and the beginning of the course. There we tumbled out into the snow and put on our skis. They were different from those to which I had been accustomed as a lad, but I soon mastered the technique for Tsano was an expert, and of course they were on the whole easier to control than ordinary skis. They were particularly well adapted for the upward climb, but when I turned to take a short run down just for the pleasure of it, I found that they were much slower and rather more clumsy to manipulate. However, Tsano assured me that I could easily borrow a pair of racing skis once we arrived at the course if I wished to try them out, though he warned me that they were rather dangerous for the inexperienced.

In spite of our keenness to see the sled racing, which was the first event of the day to start, we could not refrain from larking about like a couple of boys. We snowballed one another; we had little downhill races, which meant, of course, that we had to climb up again; we challenged one another to absurd feats of balance, and I was delighted to instruct Tsano in the art of ski jumping, for this sport was unknown in Capovolta, so he said. Of course, I had only jumped as a young lad and the length of the jump would have caused any real ski jumper to laugh with scorn. Then, too, our skis were not exactly ideal for the sport—but having found this piece of terrain which had a natural little jump, I could not leave it without having a try myself and then instructing Tsano in the art. So it was that we had whiled away a good half of the morning in spite of our early start before we reached the bottom end of the course. When we realized this, we began the climb with a will by as direct a route as Tsano's knowledge of the course layout would allow us to do. Such was our concentration now because we feared to miss the very thing we had come to see that only when we heard shouts and halloos did we realize that away to our left and our right were people calling and gesticulating frantically.

"Oh Mother Earth!" ejaculated Tsano. "We must be on the course!" And as he said it, a great magnified voice came trumpeting out from somewhere: "Clear the course! Clear the course!"

"Quickly, this way," cried Tsano, changing direction and making off laterally to our right.

I hesitated because I could see that the distance to the left where the spectators were was shorter than that to the right.

"Klemo, come!" shrieked Tsano, flinging himself flat below an overhanging rock. I realized then that he, more quick-witted than I, had seen that the competitors, if they knew the course well, would be steering clear of this natural hazard. I tore after him as I saw a great black line bearing down toward us like an oncoming breaker.

Hearts pounding, bodies quaking, we lay pressing ourselves into the snow below the overhang. Now we could hear the sibilant hiss of the runners of the oncoming sleds—and suddenly they were upon us. The earth shook beneath our bodies as we were caught up and almost smothered in this sinister sibilance and the clanging resonance of metal as they swept over and around us. Then they were gone, and immediately there was a sickening thud and a great cry from the crowd. Tsano recovered himself and thrusting his head out saw that the skyline was clear above us, so he seized me by the leg and hauled me out, muttering, "Come *on*, Klemo! For the Great Mother's sake, come *on*!" Floundering and slithering I followed him across the slope, and we flung ourselves, trembling with shock, among the spectators. Only then did we see the sprawled bodies lying in the snow below where we had lain. I was sick with horror for I thought the accident must have been our fault. A bevy of course officials was already moving to haul these people to safety, and another group pounced upon us with countenances so angry that I looked about for some support or help. There was Tsano, standing over me and squaring himself to take the blame. I could hear him reiterating that it was his fault: he had brought me, I had only followed him, and so on. I suppose I must have fainted momentarily, for the next thing I knew was Tsano shaking my arm and saying with a desperate note of appeal and alarm in his voice, "Klemo, Klemo—what is it? What's wrong?"

In fact, I could have done nothing more helpful if I had been able to calculate it, for now the mood of the people round changed from anger to concern and sympathy. Tsano told me afterward that my face had gone a deathly greenish–white for a moment, and then as I recovered I began to shudder and shake as though in a high fever, saying frantically, "Are they hurt? Oh, please don't let them be dead. Please don't let them be dead!"

No one was dead, thank God, though the injuries sustained by the crashed crew were by no means negligible—but, I must confess, my relief was even greater when I understood that the accident had not after all been our fault. Tsano's quick reaction had saved us and got us under cover before the oncoming sleds were aware of our existence. They all knew that the overhang existed, estimated its position and aimed at avoiding it, but at the same time, according to the extraordinarily unfair and unsporting practices which prevailed, each team tried to jockey its opponents into a position in which they would be obliged to go straight over the overhang and so crash unless they had the most immense skill and luck. The sleds were surprisingly large structures, manned by twelve people. Ten of them sat astride a raised central saddle, as though on a vast motor scooter, while the other two sat as it were on poop and stern respectively, wielding a pole with which they tried to push their opponents off course. The sleds ran on fierce–looking steel runners, and by the time they were coming in to the finish of the long downhill course, the speed at which they were running made accidents nearly lethal. The end of the course narrowed so that the sleds were forced to bunch together, and the final few yards was a mere passage between rocks so narrow that even if two could go in abreast, they must emerge in single file at the end. Thus there was never any dispute about the winner, but naturally the jockeying for place at that point on the course became intense and dangerous.

Now what Tsano did not know was that the layout of the latter part of the course had been changed the previous year. Then, of course, warnings and instructions had been posted everywhere to advise people of the change, but no one had envisaged the particular set of circumstances which had taken us into danger a year later. Had we come up all the way in the cable car we should have found the layout of the whole course clearly mapped and charted. As it was, Tsano, carefully avoiding the finish of the old course, had inadvertently cut straight across the new one.

The official attitude had at first been suspicious, as though we might have had some ulterior motive for endangering our own lives as well as those of the crews; the absurdity of this did not seem to strike anyone, but they saw how shocked and shaken we were, so began to treat us like a pair of criminally careless half–wits. The thing that upset us most was that they were going to send for Vrailbran and Aniad to come and collect us as though we had been a pair of naughty little lads whose mothers had to be told! We were both put into an agony of agitation about this, for varying reasons, but Tsano managed to convince them that the shock to his own wife might prove very serious. Fortunately for him, Aniad's precarious health seemed to be generally known of, and eventually they listened to his explanations and protests and agreed not to summon her.

We listened meekly to the rebukes of the course officials, promised that we would be more sensible in future, and were about to take
ourselves off when another official appeared from somewhere and
said that the course chief wished to see us. We followed with
trepidation to the pavilion that housed the officials and contestants
and were there brought before a most delightful–looking young
woman. She was attired in a tight–fitting costume which Tsano
afterward said was the normal skiing apparel for both sexes. She was
the first woman in Capovolta, except for Vrailbran, the shape of
whose body I was able to discern without much room for doubt or
speculation, and a very appealing and lovely shape it was, too.

It was an astonishing experience to find oneself harangued about
one's dangerous follies by a woman so young and so utterly
desirable. We were both duly humble and penitent, and once again
Tsano tried to take on himself all the blame and to prevent her from
sending for our wives by explaining his circumstances. She listened
intently, excused herself a moment, and when she returned, smiled
kindly at us both, saying to Tsano, "I have always heard good things
about you, Tsano–Aniad. I accept your explanation and I trust you
enough not to take the matter any further. Look after your young
friend, who is perhaps less versed in our ways and a less responsible
person than you are." She accompanied this rather critical remark
with a smile of such dazzling charm that I could gladly have stopped
there to receive further rebuke if it continued to be bestowed so
graciously. Tsano, however, had enough sense not to push our luck,
so thanking her warmly he seized me by the arm and hustled me out.
He understood that her momentary absence had been to check that
we were in fact the people we claimed to be.

So ended our escapade. Neither of us any longer had stomach for
the remaining heats of this dangerous sport; we only wanted to go
away and hang our heads in shame for a while. Poor Tsano was very
distressed at having led me into trouble, which was how he seemed
to look upon it, although I did not see that he could be blamed for not
knowing of the change, nor for the fact that I, even more than he, had
wanted to complete the climb on skis. I think both of us hoped that if
we crept away and drew no more attention to ourselves, our wives
might never know about it.

For some reason, in our newly chastened state, we both felt we should report back to our various halls, although Aniad was not expecting Tsano so early and I did not really expect to find Bran back yet. As I had anticipated, she was not there, but there was a recorded message from her, so that clearly she had been back in the interim. This message said that she hoped I would not mind if she went straight on to the body competitions without me, as she had understood that I did not much wish to attend. This would mean that she would be very late back so she hoped I would go to bed and not wait up for her. A little earlier I should have been very pleased at this extension of my freedom, but after the recent fiasco I should, I own, have been quite pleased to have Bran's company and to escort her wherever she wanted to go. I felt disconsolate and wondered how I should spend the rest of the day.

Before long, however, Tsano was back to say that Aniad was resting and was quite content for us to go off again together if I wished. He was very tentative about this because, feeling responsible as he did for our earlier trouble, he thought perhaps I should not care to trust myself to his society once again. Of course, I was much cheered at the prospect of his companionship, and we decided that we would go and see some of the team fighting, which was due to begin in the late afternoon. Four huge arenas were reserved for these miniature battles, so that eight teams were engaged at the same time. It was clear that partisanship worked up to an even more feverish degree for this event than for the others we had witnessed, but I found it a less thrilling spectacle than I had imagined. It was all on too large a scale: one hundred flailing, punching, kicking bodies do not make for finesse as a spectacle, and there seemed to be something barbarous about the whole thing. Reluctantly I was forced to agree with Bran's judgment on it. Tsano, the gentlest and mildest of men, I should have thought, surprised me by saying that he had never cared for it much as a spectator, but that to participate in it was the most exciting thing he had ever done.

"Tsano, do you mean you actually were a team fighter in your time?" I exclaimed. "You must have tremendous guts as well as stamina."

"That was years ago, of course, before I was married. I was very fit in those days and had time for training. You get a tremendous feeling of fellowship and loyalty in a team, you know. It's something one never finds anywhere else as strongly. It is amazing what chaps are capable of not only in their own defense, but to defend a teammate. You come out of the thing more in harmony with other people and more at peace inside yourself, whether you win or lose, than at any other time in your life—or at least I did. You feel wonderfully purged and clean somehow.''

"That does surprise me, Tsano. I should have expected a lot of bad feeling between the teams which would spill over into ordinary life. I saw the fight that started between the supporters at the horse racing yesterday, and how much more would one expect that here.''

"It is true that very bloody fights do take place between the supporters, but the teams don't feel that at all. Whatever happens, you know you've done your best—proved yourself in a way, I suppose, and you feel no animosity toward the others. Watching is quite a different thing: it leaves you feeling that you have *not* proved yourself and somehow wanting to take it out on someone. The Guardians are very concerned about this, I believe. It is so exactly the opposite from the effect which the Games are meant to have.''

I had already begun to ponder upon this phenomenon, that is, the existence of what amounted to licensed violence within a society whose standards of conduct at other times were of the highest moral tone. It reminded me of what I had read of the Saturnalia of old, and I suspected that the Guardians had some specific motive in not only allowing it but appearing to encourage it. It suggested to me, however, a chilling comparison with a battery of tame fighting cocks, and I resented the base view of human nature that it reflected.

Neither of us was particularly keen to go on watching or to risk entanglements with the vociferous and aggressive spectators. Perhaps we might have felt differently if either of our district teams had been engaged, but as it was we decided to go into one of the pavilions for some refreshment. Normally the Capovoltans are a very abstemious and sober people, and the sale of alcoholic beverages is strictly controlled, but during the period of the Games, the regulations are relaxed, and various types of ales, wines and spirits were being sold, and with Tsano to counsel me I had my first drink of a delicious drink called Acumba.

Tsano warned me not to drink it too quickly since I was unused to it, and suggested that it would be well for us to eat here, too. There was a great deal of noise and gaiety, and the atmosphere seemed very welcoming, so we decided to stay rather than to return to our respective halls. Perhaps our tongues were loosened by the Acumba more than we either of us realized at the time, but we talked more intimately than ever before, and at last I heard the story of the quarrel between Bran and Tsano's wife, Aniad.

It was clear to me that Tsano's feeling for Aniad was very different from mine for Bran. He worried about her, and his attitude was a very protective one. Whereas when I came to analyze what I felt for Bran, I knew that it was the most improbable thing in the world that she would ever need or desire protection from me. Indeed the boot was very much on the other foot, for as a stranger, and a sick one at that to begin with, I had lived under her protection and that of her family ever since my arrival in the place. Because of the particular circumstances, I had come to accept this dependence with less questioning or surprise than might have been expected, for after all it was her country and it was she who knew the rules and knew how things were done. She was of a determined, decided character, not given to self–doubt or any kind of tentativeness. Aniad, on the contrary, was filled with a torturing sense of her own inadequacy— sadly misplaced, said Tsano, for she was most gifted and brilliant. She and Bran, who was a year or two the younger, had both worked in the same department of the City Magistracy, Aniad being senior to Bran.

Temperamentally the two did not understand one another nor get on well together, for Bran was wont to take on herself decisions which should have been made at a higher level. Sometimes this did not matter, except that if the decision proved a good one, Bran would boast that the idea had been hers, but when on occasion it created trouble, Aniad took the blame, for she was the senior of the two. She had had to reprimand Bran more than once for not coming to her for the final O.K., but she had never put the blame on Bran as far as her superiors were concerned, because it was a recognized code that one took the responsibility for the people under one. The whole thing had worried Aniad greatly. She tended to suffer from ill–health, and I think Tsano felt that this was largely a consequence of the stresses she found in her work. During one of her periods of absence, Bran had been promoted over her head, and Aniad returned to find Bran in the job that she by right of seniority should have had. This in itself was irking, but she was only too conscious that her periodic absences were hardly a recommendation for promotion, even though she always brought work home and never in fact failed to make up the time lost. Although she personally thought Bran's promotion a mistake as she did not trust her judgment, she was prepared to accept it and do her best to work amicably under Bran. But Bran for some reason seemed unable to accept this and made Aniad's life wretched by unnecessary criticism and complaint, and did not rest until she had secured her transfer from that department. This had, in effect, been a kind of demotion for Aniad and she felt very bitter about it.

Had we not both drunk several glasses of Acumba I do not think Tsano would ever have told me this story. He told me, moreover, that when I was first put under him to learn the work, he was furiously angry and prepared to dislike me on sight. My utter innocence in all this, my obvious lack of guile and my gratitude to him had made him feel differently, fortunately for me.

I suppose, too, that this story might have caused a quarrel between us if I had been sober, for I might have felt bound to disbelieve him and to defend Bran, but now we sat together sympathizing about our lot and our relationships to our women as though we were blood brothers. It seemed clear that Tsano had a temperament much more suited to the rough and tumble of the working world than his wife did, and I would certainly have found greater satisfaction in Bran's role than in my own, yet here we were, typecast one might say, simply because of our X Y chromosome— and so we repined together about the injustices of the system. How Bran would have felt about this role reversal is another matter, and at that moment it did not occur to me to consider it.

The protective feeling that Tsano had for Aniad was proof even against the alcohol he had consumed, for he suddenly decided that he was a brute to be out here, enjoying himself with me, while she, who had come up here solely for his sake, was alone in their room back at the hall. That she was so by her own choice was an inadequate excuse. He must go back to her.

Now I was very happy here in a sentimental, slightly maudlin way. I felt that all these people round me were my cherished friends, Tsano, of course, first and foremost among them. I did not want to leave. Let him, I suggested, go and fetch his dear wife, and we would finish the evening together. I would wait for them here.

Tsano thought this a reasonable proposition on the whole and went off to fulfill his part of it. I in my turn was convinced that somehow I should be able to heal the breach between Aniad and Bran, and we should all become good friends and live happily ever after.

CHAPTER
12

As I sat there, beaming at the company and filled with goodwill to all, I became aware that the people around me had assumed different clothes: some had even grown strange animal heads and curious faces. It did not seem at all out of place, though, and I peered with interest at all these unusual creatures at nearby tables. The noise reached a deafening crescendo, and a cacophony of sound broke out as a group of animals at the other end of the room began to beat drums and to pluck and blow an assortment of strange instruments. They produced a most intoxicating rhythm and I felt my body twitching in rhythmic response. Suddenly a delightful little cat came and sat beside me; it did not surprise me at all when she spoke in perfect Capovoltan.

"What are you doing here all alone?" she said in a beautiful purring kind of voice, which I seemed to recognize from some distant past meeting, though I could not remember talking to a cat before. Her question struck me as the most sympathetic and interesting remark anyone had made to me all day. I thought for a moment before replying.

"Waiting," I said. "Waiting." That suddenly seemed very sad. "Yes, yes," I said, almost in tears, "I'm just waiting."

"Who are you waiting for?" said the lovely purring voice. Well, who was I waiting for? Now I couldn't quite remember, but then it all became clear. Of course, I had all along been waiting for this sympathetic, charming cat!

"For you, of course," I said triumphantly. The cat laughed and said, "In that case, perhaps you'd like to dance with me?"

"Oh, I should, indeed I should!" I said. I could think of nothing that I would rather do. It did not occur to me that I did not know any Capovoltan dances, but the rhythm of the music was so potent and my partner so proficient that I found myself in the most intoxicating whirl of movement I had ever experienced. Unfortunately it was intoxicating in more senses than one, and it was with some surprise that I found myself sitting on the floor against the wall while my lovely cat tried to help me up, saying, "We'd better find something to sober you up, I think, my little skier."

Skier, I thought. How does she know I am a skier? She led me over to where the refreshments were being served, spoke to the attendant there in a low tone and he in his turn handed her a full glass. She held it out to me and said, "Drink it." I felt like Alice after going through the looking glass, presented with things labeled "Eat me!" or "Drink me!" I looked at it doubtfully, still thinking of Alice, and said, "Will it make me grow, do you think?"

The cat laughed delightfully and said, "I don't think you need to grow any more, do you? You look just the right size to me." The cat herself was rather small, but made with the most lovely curves here and there. I put my hand on one and said, "So are you. See how it fits into my hand."

"Now that's just a little bit forward of you," said the cat, removing my hand and putting the glass into it instead. "Be a good boy and drink it up."

"I have never," I said earnestly, "met a cat I liked so much, I do assure you, and if you promise me it will do me no harm, I'll have it." At least, that's what I *thought* I said, but perhaps I did not say it in Capovoltan, for the cat looked rather startled. It is true I was a little confused between the glass and the cat. I was thinking of the nursery rhyme which says,

> I love little Pussy
> Her coat is so warm,
> And if I don't hurt her
> She'll do me no harm.

It may be that that is what I actually said. I do not know. But the cat with rather more urgency than before gently lifted my glass–filled hand toward my mouth saying, "Come now, little skier, drink it up."

So I did. It was a bitter, stinging fluid which was so unexpected that it almost caused me to choke. But enough of it went down the right way to do its work, for in a few moments things seemed to have clearer outlines, and there, watching me anxiously was the Cat—not a real one I now saw, but a young woman with a cat head worn above a delightfully close–fitting skiing costume.

"Hw–er–ugh!" I said, trying to clear my mouth of the horrible taste and shaking my head vigorously to make sure I was still in one piece. "Very nasty."

"Yes," she agreed, "but you needed it, you know. What are you doing here all alone? What are your—friends—thinking of to leave you here all by yourself?"

"There was only one of them, and he's gone to fetch his wife."

"Are you sure about that? If Tsano is coming back, then you should be quite safe."

"Quite safe? Of course I'm quite safe. I'd only had just a little too much Acumba, that's all. I'm quite all right now."

"Are you sure? Do you really think you're safe to be left?"

"Safe to be left? But you aren't going to leave me, are you? Oh, please, don't go. I'm sorry if I behaved badly, but I'm not used to Acumba, you see. It's the first time I have ever tasted it, and it really is so delicious that I drank more of it than I should have done."

"Yes, I do see. But Tsano—or someone—should have warned you about it."

"Oh, he did, he did!" I assured her. "He told me I must drink it slowly and not have too much of it—but I suppose I forgot."

"I don't think you should have any more of it this evening. Don't you think you'd better go back to your hall?"

"Oh, no, please don't let's do that. I am enjoying myself so much. I must wait for Tsano and Aniad anyway. I can't go until they come back!"

"All right. Do you think you could manage another dance

perhaps? You seem to be a very good dancer, even if the Acumba did knock you out!''

"I don't think I can manage this kind of dancing now that I'm sober," I said. "I've never done anything like it before."

"That is very surprising. You followed me beautifully before until—well—until! You have a very good sense of rhythm. That's all that's needed, really. Just follow me as well as you can."

I did feel a trifle nervous about embarking on the dance floor again, but the thought of quite legitimately embracing my Cat and perhaps of being able to touch and trace those lovely curving surfaces that looked so enticing decided me. I threw myself into it with rather less abandon this time, but the Cat was right: the insistent, compelling beat that was being pounded out carried me with it, and my feet seemed to follow of their own volition the swirls and arabesques of the Cat's intoxicatingly rhythmic steps.

In the brief pauses at the end of each dance, neither of us made any attempt to break up the partnership: we simply waited, hand in hand, until the beat started again. We moved as one person, drunk now both of us with the heady rhythm of our movement. At first the Cat had maintained a fractional distance between us, but soon our bodies seemed to flow together as if magnetized, and I felt every curve and surface of that lovely shape as though I had been molded round it, gently, gently, with the lightest of pressures.

And so in a kind of dreaming daze, we danced the time away. How long we should have continued I do not know, had not Tsano suddenly erupted into the room again, looking very anxious and distressed. It was the Cat who saw him and broke away from me, leading me over to where Tsano stood.

"Here's your friend," she murmured with a gentle, sighing breath, like one just wakened.

Tsano was full of apology. When he left me he had boarded the car to return to his hall, but the cold night air on top of the Acumba had sent him to sleep—and there he had stayed, making circuit after circuit in the car until at last someone had roused him. He had come straight back to find me. He did not really know how long he had been away, but he saw that it was very late and was very worried about me. His relief when he found me in good hands was enormous. The poor fellow was very contrite, and distressed that twice in one day he had, so he felt, landed me in trouble. I did my best to reassure him that this was not so, that all was well and there was no need to worry. Many of his apologies and remarks, I realized, were being addressed to the Cat as much as to me, and I thought he was being unnecessarily deferential: utterly delightful and desirable though she was, she after all was not really concerned in the affair.

Now Tsano, with further profuse apology toward the Cat, asked me if I were ready to leave. He would take me back to my hall, but then he wished to get back to Aniad as quickly as possible.

To leave the Cat now was the last thing I desired. I assured Tsano that he had no need to worry about me at all; let him go back to Aniad immediately to relieve her from worry and I would find my own way back to my hall when I was ready to go.

"Oh, no, Klemo, you can't possibly do that," said Tsano in a tone of shocked surprise, which rather irritated me, I must confess.

"Why ever not, Tsano? I know my way about pretty well now, and, anyway, I can always ask someone."

"Klemo, you don't understand. It would be quite wrong for you to be alone up here tonight any later than this. Please do come now—that is if Madam will excuse us both," with a bow toward the Cat.

So far she had taken no part in the conversation, except to acknowledge Tsano's presence and to listen to his story. Now she said, "Do not worry about your friend, Tsano–Aniad. You have done well to come back to fetch him and I understand your desire to look after him, for he is still not altogether acquainted with our ways. I promise that I will see him home myself. Will that do?"

Tsano again became profuse in his thanks, in a way that seemed to me quite uncharacteristic. Why did he need to be so placatory toward the Cat all the time? Her suggestion struck me as absurd, but nevertheless delightful, and I was quite happy with it. Tsano still seemed unsure as to what he should do, and perhaps I hustled him off rather unceremoniously, for I did wish to be left alone with the Cat once more.

"Tsano, my dear chap," I said, "you heard what the lady said. Now get along home quickly before Aniad sends out a search party for you."

"Well, if you are quite sure," he said uncertainly, looking from me to the Cat and from the Cat to me.

"Really, Tsano, it is quite all right. You may go with a quiet mind, I assure you," said the Cat kindly.

"Thank you, Madam. You are very good. I am sorry we have caused you so much trouble today. Goodnight, then, Klemo. I'll come round tomorrow if I can—and with that he was gone.

"What did he mean about our having caused you so much trouble?" I asked the Cat.

She made no direct reply to this but took up my earlier remark to Tsano by saying, "I don't think Aniad will send a search party for Tsano. She trusts him, and with reason. He is a good, sensible man. But are you sure that Vrailbran–Zenhild will not be sending a search party out for *you,* young man?"

It game me quite a shock to realize that she knew who I was and of my relationship to Bran. I suppose I must have looked rather stupefied for she laughed in her delightful way and said, "Don't look so surprised and so caught out!"

"But how did you know who I was?"

"There are many possible replies to that," she said enigmatically, "but if you look in a mirror you must be aware of one answer."

"You mean that I am obviously a foreigner, I suppose?"

"Yes—that, and other things." There was a teasing note in her voice that made her seem even more bewitching.

"What other things? Please tell me" I begged.

"That, Klemo-Vrailbran, might make you rather more conceited than you already are, so I think I won't."

"Do you really think I am conceited?" I asked in some surprise, for really I had been so much humbled in this land where I did, it is true, feel that no one recognized my worth, that I had almost come to revise my own opinion of myself.

"Well, perhaps not conceited, if you don't like the word, but let us say rather challengingly self–confident for a young man."

This criticism cast me down somewhat and I said sadly, "I'm sorry. I see that you do not like me after all, dear pretty Cat. And I had thought we were getting on so well together. I suppose I must be conceited to have imagined that."

"Klemo, Klemo, don't be hurt. Of course, you are quite right. I like you very much and of course I don't think you are really conceited. The truth is that I find that self–confidence of yours extremely attractive. There, now, have I made amends?"

"Ah, lovely, lovely Cat," I said, "you have made me very, very happy!"

"That's all very well," said the Cat in a more practical tone, "but really it is time I took you home, or your wife will be extremely worried about you. I know I should be if you were *my* husband."

"I don't think Bran will be home yet," I said, and explained about the message she had left me.

The Cat seemed to think this over. Then she said, "Do you mind if I remove my head?" and while I was stupidly pondering on the meaning of this odd, Alice–in–Wonderland question, she peeled back the furry covering on her face and head, and then I understood why I had felt that I already knew her. My Cat was now trans-mogrified into the young woman official on the sledding course who had given us our final scolding that afternoon before letting us go.

Again I must have looked my astonishment for she said, "Did you really not recognize me?"

Now I was amazed that I had not done so. That entrancing shape revealed by the skiing costume should have been enough to tell me, apart from the unusual, rich timbre of her voice. How could I have been so stupid?

"It must have been the Acumba," I said apologetically.

"Ah, yes, the Acumba—mm—Did your wife not warn you about it?"

"No—but then, of course, she did not know that Tsano and I would go in there, after all, did she?"

"No, but she should have warned you all the same."

"I'm glad she didn't, for then perhaps I shouldn't have met you," I said rather daringly.

"That's true. You would not. I came over to keep an eye on you when I saw you were alone."

"Oh," I said in a flat tone. "You mean you actually didn't want to come and talk to me?"

"I didn't say that, now did I? Anyway, we didn't talk very much, did we?"

That was true. For most of the time we had danced together wordlessly, communication being made by our bodies, with no need of speech.

"May I know your real name?" I asked.

"Why, of course. It is ————." Here she reeled off a name of such inordinate length and complexity that I knew I should never succeed in saying it correctly. I made a shot at repeating it, but all it did was to make her laugh. (Here I might explain in passing that I have had to make very rough approximations of Capovoltan names throughout my narrative, for not only do vowel qualities differ from our own, but consonants occur in unfamiliar "clusters," and the language has a number of strange palatal and velar sounds completely foreign to an Englishman's ear.)

"I shall call you Pussy then," I said, using the English word.

"Pussy?" she repeated. "Why?"

"In my country it is the pet name we give a cat, and it means we like that cat very much," I said earnestly, taking her hands in mine. "Come, don't let's waste any more time. Let's dance again."

I wanted to reduce the distance between us, both physically and mentally. I had an uncanny sense that she was having some kind of internal struggle between inclination and duty, and I was heavily on the side of what I was fairly sure was her inclination as well as mine.

She came to me and we began to dance, and again the music and the movement generated a current of such force between us that our bodies seemed to be held together in this marvelous unity of touch without our even willing it. And now I began to caress her and to whisper to her in praise of her beauty. Without any preliminary word between us, our dance took us out of the crowded room and into the kind, enveloping dark. There with trembling hands I began to try to peel off the clinging layers of wool that were a barrier between me and her perfection. She took my hand in hers, however, and led me quickly and silently through the night, threading her way between buildings by what I imagine were alleyways and passages, and then unlocking an anonymous door, drew me gently in after her.

There we did not waste words. She only said rather doubtfully, "Klemo, I hope this will not make trouble for you, my dear. Are you quite sure about it?"

I did not understand the real meaning of her words at that time. Yes, I was sure about it. It was the only thing that I was sure of—that I wanted my lovely Cat with more passion than, I then felt, I had ever wanted anyone or anything in my life before.

Afterward we lay curled up together while we briefly slept. When we woke, she sat up quickly saying, "Klemo, Klemo, I must take you home or things will be bad for you."

But the feel of her against me had made my little man greedy, and there he was, nuzzling and searching her out again.

"No, no, Klemo," she exclaimed, trying to put him away, but I stopped her lovely mouth with my kissing tongue, and he and I together finished our work yet again.

"Klemo, Klemo, the Great Mother help you if you ever get into the wrong hands!" she said, when at length I released her and withdrew.

"You think I need some help in the matter?" I asked, preparing to answer the challenge with a third round if need be.

"Don't be absurd, Klemo. You are quite mad and reckless. Come on—get dressed and let me take you home."

"Ah," I said, "no need. You have taken me home already, here and here and here," and I kissed her in each place.

She pushed me away with an exclamation and put on a light. She shook an admonishing finger at me, saying, "Now, Klemo. You must be serious and sensible. We must hurry or there really will be a scandal. Now are you sure you have got everything? I don't want any incriminating evidence lying about my office in the morning!"

She was quite right, of course, but I could have wished that she had been a little less brisk and commonsensical about the whole thing.

As we made our way to the car–rail to take us back to our

respective halls, I was surprised to see that in spite of the lateness—or by now the earliness—of the hour, there were groups of people wandering about, sometimes singing, sometimes creating much more of an uproar, many of them in strange costumes, as my companion had been earlier in the night. I commented on this to her.

"Yes—there are always lots of fancy–dress parties on the night of the body competitions. It is an old tradition. Didn't your wife tell you about it?"

"No, I don't think so—or if she did, perhaps I didn't quite understand what she was talking about." I was beginning to feel a bit defensive about what Bran had or had not told me, not so much because it seemed to imply a criticism of Bran, I must confess, as that it hurt my pride to have it assumed that she did not care enough about me to bother—not even quite that, perhaps, but there was an uneasiness that I could not quite define.

The halls, too, were still ablaze with light, and little clumps of people stood about as though they could not bring themselves to part for the night, although whatever festivities there had been now seemed to be over. I was rehearsing in my mind the story that I should tell Bran, part of the truth but not all of it, as my Cat delivered me briskly at the entrance to my hall. I suppose it was for the benefit of any party who might be listening that she said, "Here is your hall then, Klemo–Vrailbran. Give my greetings to your wife, won't you? Good night." And she was gone before I could decide how to salute her.

I went quickly up to our room and entered as silently as I could. I put on the small vestibule light so that I should not fall over something and wake Bran by making a great racket. I need not have bothered, however, for the room was empty and there was no sign that Bran had been in it since I had left it to go out with Tsano all those hours before. I will confess that I felt a certain relief when I realized that perhaps I need never explain to Bran how it was that I came to be quite so late. I made great haste to get to bed so that if she came in she would have no idea of how long I had been home. I lay there rather tensely for a while expecting her to come in, but my exertions during the course of the evening and night had been quite considerable and soon sleep overtook me.

CHAPTER

13

When I awoke it was to the light of full day. The place in the bed was still empty, but the bedclothes were in disarray and the pillow bore the imprint of Bran's head. I felt quite guilty that she had come to bed and got up again without my waking.

"Bran," I called. "Bran?"

But there was no Bran. Now I began to worry. Had she somehow found out about my escapade of last night, and gone off in anger? Perhaps she had actually been waiting for me somewhere in the reception area of the hall and I had not seen her? But, then, she would not have waited to come to bed after I had fallen asleep. No, I could make nothing of the facts, except that I felt guilty and thought her absence a rather sinister thing that boded ill for me.

As I was dressing, I saw that Bran had left her little recorder behind with its light still on. It was such an unusual thing for anyone to go out without their recorder that I played it, although normally we left messages for one another on the room machine. It was indeed a message from Bran, to say that she did not want to disturb me, since I was so deeply asleep that I had neither heard her come to bed nor get up, so she had left me to have my sleep out and would be back later. She was so glad that I had been sensible and not waited up for her but gone to bed as she suggested, as she had met some old friends and had come back much later than she intended to do. Her voice sounded perfectly friendly—and even rather apologetic—and so I threw off my feeling of guilt and with a much lighter heart prepared to meet Bran face to face. Catching myself humming gaily and smiling to myself at the memory of last night as I went downstairs, I reflected wryly that my heavy heart had been due not to a feeling of guilt but to the fear of being found out. I was still ruminating on this when I almost walked into Bran as she came hurrying in, as I in turn was about to go out.

"Oh, darling, there you are!" she said warmly, but as if something had put her into a bit of a flurry. "I am really so sorry about last night. It was so unexpected running into————" (here a list of names I did not grasp). "I hadn't seen any of them for years, and you know how it is, we got talking and didn't notice the time."

It was unusual for Bran to be so apologetic, and it gave me a slight pang again at the knowledge of how basely I was deceiving her when I said, "Why, that's all right, Bran. I'm so glad you had a good time. I wasn't in very early myself actually, and went off to sleep very quickly."

"Oh? What time did you get in then?"

"Well, Tsano went back to fetch Aniad, but she didn't come in the end, but, of course, by the time he'd been home and come back again and one thing and another, it was quite late. Probably after the twelfth twelfth" (that is after midnight, the day as I have explained being divided into twelfths). I knew that I had been much later than this, but it would have been rather difficult to explain what I had been doing after Tsano left me if by some ill chance the subject should crop up again in front of him.

"Ah, well, I must have come in very soon after, I should think," she said, smiling at me brightly.

Now that struck me as rather strange, for I well knew that it must have been at least the first twelfth or later before I got to bed myself. Then I was sure I understood what had happened and why she was being so placatory. She, too, had drunk too much Acumba, and like Tsano had fallen asleep, but of course this she did not want me to know. She wanted me to think she had come in earlier than she really had. Dear, transparent Bran, I thought. She would be no good at carrying off any real deceit.

"What are we going to do today?" I asked.

"What would you like to do, my dear? Do you want to spend the day with Tsano once again? I should not mind at all, for I quite understand that you boys have different interests from mine. I really do not care for the rougher sports now, although I suppose I watched my share of them years ago."

"I think I saw all I wanted to yesterday. I should like to spend today with you, Bran. What are you going to watch?"

"I'm afraid it would bore you, Klemo. I want to watch the acrobatics and gymnastics."

"No, I shouldn't be bored. I'd like to come."

"Didn't you make any arrangement with Tsano for today?"

"He said he'd come round this morning and see if I was free. But it doesn't matter, I'm sure."

"It's not like you to be selfish, Klemo. Don't you think it would be unkind to let the poor fellow turn up and not find you here?"

"Couldn't we wait for him and then he could come with us?"

"All right. You wait for him, dear, and follow me on to the gymnastics arena. I do very much want to see the first event and I'm rather late already. If Tsano would rather do something else, do feel free to go with him, though, won't you?"

She kissed me hurriedly and was gone. I did feel a little as though she were washing her hands of me, but reminded myself how lucky I was that she had no suspicions about last night.

As soon as she had gone, Tsano came in very conspiratorially, glancing about him as if he feared to be observed. When I hailed him, he looked so relieved that I wondered what he had been worrying about now. The poor fellow always seemed in a state of worry about something or another.

"Something wrong, Tsano? You looked quite bothered."

"Klemo, dear fellow, I *am* pleased to see you. Did you get home safely last night? I suppose you must have done, but afterward I was so worried about you."

"My dear chap, why ever?"

"Well, you know—you really are such a trusting fellow that one can't help being afraid that someone will take advantage of you. I came round early this morning at three–twelfths to find out if you were safely home, because Aniad thought I shouldn't have left you when I told her about it—and then of course I saw Vrailbran and I was afraid she'd been out looking for you all night. But I didn't dare ask her about you then. Anyway, I waited until she came out again and I could see then that she wasn't worried, so I asked her if you were up and she said you were so fast asleep she decided not to disturb you. So I went home."

I tried to digest this story which Tsano had poured out rather incoherently. I thought I must have misunderstood him—but no. He was quite clear when questioned that he had seen Bran returning from somewhere and entering the hall at three twelfths or thereabouts (that is about 6 A.M. our time), that soon after she had come out again in different clothes and that she had said I was sleeping so deeply—etc.

I felt slightly stunned by this revelation and could make no sense of it at all. Tsano said, "Madam took you safely home, then?"

"Madam?" I said foolishly. "Who do you mean?"

"Why Klemo, ————," and then the impossible name that I recognized as belonging to the Cat.

"Oh—you mean the Cat," I said.

"Great Mother, Klemo, don't speak like that about her. Someone might hear you and I don't know what they might think."

"Well, I simply can't get my tongue round that name. It's simpler to call her the Cat. After all, she was wearing a cat costume, and a very pretty one, too, I thought!"

"You're hopeless, Klemo. What is one to do with you?" But he laughed all the same, and we seemed to have got away from the subject of Bran's strange behavior and my last night's escort, for he went on, "What are you doing today, anyway?"

Bran suggested that we might follow her on to the acrobatics and gymnastics, but she doesn't mind if we do something else. As a matter of fact, I'd like to go and see some skiing today after messing everything up like that yesterday." I thought you see that up on the ski slopes I might track down the Cat again.

Immediately Tsano was conscience–stricken again at this reminder of yesterday. Of course I had not intended any kind of reproach, but he was upset because yesterday had been the climax and finale of the snow events, and not the beginning as I had thought.

I certainly felt disappointed, for I had now no idea of how I might find the Cat again. But there was no use in letting Tsano see that, so I pretended not to mind at all and we decided that we would follow on after Bran.

We walked to the car–rail in silence. I was turning over and over in my mind Tsano's account of Bran's movements and trying to make some sense of it. It did not tally at all with what she herself had said, nor had that, I remembered, quite coincided with what I myself knew. She had tried to imply that she had been back soon after midnight, when—and now the enormity of it struck me—she had been out all night. Great Mother! She had been out all night and was lying to me about it. What on earth could she have been doing all that time that she did not want me to know about? I repeated this insane question to myself, trying not to accept the only reply which seemed to fit: she had been doing exactly what *I* had been doing all that time that I did not want her to know about! But she had been worse than me, for she had been out all night. I was astounded at her behavior and filled with indignation. That a young married woman who professed to love her husband as Bran professed to love me should behave in such a way was absolutely shocking, disgraceful, and terribly, terribly hurtful. I was deeply miserable as I thought about it.

We had boarded the car by now, and suddenly Tsano turned to me and said in a rather strained voice, "I've simply got to talk to you, Klemo, for your own good."

It was like a knife in the heart, for I was sure he was going to tell me about Bran. It was one thing to know it and to have to face it within myself, but it was quite another to have it confirmed and rammed home. I did not think I could bear it and I said, "Please don't, Tsano. I don't want to hear about it."

"No, no, you mustn't think I'm criticizing you, Klemo. Don't take it like that. It's just that you are such a dear innocent, and I could not bear to see you get into real trouble. From what you have told me, you grew up in such a different world that to me it sounds almost like a fairy tale, and I really don't think that anyone except me understands quite how innocent you are. I *must* warn you."

The word "innocent" struck like a knell. Neither Bran nor I were innocent. What could this good man know of the lustful workings of my heart? What would he think of me if he knew the truth? I felt I was a hundred times more soiled, a hundred times more worldly wise than he—but how could I tell him so without revealing things I did not wish to reveal?

"You see, Klemo," he went on, "I find it difficult to talk about these things, but I must. You are too trusting and too good. You think that all women are as honorable as your wife, but it isn't so. There are many who because you are young and attractive and—forgive me for saying it—foreign, would take advantage of you and use you and bring disgrace and misfortune upon you only then to abandon you. No young, attractive man can be too careful. I should never have let you go off with [and here was the name of the Cat]. I think she is an honorable woman, but it could get you a bad reputation, and that would expose you to real danger from unscrupulous women."

I felt embarrassed that he should, as I thought, have guessed at the relationship between me and the Cat, but I thought there was no use in trying to brazen it out, so I only said, "But I don't understand, Tsano, how such a thing could expose *me* to danger. It is surely the woman in such an affair who is at risk."

"Yes, but who takes all the blame for it, Klemo? Don't you know that a woman has only to name a man about whose reputation there is the slightest doubt, and her word will be taken against his?"

Well, I will not weary the reader with repeating the whole of this conversation, for I gave the gist of it much earlier in my narrative, explaining how unfairly the male partner in such a relationship was blamed, and how unscrupulous women could take advantage of this. It was Tsano who now for the first time made me understand fully how fraught with danger to a man here in Capovolta are his relations with the opposite sex.

Now many of the slightly obscure warnings I had received began to take on a new meaning, as did the Cat's implied strictures on Bran for, I suppose, not warning me adequately and not supervising me properly. Although the whole idea of it seemed ridiculous at first, I began to see with a cold, creeping alarm that if the Cat were *not* an honorable woman, I could easily find myself named as the father of a child whom I would have to nurse and tend, perhaps entirely on my own, and for whom I should have to suffer social ostracism as one of the loose and lustful kind. I could hardly expect Bran to accept another woman's child in the home after all—the idea of suggesting it filled me with panic. If only I got out of this affair safely this time, I vowed to myself there would never be another.

By now we had reached the arenas set aside for the gymnastics and acrobatics, but any idea of finding Bran was quickly shed when I saw the great concourse of spectators everywhere. I did not even know which particular events she had intended to watch. My feelings about this were extremely mixed: with one part of myself I wanted to see her immediately and, if not to confront her with what I had learned of her behavior last night, at least to look on her with new eyes, to test out somehow or other the validity or otherwise of the conclusions to which I had been forced. But another, more calculating side of me was glad to postpone the meeting, to have time to think out all the implications for myself as well as for her, and to decide on the line I would take.

Tsano and I looked in on various events, but unfortunately we were too late to find good places for anything we particularly wanted to see. As we drifted round rather aimlessly among the crowd, Tsano suddenly said, "Why, of course, Dinad–Vlebig will be competing in the individual acrobatics this morning. He is rather a silly fellow, but after all he is a colleague, so perhaps we ought to go and support him. What do you think? I suppose he'll be quite unbearable in the office now that he's won the body competition."

"Won the body competition? Dinad–Vlebig?" My surprise must have been obvious, for Tsano said, "Yes, he was the Supreme Winner last night. Didn't Bran tell you?"

"No—no, she didn't mention it, but, of course, I didn't ask her. Really I'd forgotten about the body competition."

It is true that Dinad was a very handsome boy, but he was far from being a favorite of mine. He worked in the receipt and dispatch department, with which we had close dealings, and I had a poor opinion of his ability and an equally low one of his personality. He had a loud, mindless laugh and a habit of playing incredibly stupid, childish tricks. My foreignness had been a subject of feeble jokes, repeated each time I came across him until I should have liked to hit him—but, of course, I was obliged to laugh, albeit a very forced laugh, in order not to be thought incapable of taking a joke against myself. Loud and boisterous at all times, he became even more so when any of the women entered the dispatch room. It angered me to see how indulgent they were, with few exceptions, instead of reprimanding his foolishness and his affectations. Like Tsano, I was appalled to think of the effect this public tribute to his physique might have on his behavior in the office.

It was curiosity to see how he performed that now made me agree with Tsano that we should go and watch his performance in the individual acrobatics. Once again we were too late to secure very good places, but we could see well enough, though at a distance. The acrobatics routine was a very demanding one, involving a high degree of muscular coordination and agility, and I marveled at each competitor's skill. When, however, it was Dinad's turn, even I realized that he added to the performance something that none of the others had exhibited: this was an extraordinary fluidity, so that one part of the routine flowed into the next with a beautiful rhythmic grace that was aesthetically pleasurable to watch. His body, clad only in a small loincloth, was as handsome as his face, and, now, exerting the discipline and control necessary to perform these remarkable gymnastic feats, he seemed a different person from the callow youth we knew at the office.

The applause that greeted him when he finished was just homage to his faultless and elegant performance. Clapping, shouting, stamping, the crowd roared its approval—and then it was that I saw Bran. She was seated in the front row of the spectators, leaning forward intently, gazing at this beautiful boy, her face wearing the expression of open, sensual pleasure that it took on during our lovemaking. And as I watched, the boy, turning to bow here and there to his supporters, made to her a particularly long and low obeisance. I am sure my eyes did not deceive me, for Bran in her turn kissed her hand to him. It was only a moment's exchange, and no one who was not both watching closely and positioned as I was so that I looked down on both of them could have been certain of it. I *was* certain, and the certitude pierced me with shock and anger and furious jealousy.

It seemed impossible that things around me should go on exactly as before, that Tsano should be commenting interestedly on this boy's performance and his chances of winning yet another contest, that the next competitor should now be appearing amid the clamorous applause of *his* supporters to begin the routine again. I wanted to be alone. I could not bear even the companionship of good, kind Tsano. I muttered to him that I was not feeling too well and began to blunder my way out between the rows of spectators. I should have thought of some better excuse, for of course Tsano followed me and nearly drove me mad with his anxious solicitude, before I was able to persuade him to return to the arena and leave me to find my way back to my hall. I came very near to offending him before I convinced him that for some unfathomable reason I wanted to be on my own and that the greatest kindness he could do me was to leave me alone and go back to the competition. It was, therefore, only much later that I learned that the burst of ecstatic applause that seemed to follow me with ironic mockery as I walked away was for the performance of Dinad's rival and nearest challenger of the previous evening. This young man had a physique of matching, or some thought even greater, magnificence than Dinad's, but the beauty of his face was marred by a slight flattening of the bridge of the nose during a training session. While this had counted against him in the body competition, it had no bearing on his performance in the individual acrobatics contest, and it was he who was finally declared the winner.

Once I was alone, every remark Bran had made, every slight nuance of her voice ran themselves endlessly through my head like a sound track repeating itself, while I examined each one for any underlying meaning that it might have had in the light of what I now

knew, but for which I wished to find some excuse for refuting.
Everything did indeed acquire a new undertone, one which made the
case more certain and more damning. The surprising alacrity with
which she had acquiesced in my spending the previous day with
Tsano, her placatory tone this morning, her suggestion that I should
wait for Tsano and follow her when she must have known how
impossible it would be to find her—although in the end it had proved
less so than she might have thought—all, all fell into place and
completed a picture I did not wish to contemplate, but from which I
could not switch my internal gaze. With what innocent stupidity I
had played into her hands! How she must have congratulated herself
on the ease with which she had deceived me! Was she even now
laughing at my gullibility with her new conquest? This last thought
was a peculiarly bitter one: it was gall and wormwood to think of that
hateful youth accepted in my place and thinking of me with
condescension and amused contempt. The thought of returning to
the office after the holiday and meeting him face to face, each of us
with our secret knowledge of the other, was more than I could bear. I
thought of my own complaisance in making it so easy for her; never
for one moment had it occurred to me to doubt her fidelity or imagine
it to be any less than my own. Here for the first time I thought about
the Cat again. My own fidelity! What had I to say about that? But I
knew that however it might look to an outside observer, the
relationship between the Cat and me was something quite different
from that between Bran and me. The one did not menace the other at
all. Yes, I would gladly have seen the Cat again before I knew about
Bran; I thought of her with great remembered pleasure that had the
power to stir me even now. But compared with the totality of the
way in which I was committed to Bran, my feeling for the Cat was
insignificant. There really had been no true infidelity on my part.
How different it was on Bran's side. How could she, professing to
love me as she did, have deceived and wounded me in this way?

My pride demanded that I should not reveal to her the depth of my
hurt and my jealousy. The more I thought about it, the more I
became convinced that I must not let her know I had found out. I
should be very casual, behaving as though I knew nothing, but I

would not let her out of my sight for one moment from now on.

I had got so far in my miserable self–communing when Bran came hurriedly in. I was quite unprepared for this, in spite of the time I had spent probing the wound and trying to decide on the treatment. So I sat and stared at her miserably, saying nothing. She came over to me with a face of concern, saying, "Klemo, darling, what is the matter? Tsano told me that you were not feeling very well and had gone off home, but wouldn't let him come with you. He was so worried he came and found me. What is it, my love?" and she put her arms round me.

Gone were all my resolutions to be calm and casual and not to reveal my hurt. I flung her off saying savagely, "You know very well what is the matter. Do you think I'm such a fool that I didn't know that you were carrying on with that wretched little pin–headed twit? Body competition winner, indeed! How could you demean yourself to the level of that bit of mindless, jumped–up scum? I thought you had more taste."

Bran stood looking at me with an expression of surprised dismay, as well she might at the unexpectedness of this onslaught. I do not know what I had expected her to say or do, but her silence added fuel to my fury and I poured out fresh accusations with a violence that surprised myself. When I had finished, I stood there shaking with emotion, waiting for her reply. I suppose I really hoped she would deny it, that she would in some miraculous way explain that it had been a complete misapprehension. But she said nothing. She simply turned away as though to walk out of the room.

"Can't you say something?" I almost shouted at her. "Are you dumb as well as false and treacherous?"

She turned slowly. "What can I say? What is there to for me to say? You have made your mind up and have condemned me unheard."

"Can't you even say you're sorry? Or does it amuse you to make me more unhappy than I have ever been in my life?"

"I have behaved badly, and of course I am sorry, Klemo, but what difference does that make, since you are determined to exaggerate the importance of the thing out of all proportion? Yes, I did deceive you about the time I came home and all that, but I didn't want you to know because I thought it would make you unhappy. And how right I was. Of course I wouldn't have done it if I'd thought you'd find out."

The extraordinary sophistry of this argument almost silenced me. How could one begin to attack someone who thought in this way? I was outraged.

Finally I said, "Bran, are you trying to tell me that if I hadn't found out, you don't think the thing would have mattered at all? How *can* you think that when you have hurt me so much?"

"But, Klemo, that is just my point. If you didn't know about it, it wouldn't have upset you like this!"

"How could you do such a thing," I burst out, "when you say that you love me? And to lie to me about it, too!"

"I do love you, Klemo," she said in a flat, tired tone. "You may not believe it, but I do. This other thing means nothing to me in comparison with the feelings I have for you. That is the truth, whether you believe it or not."

Of course, I longed to believe it. She went on in the same sad, tired voice, "I am an absolute fool to have risked losing something so precious for the sake of something so utterly trivial. I don't suppose I can make you understand, because I don't really understand myself why I did it. But I can only assure you that my feeling for you is something deeper and more important to me than anything else in my life."

"Oh Bran, Bran!" I said, taking her in my arms and in some strange way finding myself now the comforter instead of the comforted. And so we were reconciled and, like a spring that had been stretched and then released, we seemed even closer for the time than we had ever been before. It was a mutual decision, taken without any discussion, that we should leave the Games and go back home for the rest of the holiday. I left a message for Tsano to tell him this, and we were off early the next day.

CHAPTER
14

The rest of the holiday passed in a happy and peaceful way for the most part. From time to time, the thought of Bran's perfidy came back to prick me like a goad, but she herself seemed more loving and more thoughtful toward me than ever before. There were times when I would find her gazing at me with a particular, loving intensity of expression that I found very engaging, and she would smile at me warmly when I caught this gaze, but she said nothing, although I had a feeling that there was some unspoken statement or question in the air. Finally one evening when the holiday was nearly over and we had been making love on a thick rug on the floor, luxuriating as it were in our leisure to make love exactly when we wanted to instead of having our times dictated by the work routine soon to begin again, she said, "Klemo, I want to talk to you seriously. I have been thinking a lot about us, and I feel that it is about time we decided to begin our family."

For a moment I did not understand the import of what she said, but when I did realize it, I found myself quite unprepared for it. I had been wondering what was on her mind, sure that she would tell me in her own good time, but *this* had never crossed my mind as a possibility. Of course, I knew that we had been granted permission for a family marriage and I must have accepted that at some future time we would have a family, but somehow I was quite unable to envisage Bran as a mother—and, too, the thought of assuming fresh responsibilities here in Capovolta frightened me, truly.

"Isn't it a bit soon, Bran?" I said. "We haven't been married very long. Wouldn't it be better to wait, say, a year, at least?"

"Why, Klemo? I don't want to make the mistake that some people make and put it off until we are too set in our ways to want to have children. And then, too, medical opinion here emphasizes that children of young mothers and fathers have the best chance of being born perfect in every way. We may not be lucky immediately, you see, and it may well take us a year or more before we actually have our first child."

That consideration seemed to distance the prospect a little and my alarm subsided. After all, Bran was quite within her rights to want a family; the fact that I already had one could hardly be expected to weigh with her.

"Well, then," she said, "you won't take anything from now on, will you?"

"Take anything?" I was rather bewildered.

"You know, to prevent us having a baby."

"Great Mother, Bran. Of course I won't. What did you think I might take?"

"Don't be silly, Klemo. You know what I mean. Whatever it is that you have been taking so far."

Again that horrid cold shock of the unwelcome and unexpected. I was ignorant of so many of the unexpressed and silent assumptions here that I was slowly learning to be wary in my responses. Of course, after what Tsano had told me, I should have realized that I was the one on whom rested the responsibility for taking birth control measures, but I simply had not applied this knowledge to Bran and myself. She it was who knew the rules and regulations and gave me the necessary guidance. Probably she assumed that her father would have told me, but he certainly had not.

Now, in response to this remark of Bran's, I simply said, rather noncommittally, "Yes, of course." For, after all, if she had not yet become pregnant, then she need never know of the risks she had unknowingly run. It did fleetingly cross my mind to think that I might in fact delay the whole thing if I could get some information and advice from Tsano. But then I thought that it was hardly fair to Bran and that I would simply accept whatever fortune might send.

All too soon we were back at work. I say "all too soon" not because I wanted the holiday period prolonged for its own sake but because I hated the thought of having to see and even greet the loathsome Dinad–Vlebig. He would be a constant reminder to me of what had happened that night up at the Games. At first, in the general outburst of congratulation on his victory, there was no need for me to address him directly, for he was always surrounded by an admiring coterie, although he himself continued to feel injured that he had not had a double victory. He was sure that his rival's victory in the individual acrobatics was a dire miscarriage of justice and proof positive of the veniality and corruption of the judges. Eventually one of the senior women heard of this and reprimanded him severely, so that from then on he sulked about it instead. After the first week or two, when I had occasion to go into the receipt and dispatch room, I saw that he was no longer so feted and acclaimed, for the normal tenor of life was very quickly resumed, almost as though people had had their fill of thrills and excitement and were glad of the return to order and routine. Now I could no longer avoid a face–to–face meeting. It seemed to me that he treated me with a kind of scornful condescension that I could hardly tolerate, and I made every possible excuse for asking others to go to the dispatch room for me, instead of doing my own errands. On one occasion he had the nerve to ask me how Bran was and to send her his greetings. I could hardly keep my hands off his throat, I can assure you.

I do not know whether Tsano knew or suspected anything, but the good fellow saw that for some reason I hated going into that room, and whenever he could, he sent someone else instead of me. Apart from that, I began to find his general solicitude a little galling: he so clearly seemed to feel that I needed support or protection against someone or something that he made me feel as though I must be more vulnerable than I knew.

The holiday had only been over a few weeks when Bran gave me the news that we had in fact begun our family. I was glad for her sake, of course, but if the truth be told, I had hoped for a longer respite. At first she felt rather wretched, and was given leave of

absence, which necessitated my taking it, too. Fortunately, she
soon recovered from these early disturbances and was thenceforth
wonderfully well and blooming. The months slipped by too quickly
for me, and when she was five months pregnant she began upon her
maternity leave, for it was considered very important that the
mother–to–be should lead a life as free of stress and worry, and as
healthily spent in resting and taking enough fresh air and exercise as
paid leisure would allow. I had not foreseen that I would so soon be
involved in the care of my wife and our future baby, for my real wife
had worked until just before the baby was born, and afterward had
continued to run the house and look after me as before. Now I found
that from the moment Vrailbran gave up work, I was expected to do
the same. My duty henceforward was to look after her and wait upon
her with even greater devotion than before, to accompany her upon
her daily walks, to time her exercises, to buy and cook her special
diet–in short, to take on every possible task except the one I could
not, of actually bearing the child. While I was prepared to perform
these duties willingly out of my affection for Bran, it was a bitter
blow to me that they should necessitate leaving my employment at
the City Transport Company, and at first I resisted the tacit
assumption that I should do so. Then shortly before her maternity
leave began Bran said, "Won't it be lovely to be at home together all
day and every day for a while? I am looking forward to it so much."

"It won't be quite 'all day' yet, will it?" I said. "But I'll go as late
as I dare and leave the office as early as I can. Do you think I might
be able to get special permission perhaps to leave early?"

"What do you mean, Klemo? You will not be going to the office
after the next full moon."

"Why not, Bran? I have been running the house as well as doing
my other work for a long time now. Surely there is no need for me to
give up work yet?"

"But *I* am giving up work after the next full moon, you know
that."

"Of course I know that, Bran, but I cannot see what difference
that will make."

"Cannot see what difference it will make? What *do* you mean?

What about me? You can't seriously be suggesting that I should be alone at home all day and have to look after myself?''

"But I should look after you, Bran, as I do now. I don't need to give up my work just for that.''

"Don't be ridiculous. Of course you must give it up. I need you at home, you silly fellow.''

"We should find it difficult to manage without my earnings, Bran.''

"Klemo, dear, you are really a feather–brained lad, sweet though you are. I've explained to you that from next moon I shall begin to earn the special maternity bonus, and that will make us far better off than your miserable little earnings, my dear.''

"But none of it will be *mine*. Don't you see that I shall have to come to you for everything then?''

"You don't think I mind that, do you my dear? You *know* that I regard everything as *ours,* not *mine,* and whatever I earn is equally yours. Don't give all that another thought. The loss of your earnings is a very small sacrifice to make in return for your presence here, for you are very important to me, you know that.''

What could I say in reply to such a well–meant, loving declaration? It would be impossibly ungracious to point out how she had misunderstood my real meaning. And so it was that with a heavy heart I told Tsano that I should have to leave at the next full moon. I discussed with him the chances of my being able to resume work there again, if ever I should be able to free myself from my domestic ties. Tsano could see no possible chance of this for many years if we were going to found a family, even if of only two children, for Capovoltan opinion was greatly against single–child families. It was thought very important as a part of a child's social training that it should from an early age grow up learning to adjust to the claims of others, in the shape of its siblings. I, however, could not bring myself to contemplate year after year of such a life as seemed my immediate prospect. Like an entrapped creature, I scrabbled round in my mind for some way out. Surely, I argued with myself, if I were able to return to work, it would be possible to hire someone to discharge the tasks that otherwise I must perforce perform at home;

therefore it was of paramount importance to me that there should be a possibility of my resuming work at some future time. I will confess that I gave no thought at all to the person upon whom I hoped eventually to unload my personal domestic burden. Tsano promised to do his best as my ambassador, first with our immediate superior and then with Avgard. I hesitated as to whether I should plead my own cause with Avgard, but in the end I could not bring myself to do so: I felt foolish and ashamed, for Avgard had so clearly foreseen the situation in which I should find myself and had offered me a way out, which I had refused. How could I cast myself again on her mercy?

Tsano, however, was indeed a good friend to me once again and must have pleaded for me with all his persuasive force, for a couple of days before the dreaded day on which my employment with the Transport Company was to be terminated, he came with a beaming face to tell me that I had been granted indefinite unpaid leave instead. I felt like a condemned man reprieved, such was the relief that engulfed me. Perhaps only then did I realize the full measure of my unwillingness to accept the role which the structure of Capovoltan society was inexorably thrusting upon me.

The months at home with Vrailbran before the birth of the child were a strange "limbo" period for me. I felt all to be in suspension; what was past had vanished almost as if it had never been, while I could only dread, but not imagine, the future and consequently pushed away all thought of it from my conscious mind and lived as much in the present as I could. My nights, however, were full of sleepless worry alternating with evil dreams which I could not recall on waking, but which left me with feelings of foreboding so intense that each morning it was hours before I could shake them off. I looked back upon my old habit of deep, peaceful sleep and an untroubled awakening as on a time of childlike innocence and trust, although it had been the pattern of my life until now. Superficially this was a tranquil and happy interlude in our life: for Bran, I think, it probably was genuinely so—a restful pause in the even progressions of her days, not a complete disruption of her whole life as it threatened to be for me. Although on leave, Bran retained some connection with her working life, for she was still consulted and gave advice about any development or problem which particularly concerned her department. Moreover the interruption, far from holding up her career, appeared rather to be forwarding it, for the young woman who was deputizing for her now would, if she were judged successful in discharging her new duties, replace Bran eventually, while Bran herself was destined to take a step up in the hierarchy. Relieved of the day-to-day routine work, she had time to consider general policy and its attendant problems in a more dispassionate way. I envied her the happy absorption with which she would listen to the cylinders sent her from time to time and then bend the by no means negligible powers of her mind to finding solutions for the problems contained therein. The rest of the time she spent carefully and painstakingly carrying out the regimen laid down for her.

About a month before the baby was due, when Bran went for her regular routine examination, the doctor asked her to go into the hospital for a few days for further examination and certain other tests. This put me into a state of great apprehension for Bran, although she herself seemed not unduly perturbed, as the doctor assured her there was no need for worry. It transpired, however, that the doctor suspected the birth was nearer than we had reckoned, for a reason which she suspected but did not wish to confirm until she was certain. Indeed, she had barely time to confirm her suspicions and to advise Bran and me of it before we found ourselves the parents of twin girls! I will not deny that after my jubilant relief that Bran was safe and well, my immediate feeling was one of incredulous alarm. I had never imagined being the parent of more than one baby at a time and, I realized, somewhere inside me I had assumed it would be a boy. Why, I do not know. But here I was, lumbered with two instead of one, and girls at that. The doctor congratulated me as she went off to her next delivery with an amused condescension that I found extremely galling. The medical aides were, however, obviously genuine in their praise and congratulations on the babies. They were two middle–aged men and they cooed and gurgled at the creatures with as much pleasure, I do believe, as if they had been their own, while I gazed at these two minuscule human beings as if they had been a pair of puppies. I only felt a slight pang of disappointment when I saw that neither of them had inherited any physical characteristic from me, as far as could at that time be observed. Of course, I should have known that it was genetically improbable if not impossible, since dark coloring in hair and eyes is dominant to fair—and since the Capovoltans could have no recessive genes for fairness, being of pure racial stock as I have explained; nevertheless somehow I must have been irrationally expecting some modification in feature or coloring caused by their genetic endowment from me. I was ashamed of my lack of feeling and tried to make up for it by lavishing my relief and my love upon Bran.

I had, however, little time for that or for repining, because I now found that I was considered by the aides to be a kind of nursemaid in training, for once we were home again the care of these two new beings would be my task. I suppose it was lucky that my probationary period was longer than it would normally have been because the premature birth of the twins meant that there would be a prolonged period of intensive care in the maternity unit before the twins and Vrailbran would be deemed fit to go gome—and be left to my inexpert attentions.

I had handled my other children before, of course, but never more than the briefest and most gingerly executed embrace while they were so tiny and so vulnerable. Now I had to learn to bathe and change them, to exercise their tiny limbs (for the Capovoltans believe in this and begin almost from the day of birth), to diagnose the reason for their wailing and crying, to massage them to relieve digestive discomfort, to lift them safely, supporting the weight of their surprisingly heavy little heads dangling on the thin stalks of their necks, and to lay them down comfortably. Their vulnerability and fragility terrified me, and I looked with envy and admiration at the confident handling of the aides, but felt I should never dare to emulate them. Slowly, slowly, however, I began to gain courage and even to take some pleasure in my growing ability to assuage the distress of these tiny creatures, and by the time we were able to take them home, I was anxiously watching Bran when she fed them to make sure that she nursed them properly, supporting the little dangling heads and holding them gently but firmly enough to make them feel secure. I weighed them before each feed to check whether they had had enough and became obsessionally anxious when for a time I found that one of them was consistently taking less nourishment than the other. My nights and days were dominated by their needs and by my anxieties about them. Bran, on the contrary, seemed to me very casual, sleeping peacefully through their crying, and laughing at me for being so preoccupied with their well–being. It was some time before I realized that I loved them with a passionate absorption I had never felt for my other children. It was as though the anxiety and exhaustion that they caused me had bound them ever more closely to me. Now, too, I rejoiced that they were so unmistakably little Capovoltans, for I found myself thinking about their future, hoping desperately for their happiness, and I realized then that they could never have been completely integrated into Capovoltan society if they had borne with them everywhere the recognizable signs of their foreign parentage. And I was glad for their sakes, now, that they were girls.

Vrailbran was toasted as a veritable heroine by her family and by our friends and acquaintances, as though she had by personal merit achieved the astonishing feat of having produced twins, and especially girl twins, as her firstborn. I never met a family at home who had had boy twins to start with, but I cannot believe that there would have been such obvious male chauvinism about this as there was here female bias (although it is true that I have heard a note of commiseration among the congratulations on the birth of a girl in my own country). However, since our children had to grow up in this very unequal society, it was truly lucky for them that they were of the privileged sex—but my personal feeling for them would have been no more and no less had they been boys.

By the time Vrailbran's leave was up, another winter holiday had gone and the babies were beginning to delight us by their lovely smiles of recognition as we fed and tended them. My one regret at that period was that I could not spare as much time as I would have liked to nurse them and play with them, for my life was a busy one. I had three people to look after and wait upon, and there were times when I felt that Bran need not have been quite so helpless, but there seemed to be a great mystique of motherhood here in Capovolta which it was difficult for me, a foreigner, to challenge. I could hardly expect Bran to accept an unfavorable comparison with my real wife in the matter of her role in childbearing and rearing, but naturally I could not help a mental comparison which made me feel rather critical toward Bran, who did not lift a finger to help except when she fed the babies. This was considered such an exhausting business for the mother that nothing else was expected of her. At first I had dreaded the time when Vrailbran would return to work and leave me quite alone with the twins, to feed them as well as tend them during the day, but gradually I began to feel that it would perhaps prove easier when I had only the babies to look after and had no need to prepare food and fetch and carry all day for Bran as well.

In some ways this proved to be so, but one thing I had not taken into consideration was that I could not leave the house now to make the necessary purchases and so on without taking the children with me. This involved the lengthy business of stuffing their flopping limbs into special outdoor clothing, so that the whole procedure took at least twice as long as when Bran was still at home and I could leave them in her care for the time that I was out of the house. In addition, the babies were now having artificial foods during the day and only being fed by Bran morning and evening. They did not take kindly to the change at first, so that feeding one, let alone two, took an inordinate amount of time. Moreover, one or the other of them was much more liable to vomit up part of the feed again, so that as soon as I had them dressed and ready in their little wagon to go out shopping, one of them would discharge a messy milky fluid over herself, and her sister—fortunately with great good humor as a rule—but it meant that I had then to take off the soiled clothes and start again the whole procedure of encasing their vaguely wandering limbs in a fresh set of outdoor clothes. Sometimes I felt as if they each had as many limbs as an octopus instead of only eight between them, and I called them collectively "my octopus." By the time we got back again, one or the other would be wailing with discomfort from a wet or soiled diaper and once again I would have to set to and strip and clean them. All the while the dirty linen stacked up endlessly for me to deal with when I had time. "When I had time" is a splendidly ironical phrase, for I *never* had time; I was forever battling with it, desperately trying to clear up the baby paraphernalia and prepare a meal by the time Bran came home.

At first she came home very promptly from the office and was interested in the children's progress, but she was critical if she found that I had not finished the day's chores, and was bored and impatient when I tried to explain that Sora had been sick or Tara had not wanted her dinner. Instead of helping me with the children's bedtime routine or preparing the meal, she would go off saying she had work to do, or that she was exhausted after a difficult day at the office and would I call her when the meal was ready. I felt this to be unfair, but I bore with it for some time, until the whole thing came to a head one evening, when I had had a particularly difficult day. Tara had been fretful for several days and had been sick several times. I was very worried about this until I discovered she was cutting her first tooth. The poor baby could not sleep much, and I had to get up to her several times each night. This particular day she had cried almost all day and there seemed to be nothing I could do to soothe her. By the time I had at last got her off to sleep that evening, I was utterly exhausted and longing to snatch some sleep myself while I had the chance, since I knew this respite was unlikely to last long. Vrailbran had other plans, however, for, as I have mentioned before, she had a lusty appetite for the delights of married life, as indeed I normally had myself. This same night, however, my poor fellow was so tired that all Vrailbran's persuasions could not induce him to perform, and I must confess that I myself simply wished to be left alone and allowed to sleep. Finally I said apologetically that I feared he was too tired.

Bran flung away angrily saying, "Too tired! You are *always* too tired these days. Do you know how long it is since you made love to me? Not since the New Moon!"

Now that was about nine or ten days before—certainly a record period of abstention in our relationship, but I could hardly believe that it had been so long. However, I reiterated my apology and pointed out that I had been up several times each night, apart from the exhausting days I was now having to endure. At this point Tara began to wail again.

"Great Mother!" shouted Bran. "There's never any peace in this house. Either the wretched children are crying or you are complaining about being tired or their being sick. What a place to come home to!"

"They do happen to be your children as well as mine," I said angrily, "and if you were to stir yourself and help me a bit instead of being so damned lazy, I shouldn't be so tired."

And with that I rushed off to soothe Tara.

When I came back again, feeling a little ashamed of my outburst, Bran said in a voice of steel, "I have had enough of your whining, Klemo. I work hard to keep you and the children in comfort, and what thanks do I get for it? None. Instead I come home to an untidy, ill-kept house, to the noise of crying children, which after a day at the office gets on my nerves unbearably, and to a husband who instead of appreciating his luck and being grateful is late with the meals and complains about being tired. What do you think *I* feel like after working all day—full of energy and ready to do *your* work? If you think that you are very much mistaken, I can tell you. I come home tired out and I expect some comfort from you, who are at home all day with nothing else to do except look after two small children. What on earth is the matter with you?"

"I don't know how you have the nerve to compare your day with mine, Vrailbran. *I* know very well how exhausting or otherwise an office day is in comparison with mine here at home, and I know that when I was running the house and working at the Transport Company all day as well—something which you have never done, after all—it was not one-twelfth as wearing and tiring as the way I live now. I love the babies dearly and I look after them willingly, but you must recognize that you have some responsibility for them also. May I remind you that it was your decision to found a family just now, not mine."

"I thought when I married you that you were a normally fit and able young man. It seems I was mistaken. If you are unable to carry out the normal duties of a houseman . . .''

"How dare you talk like that?" I cut in furiously. "You know very well that I have in no way failed in my duties toward the children, or the house, or you . . ."

The moment I had said that I regretted it, for Vrailbran simply looked at me with raised eyebrows, letting her gaze travel over my person until it rested upon my groin. "Indeed? You think not, do you?" she said with an insolent coldness that stung me like a lash.

I flung myself at her and would have seized her beautiful throat with my two hands had she not raised her arms in a defensive gesture so that I was taken off balance and we crashed to the floor. My anger and the feel of her writhing body under me did what all her earlier coaxing had failed to do, and now I did not care whether she were willing or not but took her with a force I was afterward ashamed of, ramming home again and again as I did so every word of that insulting phrase "the normal duties of a houseman."

She lay very still when it was over, and I rolled off her no longer angry but ashamed and unsure. "Bran," I said. "Bran, darling. I am a brute. I am sorry, but you provoked me so. You shouldn't have spoken like that, you know, you really shouldn't. But I am ashamed of myself and very sorry."

She lay there staring up at me in such a strange way that I suddenly felt a sick fear that I had hurt her in the scuffle without realizing it. "Oh, Bran dearest, what is the matter? Have I hurt you, my dearest love?" I said, lifting her tenderly and gently in my arms. "I'll kill myself if I've done you any harm."

She lifted a hand and traced the lines on my forehead saying, "Don't look so anguished. It's all right. But I am not sure that I really know you at all. You were rather magnificent as a matter of fact." She smiled with the old endearingly mischievous smile and added, "You carry out the normal duties of a houseman splendidly. I will write you a testimonial to that effect any time you like!"

So the rift between us was healed temporarily at least, and each of us tried harder to understand the other. I tried to voice no complaints to Bran about the problems of the day, and she in her turn came home somewhat later, to give me more time I suppose to get through my daily routine; she even took on several small domestic duties that she normally never did, such as preparing the table for our evening meal or clearing it afterward, or sometimes emptying and cleaning the bath after I had bathed the twins.

I had been thinking a great deal about the effect these delightful and beloved creatures had had upon my relationship with Bran, and I was sadly forced to conclude that it had been a bad one. I set myself therefore to trying to envisage some remedy. I loved the babies, but I could not deny that they often exhausted my patience as well as tiring me physically. This made me less ready to understand and sympathize with Bran and her problems. Moreover it narrowed my vision, so that my life seemed bounded and circumscribed entirely by the small domestic environment. I had to acknowledge to myself also that I much disliked my complete dependence upon Vrailbran. I now possessed no resources that were truly my own. Surely it would be good for us all if I were able to widen my horizons once again—if, for example, I could persuade the Transport Company to give me part–time employment and we were to hire some competent person to look after the twins while I was at work. I did not know if this would be possible, but the more I thought about it, the more it seemed a sensible idea. Of course, with a part of myself I could not believe that anyone could look after the children as well as I could, but I realized that this was probably an emotional point of view— and anyway if it were for only a few hours at a time, this surely could do no harm. I decided therefore to broach the matter to Vrailbran.

She listened sympathetically, but her reply was sadly dashing to my hopes. "There is something in what you say, Klemo, and there are times when I, too, cannot help looking back nostalgically to the past. But you must see that in a truly democratic society such as ours, it is not considered right to employ other people to perform for us the tasks which should be the personal responsibility of each individual to do for herself. Of course, there are some people who shirk their share and do employ others, but they are few and I could not honestly approve of such a course for ourselves. Our society has moved forward a great deal since the days when these labors were

performed by lowly paid drudges. Nowadays each of us must do our
own individual share, and rightly so.''

"But Bran, you and your mother do not. It is I and your father
who do this work, and for no pay at all.''

Bran laughed her charming laugh and said in an indulgent tone:
"You really are a dear featherbrain, Klemo. Of course you are paid,
my love. Have you not a delightful house and the best food and
clothes that money can buy?''

"Do the few people who earn their living at domestic work receive
no money, then, but only their keep? Surely that is almost equivalent to slavery?''

"Of course not. Don't be so absurd. It is so difficult to find anyone
willing to undertake such work that they are now very highly
rewarded indeed. One must give them good living quarters and good
food, provide them with good quality working clothes, allow them
much time off and pay a good salary in addition. I must say that in
this respect I do feel that these things have gone almost too far.
However, one must pay what the work is worth, I suppose, and I
could not afford it even if I did not disapprove, as I do, of the
principle of the thing.''

"So actually such people are considerably better off than I am, for
I have no time off and am not paid.''

At this Vrailbran turned upon me a face of such displeasure, her
eyes flashing, her brows drawn into such an angry frown, that my
heart misgave me and I wished unsaid all that I had said.

"Do you put monetary value upon everything, then?'' she said.
"This is the kind of pernicious nonsense which cuts at the root of our
feeling for one another. Of course, no husband is paid in the way you
mean for the work he does: he does it for love of his wife and family
in this country. I am immeasurably distressed that you should bring
with you the mean and mercenary calculations that must pertain in
your country. Such an attitude undermines the whole foundation of
love and trust upon which our relationship is built.''

"Bran, darling, please try to understand. Of course, I do not mean
that I want to be paid for what I do here. But I am not accustomed to
the position of complete dependence upon another as I am upon you

and I do find it irksome. I am only trying to point out that in true democracy of the kind you assume you have in this country, if you truly believe that each individual should be responsible for his or her own share of the absolutely basic household tasks, then you should indeed take on your share, and I in my turn would be happy to take on my share of helping to earn a living. I see that if you do not think it right to employ help, then this would be difficult to do, but you yourself have often commented upon my intelligence and my abilities and surely you can see that it is hardly just that I should be denied any opportunity of exercising them simply because I am a man."

"I have never heard such illogical, back–to–front argument. What more worthwhile task could you turn your abilities to than the bringing up of our children? It is far and away the most important work in the country. The future of our whole civilization depends upon the training of our future citizens."

"In that case, Bran, it is strange that this highly regarded occupation is neither paid nor done by women. Surely the mother should take on this work, since your whole civilization is built on the assumption that women are wiser, more mature, less aggressive beings than men and are the natural guardians of all moral values? As it is, mothers here see almost nothing of their children, as far as I have been able to observe."

"You know very well, Klemo, that the business of the state and the top organizational levels of all enterprises absorb the energies of women. I dare say it would be as well if we had more share in the upbringing of our children, but unfortunately we have no time. Since *someone* has to undertake it, it is better that men, who are much more adapted to it because of their superior physical stamina— which no woman disputes—should do so. Surely you can see that?"

And so we had argued round in a circle without Bran ever once understanding the real points I wished to make. First, if one did these things for love of another person, then it must never be regarded as one's duty, as though one were some natural underling, and, equally, love should guarantee that the partner should be prepared to share the tasks. Secondly, one might love one's children dearly but not find a life led in their company exclusively, and wholly devoted to them, entirely fulfilling. Thirdly, in a society which did put monetary value upon any work or service except that which husbands carried out in the home, and which still to some extent measured the importance and the "status" of the work and its performance in monetary terms, it was illogical and unjust to expect the task which, with lip service, was said by all to be one of the most important in society, to take up the whole of a person's time and yet be without tangible reward. Perhaps in a more equitable social structure, the solution would be to arrange working times and loads so that the work in the home could be more equally shared and both parents could work outside the home as well as in it.

So there I was, back where I had started from, and the only result was a further slight alienation of Bran, who was incapable of seeing things from my point of view and who simply felt that she was being unjustly attacked and criticized by a carping and ungrateful husband.

chapter 15

It was with deep sadness that I watched this rift between myself and Bran widening slowly, very slowly at first, but perceptibly, and yet I seemed powerless to do anything about it. I felt some resentment that this doing of things "for love" was expected of me only, but I tried very hard to see matters from Bran's point of view, and not to let my resentment appear. I often felt extremely isolated and miserably depressed as well, and I suppose this must to some extent have colored my behavior. I made a conscious effort to try to be alert and cheerful during our brief hours together in the evening after the children were in bed, but often without much success, I own, for Bran would comment on my tired and dispirited air from time to time or would even say how much I seemed to have changed. She herself, on the contrary, seemed to be more beautiful and blooming than ever; although her latest promotion had caused her to extend her working hours and so to come home later than before, it seemed a stimulus to her rather than otherwise. Had she been prepared to discuss her work with me, or recount to me the happenings of the day, things might have been different, but although she was for me my one contact with the adult outside world, she did not, she said, want to talk about the things that had been occupying her whole day: she came home wanting to relax and be entertained. Thus we were at an impasse, for how could I conjure up out of my dull daily routine the material for entertaining chatter? For my part, what I needed was the exchange of ideas with another intelligent mind. Thus gradually a wall of silence grew between us, and we took refuge in listening to programs of music or drama, either recorded on cylinders or sent out on the country's broadcasting system. These programs were very limited because they were felt to discourage initiative and individual creative activities. For these there were many opportunities, but, of course, the care of children took precedence for most fathers.

There were two bright spots in my life at this time, apart from my delight in the gradual unfolding of the personalities and gifts of the twins. One was the occasional companionship of a young man whom I had met at the Child Health Center, to which I regularly took the babies for their statutory health checks. Zved and I had made friends as we waited our turn at the center, and my good fortune was that he lived quite near us. Our charming little house, chosen with such solicitude on Bran's part to make me feel at home in Capovolta, had unfortunately turned into a kind of prison for me now, since it was so far from the city that I found myself living in almost complete isolation. The other cheering factor was that my old friend Tsano had taken to visiting me after office hours and before Bran came home whenever he could. Of course this was not as frequently as I should have liked because his own life was a very busy one and his home did not lie in the same direction as mine. However, he brought me news of the outside world when he did come, and I found myself thirsting for all the absurd trivia of office gossip and office life in a way that I could not possibly have envisaged when I was working there. I was particularly pleased to hear that loathsome Vlebig had been transferred; Tsano did not know where, but that he had gone from our office was enough for me.

Bran was not at all pleased when I told her about Tsano's first visit. Had she been able to forbid a repeat visit, I think she would have done so. She was unjustly and unnecessarily incensed, and whereas in the early days of our marriage I should have argued back about it, now I simply said that I was unlikely to see him again for a long time since we lived quite out of his way. I could only imagine that to her dislike of Aniad there was now added the fact that Tsano had been an unwitting witness of her faithless conduct at the Games.

I took the obvious course of omitting to mention his later visits, for they were always short and he had gone by the time Bran came home.

For some time now Bran had been making fewer and fewer overtures to me at night, and was slow to respond when I took the initiative. I thought at first that she was behaving in this way out of consideration for me after the angry scene which I described earlier, but gradually it began to dawn on me that her sexual appetite had declined, as indeed mine had done, although I knew in my case it was pure fatigue, for an unexpected sight or touch of Bran's beautiful shape could still rouse me in an instant. It seemed very sad that even this, our deepest and strongest bond, was slowly weakening; I set myself to reestablish it in the old way, and although Bran was rarely the initiator now, as she had often been in the past, still it seemed to me that for a while our old, loving relationship was restored, and it filled me with happiness.

One day Zved suggest that we might occasionally give each other "time off" by taking charge of one another's children. I had thought of this myself before, but as he had only one baby, I had felt that I could hardly ask him to take on two more. Now that Zved had suggested it, however, I accepted the idea with alacrity, only insisting that he must be the one to have the first taste of freedom. His baby was a boy and slightly older, by a few weeks, than Sora and Tara. We agreed that the first time should in each case be a brief trial in case unforeseen difficulties developed, but both went smoothly and we planned to take a longer break next time. When my turn came, I decided that I would go up to my old place of work to visit Tsano, for there had been a rather longer period this time since his last visit than was normal.

It was with an extraordinary sense of adventure and of freedom that I set out on this utterly ordinary little jaunt and that, I think, will cast more light on the circumstances of my life at that time than any amount of reiteration of other detail. It was wonderful to have only to think of oneself for a brief time, to be quite alone instead of always a little company of three, however dear and much loved the other two were. I loitered about the streets, savoring the unique flavor of this day, no longer rushing against time, for I did not propose to embarrass Tsano by appearing in office hours, but only to catch him, always last as he conscientiously was, as he left the building. I should not have long with him, of course, for I should have to hurry back home to finish the evening routine before Bran arrived.

I clapped him on the shoulders as he came out, saying the Capovoltan equivalent of "if the mountain won't come to Mohammed. . . ." Had I not known his real affection for me, I could almost have imagined that my sudden materialization beside him had embarrassed him, but the impression was a fleeting one and the next moment he was expressing his surprise and pleasure at seeing me in the warmest of terms. I explained how it had come about, and in return he told me that once again Aniad had been ill and he had not liked to leave her alone longer than was absolutely necessary. However, he promised to come and visit me again as soon as he could.

He asked me if Vrailbran knew about my hours of freedom and seemed, I thought, rather relieved than otherwise when I said, No, I hadn't told her yet of my arrangement with my new friend. I wanted to make sure that there could be no unforeseen hitch, or consequences which would make her disapprove of it. However, I explained that if all went well this time, then next time I thought I would plan everything very carefully and surprise her by paying a call at her office.

Tsano said instantly, "Oh, no, Klemo, you must not do that. I am sure that would not be a good idea."

"Why not, Tsano? Do you think Bran would not like it? I used to go quite often you know before the babies were born. She never seemed to mind."

"No—no—but—well, I think that was different. I think she might be angry if you simply turned up unexpectedly now when she thinks you are safe at home with the children."

"What do you mean, Tsano? Safe at home with the children, indeed! Do you think that I can no longer take care of myself up here in the Big City or something?" and I laughed.

"No, no—of course, I didn't mean that, Klemo. I only meant—well—I suppose it might be a bit of a shock, you know. She'd think something awful had happened to the children, wouldn't she?"

"I don't think she would, really. Bran doesn't think like that. But you may be right. I'll think about it."

"Look, Klemo"—he was speaking with great earnestness and some agitation, more than was necessary in the circumstances, it seemed to me. "I am sure she would not like you to turn up without warning like that. Ask her first if it is all right for you to come. You know how odd women are about husbands intruding too much on their professional lives and all that."

"All right, all right, Tsano. You need not be so bothered about it, my dear chap. It wouldn't be the end of the world if she wasn't too pleased about it, but I won't do it anyway since you think I shouldn't."

"You are such an impulsive fellow, Klemo. It makes you the interesting, lively person that you are, of course, but I am often afraid that it may lead you into trouble, you know." He said it with such earnest affection that I could not possibly be offended, and to tell the truth it rather pleased me that he should still see me as the simple, impulsive fellow I once was, instead of the wary prevaricator and avoider–of–trouble I felt I had become.

However, Tsano's strong opposition to my plan made me think it prudent to break the news of my occasional spells of freedom rather gently to Bran. I simply told her about it as though it were still a project in the future and waited for her reaction.

She thought about it for a moment and then said, "It seems quite a good idea if you really think this young man is a trustworthy person—and so long as you are never away for very long. I don't think, however, that you should ever be out of reach. Some crisis can so easily arise with tiny children."

She was perfectly right, of course, but the reply disheartened me, for Bran was not given to worry about the children as I was. If she even thought this, then perhaps it would be wrong to take the thing any further, although my friend and I had great faith in one another.

Each of us knew of the children's little individual quirks and needs. We had the same pediatrician, whom we could call upon if indeed any emergency arose.

"You don't think, then, that it might be possible for me to come up to the city and visit you one day?" I asked tentatively.

I was quite unprepared for the vehemence of her reply. "Gracious Mother, Klemo, what an extraordinary idea! No, indeed, I do *not* think it would be possible. I do not understand you. Here you are saying that you find it difficult to get through all you have to do before I come home and then you seem to think you have time to take a complete afternoon off. Quite apart from involving your being dangerously long away from the children, it is clearly quite impractical on other terms. I can't imagine what you are thinking of even to suggest it."

"All right, Bran," I said meekly, swallowing down my disappointment. "I just thought it would be nice, that's all—like old times."

At this she relaxed and patted me on the shoulder, saying, "Ah, what a sentimental old silly you are. When the twins are a bit older and can more easily be left in someone else's care I'll ask my father to look after them one evening and we'll go out together. That will be something for you to look forward to, won't it?"

I cannot exactly tell you why, but I felt this to be a hateful piece of condescension. She seemed to think that she was bestowing on me some extraordinary favor and it annoyed me. I said nothing, but I vowed within myself that I should not wait until it suited Bran before having a few free hours to myself once again. I did not, however, venture so far afield for some time. When I did so, it fell out in this wise:

One day, Vrailbran was obliged to go to some great banquet or other as the representative of her part of the Ministry of Justice. As the festivities would continue very late, it was agreed that I should not expect her home that night. She had warned me of this well in advance, for it was an unusual circumstance. I decided to ask Zved if he could look after the twins that day, for with no time limit set by Bran's return I could have longer than usual on my own. By an odd coincidence he was about to ask me the same thing, for his wife would be away too that night. She had to be away at night more frequently than Bran, for she was employed by a large catering establishment, the managers of which had to take it in turns to be on duty when there was some particularly important banquet. Zved did not know what banquet it was, but we thought it likely that it would be the one that Bran was attending.

At first we were a little downcast to find our individual plans gone awry, and then, both together—I honestly do not know which of us thought of it first—we saw that there was no need for us to forgo our anticipated outing: we would simply take the children with us, putting their wagons on the mid–rail and taking their food for one meal with us. Although it would curtail our freedom of movement, the expedition taken together would be much more enjoyable and companionable. This, too, took care of objections about leaving the children too long and so on. I did not mention it to Bran, however, for I did not want some objection on her part to overrule us.

We set off in great spirits. The children were now big enough to watch the world moving past them with interest, and they behaved beautifully, charming passersby with their smiles and chuckles. We fed the water birds on the ornamental ponds, we went to the children's park and set the clockwork toys in motion, we gave the children their first alfresco meal. All together, it was a delightful day.

When at last we thought we should begin to make our way home before the mid-rail was too crowded for comfort, Zved was visited by the idea that it would be fun to pass by the banqueting hall where he knew his wife would be supervising the preparations for the banquet, not so much in the hope of seeing his wife, who would be much too busy to spare us any time, but simply to have a glimpse of the exotic plants which he said would be brought to decorate the courtyard. He was obviously very proud of his wife's taste in dictating the layout and so on. It was not far out of our way, and we were standing watching the men arranging a kind of backdrop of giant ferns with a charming little fountain in front of it when I suddenly saw Bran on the other side of the courtyard. She had just come in through the far gate accompanied by a young man. Her hand was on his arm and she laughed up at him in the charming, intimate way that I had thought was only for me before she turned away into the building and the young man came across the courtyard. It was Dinad–Vlebig. He came out of the gateway only a few yards from us, but I was screened from him by other passersby and he turned in the other direction.

I suppose Zved had been talking to me, though I was not aware of it, for he was suddenly shaking my arm and saying in a frightened voice, "Klemo, Klemo, what's the matter? Are you ill? Klemo, answer me please. Whatever is the matter?" I was trembling with shock and I sat down heavily upon the low wall as though all strength had been drained from me. I dropped my head upon my hands, so Zved declared afterward, and let out a terrifying, low keening sound. All this can only have lasted a few seconds, I suppose, for then I pulled myself together and said, "Someone was walking over my grave, I think" (the Capovoltans have almost the same expression). "It's nothing. I'm quite all right now."

Poor Zved was much upset and very anxious about me, but clearly had not seen Bran, and if he had seen Dinad, it would have meant nothing to him, except that he might have recognized the winner of last year's body competition. But by now there were a new face and a new body for the crowds to drool over.

I tried to talk as normally as possible to Zved on the way home and I think I succeeded in quieting his anxieties to some extent. I simply said that I had had an inexplicably acute sense that something terrible was about to happen, but that it had passed off and I felt perfectly all right now. I invented another occasion on which something similar had happened and said that a medical friend had told me that such a sensation could be caused by a momentary irregularity in the heartbeat. It seemed as good an explanation as any other, and he appeared to take my word for it.

Once home, I got the children off to bed as quickly as possible and sat down to think over the implications of what I had seen. It was just possible, although improbable, that I had witnessed an unexpected and casual encounter between Bran and Dinad. At first I tried to make out such a case to myself—but that Dinad should be entirely by chance at that particular place at that particular time, that is, in working hours, was exceedingly unlikely; moreover the impression came over most vividly that they had arrived there together, indeed that Dinad had been escorting Bran. That could only have been by arrangement. The intimacy of gesture and expression between them suggested something more than a single meeting; it seemed like the expression of a continuing relationship. I forced myself to think again the thought that I was flinching from. Was not the most likely explanation that Bran had resumed some time ago the relationship with Dinad which she had broken off after the Games of the previous year? I had to answer yes to that. Such a consuming, painful jealousy took possession of me at this that I could not sit still but jumped up and paced about the room. In this turmoil of emotion, I could not think clearly about anything: it was as though any area of thought was so tender and painful that no sooner had I touched upon it than I reeled away from it immediately. But one fact after another came into my mind and each one with a dreadful inexorability fitted into place like a series of pieces in a jigsaw puzzle: Bran's surprised and angrily emphatic refusal to allow me to visit her at her office; the news of Dinad's transfer; Tsano's momentary confusion when I went to the office without warning; Bran's lack of interest in the children's development; her later and later homecomings; most painful and most convincing of all, the notable change in her sexual response to me.

Round and round I went inside my mind until far into the night. Finally, when dawn was breaking, I took a soporific, and at last sleep gave me a few hours' respite. The new day brought a renewal of the night's torturing thoughts, but now there was a fresh consideration: I should have to decide before Bran came home what I was going to say to her. It did not occur to me that I had any choice as to whether I should face her with what I knew or not: I was simply concerned as to how I should do it. I wanted to be as cool and dispassionate as possible: I did not want her to realize how nearly mortal was the wound she had inflicted. This was from no heroic motive but only to protect myself; I could not bear her to see how vulnerable I was. I should speak calmly and simply say that since she did not love me anymore, we must arrange affairs so that she could marry Dinad. Of course, I still had a wild hope that she would deny it all and give me convincing explanations of the evidence against her filed away in my mind; such is the facility for self–deception of the human heart. But she should never, never know the depths of my unhappiness and my despair if what I feared were true.

As the day drew on toward evening, it became more and more difficult for me to give Sora and Tara my attention. I was restless and sick with dread anticipation, and of course the children sensed it, as children will, so that they were difficult and fretful. It was a nightmare day, and just as I was wondering how I could bear several more hours of this tension, dear old Tsano came to pay his promised visit.

His first anxious glance confirmed for me the suspicion that he knew something of our affairs.

"Tsano," I said, "tell me, do you know where Dinad–Vlebig is working now?"

The blood swept up into his face, having the momentary darkening effect on his complexion which I had observed before among the Capovoltans, and he looked at me in confusion for a moment. Then he dropped his eyes and murmured, "I'm not sure."

"Isn't he at the Ministry of Justice?" I asked.

"Possibly—I think I did hear something to that effect."

"Tell me the truth, Tsano. You are not being a good friend to me if you conceal anything from me that I should know. Is he—is he—particularly friendly with my wife?"

Tsano stared at me miserably. "I've—well—I mean—I don't really know," he stammered.

"But you've heard something or seen something, Tsano, haven't you? Come on, tell me. You only make it worse for me by not talking about it. I shall not rest until I know the truth. You may as well know that I saw them together yesterday."

"Oh, Klemo, dear fellow. I am so sorry about the whole thing. I've been miserable about it ever since I—well—ever since I first thought something was wrong. That's really why I didn't come to see you for so long. I was a miserable coward about it. I didn't want to face you in case something I said or did caused you to find out about it. And anyway, of course, I didn't really *know* anything. You see, I was away looking after Aniad when Dinad was transferred. It was only after that I heard some of the boys talking, and apparently he had been boasting about his lover at the Ministry of Justice and how she was going to get him transferred to her office and all that. Well even then I didn't realize that it was Bran. It was only when I saw them together one day on my way home that, well, that I began to think that . . ." He trailed off into silence.

"Why did you think that, when you saw them, Tsano? What were they doing?"

Poor Tsano looked desperately uncomfortable but finally said "Well, they were—arm in arm—and sort of laughing together, and when the Lady Vrailbran saw me, she stopped laughing and looked very angry. So, of course, I just bowed and hurried away."

No wonder Bran had been so hostile to the idea of Tsano coming to see me. Another piece of the puzzle fell into place. Now I poured out to Tsano's sympathetic ear the whole story as far as I had been able to piece it together, and told him how I meant to challenge Bran with it that very evening.

"Don't do that, Klemo," he said in alarm. "You must think it out very thoroughly before you decide to do such a thing."

"But I *have* thought it out. I've thought of nothing else for a complete night and day."

"But have you thought of what will happen to you and the children if you force some kind of choice on her? I think she is an honorable woman in her way, and as long as she is not forced to choose between you, I do not think she will desert you and the children. If you act as though you knew nothing about it, things may yet be all right."

"How *can* you suggest such a thing, Tsano? Can you not see what an impossible situation that would be? Imagine living with someone whom you know does not care for you! It's a horrible and shaming idea—and quite apart from that, I could not live such a lie."

"Many people do, Klemo, my dear chap. It's very sad, but what is a man to do if he has several children to look after? A deserted man with a family is in an extraordinarily difficult position, you know."

I suppose I had not thought as far ahead as that, but it made no difference to my feelings. If Bran no longer cared for me, then I could not bear to continue living with her, and that was that.

Tsano tried very hard to dissuade me from putting my resolution into immediate action: he thought that, given time, I should see that the course he prescribed was a wiser one. But it was simply not a thinkable alternative for me, and eventually he went sadly away, fearing that Bran might return at any minute and find him there.

I found a little comfort in the good fellow's protestations of friendship and offers of whatever help lay within his power to give, but the truth of the matter is that the agony of betrayed love has to be lived through alone, and no third party can bear any of the pangs for the stricken one, however close a friend he may be.

I did not stir myself to prepare a meal once the children were in bed, and when Bran eventually came, I was sitting in the half–dark, listening in a kind of eager dread for her footfall. She came in humming softly to herself, pulsating with a vibrant exhilaration which seemed callous and cruel beyond belief; when she dropped a kiss on my head and cried gaily, "Why, Klemo, my love, are you sitting in the dark?" all my resolutions to appear calm and reasonable and coolly dispassionate vanished and I jumped as though her lips had stung me. I pushed her from me and hissed—yes, positively hissed, "Traitress, base traitress!" like the hero of a melodrama, but then life does so often turn into a melodrama in which we are not properly coached for our parts.

At first Bran was all protesting, injured innocence—"Why, Klemo, whatever do you mean"—but as I poured out my indictment, she ceased protest and listened, still and silent, until I had finished. Only when this silence of hers prolonged itself did I know how much, how very much, I had been hoping that she would have some other, innocent explanation for the damning facts I had collected.

At last she said quietly, "What do you want me to do then, Klemo?"

In my fevered rehearsals for this interview, things had never taken quite this turn, but there was no doubt that my reply should have been something like, "Go to him since you do not love me anymore," but instead, in reply to her repeated question, I heard myself say in a strangled, pleading voice, "Oh, Bran, please go on loving me. Don't stop loving me."

And so I set the stage for more scenes in this torturing farce. She promised, and broke her promise—and whether she broke it or not, I lived in sick anticipation of it. I suspected her whether she was innocent or guilty, and so frayed yet further the raveled bonds between us. I do not know whether I should have had the strength to send her away, but it was taken from my hands when Dinad, without doubt quite deliberately, made her pregnant, and the children and I were left deserted.

16

And now there began for me the most wretched and hopeless period of my whole life. I do not want to recall it in too much detail, for even now the memory pains me. Had it not been for the twins, perhaps I should have contemplated taking my own life. Or perhaps I should have tried to emulate the traitorous Capovoltan of long ago and made my escape from this country in which, whatever the Capovoltans themselves might have been indoctrinated to believe, I, like all my sex, was an underprivileged, second–class citizen. I cannot fully express with what longing I thought of my own country where, I realized for the first time, I had led a life of privilege. If ever I succeeded in returning thither, I vowed within myself that I would never again be so insensitive to the subtle bias I had so casually accepted as the natural, predetermined order of things.

I say "escape" for, although there were no apparent restrictions on the movements of citizens, neither were there available means for travel beyond the shores of Capovolta. Had I been alone, I should somehow have found means, even if I were to lose my life in the endeavor, but I could not abandon these two small beings, so utterly dependent upon me and so tightly entwined in my affections, either by seeking to escape or by taking my own life. The thought that in such case they would almost certainly be handed over to the care of the odious Dinad–Vlebig would have dissuaded me even if there had been no other deterrent, for how could I expect this shallow, vain youth to give them the care that I had given, even if he had had the goodwill to try—and that I doubted even more than his capacity. For the first time since I had come here a chill foreboding began to form in my mind that perhaps I should never succeed in leaving Capovolta and returning to my own country; until then I had never come to regard it as my "real" life, as anything indeed more than a dreamlike interlude, at first pleasant and then painful. I could not but reflect how right the Guardians had been in their calculation, as I had concluded, that a family marriage would bind me more firmly and inexorably than any physical restraint on liberty would have done. What an impossible situation mine now was!

In the period during which Bran's residual affection for me and her sense of duty toward the children battled with her infatuation for Dinad, there had been many times when I had thought that any resolution of our situation, however painful to me, would have been better than the torturing uncertainty I was then enduring, but what I had never adequately envisaged was that the coup de grace to my affections would be accompanied by acute anxiety as to how to provide the barest necessities of life for the children and myself. I learned all too rapidly how right I had been to doubt if Capovoltan society, any more than our own, really regarded the care of the "new citizens" as the most important task in the country. There was, it is true, a fail–safe plan which prevented destitution, but the level of care which this could provide in this so–called caring society was minimal. Everything was based on the assumption that there would always be a stable unit of two to care for the children, one to earn in order to provide food and shelter and one to provide a permanent physical presence. This might have led me to believe that my own case was an isolated or exceptional one, yet that was very far from the truth. There existed a widespread subculture of such underprivileged families, which either lived right on the poverty line or where the husband was forced, whether he liked it or not, to forsake his care of the family to go out to work. Of course, there were also some abandoned wives, but their position, although not an enviable one, was usually slightly better, for at least they were already established in careers or in work where the pay would certainly be better than that which the men—especially those without previous training—could command.

At first my personal unhappiness was such that it was some time before the realities of the situation came home to me and I began to understand the anxiety that Tsano had felt on my behalf. Of course, Bran was obliged to contribute to the children's support, and even had it not been obligatory in such circumstances, she was not conscienceless and would I am sure have done so voluntarily—but supporting two establishments instead of one, five people soon to be six, out of the same stipend meant that our share of it was exiguous indeed. Even so, I hated accepting it.

The little house on the outskirts of the city, though small, was now far too costly, and so to loss of wife and of love was added loss of home. With Tsano's help I found the cheapest possible accommodation in the form of a couple of rooms in the house of an acquaintance of his, but it still seemed impossible to remain solvent. The "new citizen" payments which had been made on the children's behalf to Bran ever since their birth now began to be paid to me, once it had been legally established that Bran had deserted me and that I had, as was customary, the care of the children, but that simply meant that Bran's contribution to their support was cut by that amount and it became increasingly urgent for me to find some way of supplementing our income. Tsano thought it quite possible that, overprolonged though my "indefinite leave" had been, I might be accepted back into the Transport Company, though probably at a lower level than before, but what arrangements could I possibly make for the children to be cared for during my working day? They were now toddling around everywhere and perpetually getting themselves into all kinds of mischief through the inquiring nature of their dispositions. It would be ridiculous false modesty to pretend they were anything other than exceptionally intelligent as well as enchantingly beautiful. Fortunately, I suppose, given the circumstances, they had had so little of Vrailbran's company that they did not seem to miss her greatly. They continued to look up expectantly at the sound of opening doors or distant footfalls, especially toward their bedtime, but I thought it would not be long before they forgot what it was that they expected. I was both hurt and glad that Vrailbran did not wish to see the children for the time being. I suppose that the new pregnancy fulfilled such maternal feeling as she had. She had reserved the right, however, to have them to stay with her for short periods if she so wished in the future.

I turned my mind to the problem of finding trustworthy care for the children during the working part of the day, so that I might try my luck with the Transport Company, or elsewhere if I was not to be reemployed there. After all, I was not the only deserted husband with a young family, so I thought that perhaps I might join forces in some way with another such family.

Once again Tsano proved himself an invaluable friend. He made inquiries for me through Aniad, whom I was at last allowed to meet, for her sympathies with me were all the greater because of her dislike of Bran. She was a subdued, intense young woman, some-what older than Bran and with none of Bran's facile charm, but with a sympathetic gravity which was very heartwarming. Now as I have explained, she too worked in the Ministry of Justice, but because of Bran had been transferred to a different department. This proved to be a great good fortune for me, for the protection of the rights of deserted husbands came under Aniad's jurisdiction—that is, her department received appeals where wives had reneged on their obligations and so on. Consequently she was easily able to inform herself of men in like circumstances as myself, and to find out something of their backgrounds and personalities. She arranged for me to meet a couple of young men of about my own age whom she had personally interviewed in the course of her work and thought intelligent and able beyond the common run. Both of them were having great trouble in securing the support due to their families from recalcitrant wives.

At first we simply discussed our circumstances and our troubles and met one another's children. Although I did not feel that either of them could ever be as dear to me as Tsano, I found both of them thoughtful and agreeable companions. After a couple of such meetings I broached the project I had at heart—that is, that we should try to help ourselves and one another by sharing the care of our children, so enabling one at least and perhaps two of us to find work and to share the income thus obtained. Although I wanted to go back to work myself, I felt it was only fair for us all to share in the care of the children, and said that if I could get back my old job, I would look after my friends' children at the new and full moon holidays so that we should all have some time away from our "dear octopuses." This idea appealed greatly to the slightly older one, Raunau, who had three children, including a quite young baby. He had married while very young and had no real experience of anything except the domestic life. Zruchi, the other young man, had been offered some private part–time work if he could free himself for a part of each day. If only I could get my old job back, it would work out excellently, I thought.

I consulted Tsano as to how I should go about this. At first he suggested that I should seek an interview directly with Avgard, but this I could not bring myself to do after the circumstances in which we had parted. Kind though she was, how could I go crawling back to ask a favor of her now? In that case, Tsano said, I could only make a formal application to end my so–called indefinite unpaid leave and ask to be reinstated. I could see that he was not altogether confident about the outcome of this, being doubtful whether "leave" could be stretched to mean more than two years, but I had no other option.

The young woman who had been our immediate superior had been moved on, from age rather than merit, I am sure, and a new young woman had taken over. It would be up to her to decide whether my application for reinstatement went any further. It was only later that I discovered that Tsano had gone to Avgard on my behalf, for the young woman had simply told Tsano to file my appeal in the memory bank, since there were no vacancies. He did so, but went to Avgard, who recommended one of the youngsters in the dispatch department for promotion across into another department where there did happen to be a vacancy, and so secured for me a place, although on the very bottom rung.

At first I was too glad to be back and too busy organizing my new life to repine at the lowliness of my position and the mindless, boring repetition of the work, but what I have not mentioned so far in my story of my life in Capovolta is the bitter sense of wasted ability that I had. You may think this conceited of me, but I can only tell the truth. I believed myself to have far greater abilities than I was given the chance to use. You may say that there are many people who have an exaggerated idea of what life owes them, and that if they were really as able as they thought they were, they would find some way to fulfillment. I can only say that in my own country I had proved myself able beyond question, but that here in Capovolta I was trapped in other people's preconception of my capability; a sense of outrage and futility grew in me at my failure to find any way of realizing what I knew to be my own potential.

My life was now marginally better than before, but, alas, human beings accustom themselves all too soon to such changes and begin to resent the irksome restriction of their present lot instead of savoring the improvement—and I was no exception. I cast about in my mind for some way of gaining recognition, but could think of none. In the end I submitted a memorandum to my superior, asking her to send it on, recounting how my interlocutors at that famous interrogation so long ago had found my mathematical ability to be exceptional, and asking whether there was a possibility that I might be permitted to use this gift in some more profitable way than counting out cylinders. I do not know quite what I hoped for from this, but it is a measure of my desperation that I took this step.

Again, it was due to Tsano's intervention that it ever went further than the young woman who was our immediate supervisor, for she thought the whole thing ridiculous and would have destroyed the cylinder, but Tsano assured her that what I said was true, so reluctantly she passed it on.

At length I was summoned once more to Avgard's office. She greeted me with her usual kindness and expressed her pleasure that I was back with them. I could hardly restrain my eagerness to hear what she had to say about my application, but I forced myself to make this exchange of civil banalities until at last she said with a sigh, "My poor, poor Klemo. They have clipped your wings indeed, haven't they? This is what I feared for you, you know. *Then* you could have flown, my dear, and I could have helped you—but *now*—what is there I can do?"

I think that I had not realized what hopes I had placed in this interview until I heard the pitying tone in which she uttered these hope–destroying words. I had allowed expectation to overleap the bounds of reason and of likelihood, and I was bitterly disappointed and cast down. I determined, however, not to give in so easily—at least to show some fight.

"Why do you think my case so hopeless, Avgard?" I asked.

"Four years ago, Klemo, you could have made yourself a free man, but is there any chance of your doing so now? Men do not realize until too late what hostages they give to fortune when they have children. Can you see any way in which you could rid yourself of this burden?"

"I do not wish to be rid of my burden, as you call it, Avgard. What I want is the means of ensuring a better life for them and of greater fulfillment for myself."

"I will be honest with you, Klemo, at the risk of hurting your feelings. You are not the same young man whose spirit and impetuousness attracted and challenged me as much as did his physical beauty. Now you have become cautious and careworn, hardly distinguishable from any other young Capovoltan man in your situation—but I have a tenderness for you, as you are now, not only for what you were, and I would still marry you if it were not for the children. But now I am too old to be prepared to tolerate the noise and chaos of a home with two such young children in it. And, indeed, although I could offer you freedom from worry over the material things of life, there is no way in which I could procure you any other fulfillment while you still have the children to care for."

This speech upset me, not only because it was the first time anyone had commented upon the changes which the years had brought about in me, but because it seemed to me to express a complete misapprehension of my purpose in making my application. Could she really think that it had been my intention to invite an offer of marriage? Perhaps it upset me most of all because although I certainly had no conscious thought of this originally, I could not help acknowledging somewhere deep within myself the longing for someone to confide in and to share my responsibilities; had she offered to support me and the children I might for a moment have been tempted, although common sense would have seen to it that I did not in the end succumb.

"You have been very frank with me, Avgard, so I will be equally frank with you. My experience of marriage in Capovolta has not been such an encouraging one that I wish to make any further trial of it. I am grateful to you for your kindness to me in the past and for your present goodwill. I should be even more indebted to you if you could suggest to me any way in which I could use what abilities I have to better advantage than at present."

"I will make inquiries on your behalf and see what can be done, Klemo, but I cannot hold out much hope. You must see yourself that you would need a long period of training before you could be of any use at a much higher level than you are now. Your abilities would have to be quite outstanding to convince anyone that a man of your age would be worth such an investment of time and training resources. I do not say that it is impossible, but it is highly unlikely, I am afraid."

I was much downcast by this reply. If Avgard, who had at least some reason to know of my intellectual potential, was so doubtful about my chances, what likelihood was there of any less interested and informed party taking up my cause? Nevertheless I refused to acknowledge defeat and simply said, "Thank you for being realistic and not encouraging me with false hopes, Avgard. But all the same I hope you will advise me as to what steps to take next, however slim the chances of success may be."

She sighed. "Very well, Klemo. Of course I will do as I promised and try to find out where best I could recommend you, but please do not build too much upon it."

The effect of this discouraging interview was to plunge me afresh into deep gloom. Cerebrate and wrestle within me as I might, the facts of my situation remained the same, and I could see no light ahead anywhere, only a perpetual grayness. It was of no use to tell myself that I must cease to kick against the pricks and accept my present worry–fraught existence and my lack of any prospect of improvement with philosophical resignation when it was not in my nature to do so. With my intellect I could see that a calm accommodation to the restrictions which Capovoltan society and my own lack of foresight had laid upon me was not only probably the most worthy procedure but also the most sensible. But my spirit simply would not acquiesce. Castigate myself as I might for my presumption when I looked around and saw how many others accepted their lot without protest, yet I could not believe myself unworthy or the system just.

This ceaseless dialogue ran as a perpetual undercurrent below the normal preoccupations of the daily routine. Perhaps only when I was actively engaged with the children, bathing them, playing with them, telling them a bedtime story, was there a momentary pause in the perpetual recapitulation of the circle of argument. I could see that in spite of the resentment and frustration I had felt at times, the circumstances of my arrival in Capovolta had made it both necessary and easier for me to accept the restrictions of my life here at first, since my illness and the fact of my being foreign had put me into a state of dependence upon others which I had not known since I left my parents' home in my own country. I had needed the protection I was given by Bran and her family; my complete ignorance both of the Capovoltan language and of the culture it reflected had made it not unreasonable that when I sought work it should be available only at a lowly level; since I was an unknown stranger, it was understandable that I was regarded only as an appendage of my wife rather than as a person in my own right. Now, however, the monstrosity and cynical illogicality of the system became apparent to me. If the Capovoltans genuinely believed men to be creatures incapable of acting independently or of taking full responsibility for themselves, if they truly believed them to be so much less able than women that they had to be in a state of constant tutelage, first to their parents and then to a wife, how could they possibly justify the present situation of men like me and Raunau (the friend who was looking after the children during the day)? Suddenly, without warning, far greater responsibility had been thrust upon us than any woman in Capovolta had to undertake alone, for the assumption was that no woman deserted by her husband could possibly be expected to care for her children as well as earn a living. If, as happened in rare cases, the deserting husband did not accept the continued care of the children, then relations, friends, neighbors, social workers, marriageable men all crowded round with a chorus of commiseration and offers of help. On the contrary, here we were, previously treated as creatures incapable of functioning on our own or taking the ultimate responsibility for ourselves, not only deprived of protection but actually put under additional disadvantages and made responsible for the care of our children as well. However unconscious the community in general was of what was really being done in their name, anyone with an ounce of logic in her makeup could see that the ostensible reasons for men's position were not the true ones: it was simply a highly convenient assumption for the women. The more I thought about it the more I marveled that generations of men could have been taken in by this gigantic confidence trick. Why had they not risen in revolt long ago and demanded their rights? True, it was a self–perpetuating system, for if even I, with the entirely contrary assumptions of the society in which I had grown up, had succumbed in some degree to the external pressures of what was expected of me, it would be even more difficult for those born and bred here to resist them. To be regarded as undutiful, ungracious, carping, critical and unloving by someone whose approval one dearly desires is a potent deterrent; in essence, this fear of disapproval, however manifested, is the sanction most societies use for training each generation to conform to the standards desired, and it takes a great deal of courage as well as an intense conviction of rectitude to rebel.

Burdened with these gloomy and depressing thoughts, my spirits were at the nadir. An interminable period seemed to pass without news or hope. In fact it would only have been about fifteen days, for it was immediately after the next full–moon holiday that I was summoned again for interview. The good Avgard had kept her word and had secured for me the chance of putting my case at a higher level. That she had already done her best for me was obvious from the tone of the interview, for it was clear to me that the two officials who now saw me had only done so to oblige a colleague and that they thought the whole thing certain to be a waste of time. However, they obligingly went through the procedure that must have been laid down for testing out candidates for the higher level posts which they controlled, and as the interview proceeded I could sense the change of attitude which was gradually taking place.

At length they sent me to wait in an anteroom, presumably while they consulted together. Time went by with a purgatorial slowness as I waited, but when they recalled me my heart bounded in my breast with sudden new hope, for they were both smiling in the way people do if they have good news to impart. The more senior one gestured for me to sit down and began to speak.

"Well, Klemo–Vrailbran–Zenhild, I want to tell you that my colleague and I have been much impressed by your performance at this interview. Had you been a woman, we should have been in no doubt about recommending you for training, but, of course, things are not so straightforward in a man's case. One can never be sure that domestic responsibilities will not interfere with a man's dedication to his work. We have to face the fact that for this and other reasons, men are not as reliable as women in the work situation, even where they may actually be as able. It is difficult, therefore, for us to make a decision in your case. We know something of your domestic situation, but there are one or two further points we should like to discuss. First of all, have you satisfactory arrangements for the care of your children during your working hours?"

I replied to this by explaining my arrangement with my two friends. They conferred for a moment in low voices and then the younger one said, "Suppose the children should be ill, could that arrangement still stand? Could you guarantee not to be absent on that account?"

The truth of this was that I did not know. I had taken odd days off when the twins had been suffering from one or other of the minor ailments to which children seem to succumb however carefully looked after, but that was because they had missed me more and fretted for me when they were unwell and not because Raunau had been unwilling to care for them. I could not bear to let this chance slip away from me by not giving a firm answer, so I said, "Certainly the arrangement would stand, unless, of course, there were some utterly unexpected and serious crisis which in a normal two–parent family would necessitate the presence of the mother as well."

They thought about that for a moment, again sent me to the antechamber and finally recalled me to announce that they had decided to recommend me for training in the Capovoltan equivalent of my previous profession of geometer. Of course, I should begin at something of a disadvantage because of my age and because of my sex, but, they assured me, there was nothing ultimately to prevent me from rising in the profession to a respectable position.

It was with the greatest difficulty that I kept my voice steady as I thanked them and tried to tell them how much this decision meant to me. They were, I think, touched by my gratitude and my enthusiasm, which I could not altogether restrain. The younger one then explained that they would forward their recommendation to the proper department, which in turn would make arrangements for my training and summon me when ready.

By the time I was free to go, both my office and Tsano's had long been closed, and the homegoing crowds were reduced to a trickle. I walked out of the building with as much gravity and decorum as I could summon, but the moment I was out of sight of it I began to run, laughing to myself and leaping into the air like a madman. It was only when I saw that I was drawing unfavorable attention to myself that I forced myself to calm down and made my way to the nearest mid-rail stop on my homeward route. I went straight to Raunau's apartment to pick up the children as usual, and late though it was, poured out my news to him, throwing myself on his mercy for support during any future childhood illnesses which might occur. He was delighted at my delight but somewhat overawed at my prospects, for he found it hard to understand that I was genuinely confident in my ability to hold my own in what was regarded as a woman's career in a woman's world. Tsano, too, when I was able to confide in him the next day, though pleased for me was unexpectedly reserved and guarded in his response, repeating again and again in a doubtful, worried tone, "I hope it will be all right. I *do* hope it will be all right for you, Klemo, my dear fellow." Each time I challenged him with the return question (each time repeated more impatiently, I have to confess), "Well, what do you think is likely to go wrong, Tsano?" it seemed to me that there was a slight hesitation before he would reply, as though trying to convince himself, "No—of course—I'm sure everything will be all right."

CHAPTER
17

Once again I lived for weeks in a perpetual ferment of excitement and, as the time lengthened, of fear that there might have been some unexpected hitch. At last one day an officially sealed cylinder was delivered to me, and when I was able to play it in private I found that it was a record of the terms of the contract which was being offered to me. As I listened, my first transports of exhilaration and relief abated and were replaced by a bitter disappointment, all the deeper and more biting because of the high expectation I had felt encouraged to entertain. I was, it is true, being offered exactly what had been proposed, a place on a training course which would open to me the promised career, but the terms were quite impossible and unacceptable. It was to be an intensive two-year *residential* course, at a center in the depths of the country many many miles from the capital, and while I should be fed and housed and instructed absolutely free, the personal allowance for any additional expenses was ludicrously inadequate for the support of a separate establishment and two children, quite apart from the difficulty of finding anyone in the neighborhood prepared to care for them as Raunau had. To have the chance I so ardently desired offered with one hand only to be immediately snatched away by another seemed to me a refinement of cruelty; for some time I found it hard to believe that I was not the victim of some misanthropic bureaucrat whose sadistic pleasure lay in creating such paradoxical situations for the already disadvantaged.

When I went storming in to Tsano, pouring out my anger and frustration, I found that something of this nature was what he had feared and what had caused his reservations when I first told him of my "good fortune," as I then believed it to be. It was not that he was aware of these factors in particular, but long experience had taught him to be wary of the Capovoltan Establishment when it seemed to be making friendly gestures. He wryly quoted a Capovoltan saying to this effect that might well be translated as *Timeo Danaos et dona ferentes*.

We listened again together to the hope–raising, hope–damning cylinder to see if there was any loophole at all. The only mildly hopeful feature in it was that the training program was several moons away, presumably to allow the successful candidates to settle their affairs in the city and make whatever arrangements were necessary for their transfer. This at any rate would give us time to find out if there were any regulations governing people with families. Most of the candidates for such a course, said Tsano, would be young unmarried women. However, surely they must occasionally have women with dependent husbands, and maybe even families, among the successful applicants. He would ask Aniad to find out what provisions would be made in such cases. He was, however, far from encouraging about the likelihood of any help for me.

Aniad was almost immediate in her reply to this query, for cases of this nature where special appeals are made were dealt with by a department of the Ministry of Justice parallel with her own. In the case of a married woman with a family, special allowances could be granted; in the case of a married man making such an appeal—an almost unheard–of contingency—no allowance would be granted, for he was considered to be a dependent of his wife's and she would be responsible for the maintenance of the family. I was forced to wonder yet again if ever a man was more firmly trapped by a series of ironies than I now was.

Aniad suggested, however, that since no man in my particular circumstances had made such an appeal as far as she knew, it would at least be worth attempting to put my case to the appeals section of the Ministry, on the grounds that Vrailbran's contribution to the support of the family was so inadequate that I was forced to work, and was thus in the same position more or less as a woman with a family to support, and might therefore be considered eligible for the allowances she would get in such case.

No one held out much hope to me about this, but after we had considered it from every angle that we could think of, at least it seemed it could do no harm, and just possibly might do some good. I was eager to wage battle on my own behalf for I could not bear to sit down under what I regarded as a real miscarriage of justice.

Little did I foresee what further stunning blow was in store for me. While this appeal was still pending, notice was served on me without prior warning that Vrailbran was claiming custody of the children on the grounds that she could now offer them a stable home with permanent child care provided in the person of Dinad, now at home looking after the new baby. Her claim went on to maintain that I had no possibility of providing such a stable environment since I was making application to attend a residential course where no provision for children obtained. So much for my conclusion that my appeal could do no harm! Vrailbran had presumably heard of my application through friends in the appeals section. Even so, I could hardly bring myself to believe that she could take measures behind my back to hurt me so cruelly. She had abandoned the children and me, leaving us to weather circumstances more difficult than we would ever know again, without one backward glance, without one inquiry as to our welfare for more than a year. She could not really think that I would neglect the well–being of my beloved children, whatever it might cost me in the sacrifice of my own ambition, if in the end that is what it should come to.

I was so bitterly incensed by this action of hers that I would immediately have gone to see her and have it out with her, but Tsano and Aniad said that on no account must I do this. I needed the advice of a lawyer versed in that side of the law before I took a single step. Clearly they felt that somehow I might damage my own cause by my impetuousness. In the end I agreed, for I could see that I should probably end by heaping accusation on her and abuse on the hated Dinad. So instead of being confronted by an outraged and furious ex–husband, Vrailbran was civilly interviewed on my behalf by a lawyer friend of Aniad's. From her report of this interview it became clear that the appeals section of the Ministry of Justice had made inquiries as to the scale of the provision made for the children by Vrailbran as a preliminary to hearing my appeal. This had annoyed her, and had angered Dinad. Also, unfortunately without my knowledge, for I should not have given my consent to it had I known, the machinery had been set in motion for a reassessment of this contribution, with the object of securing a more substantial share of her income for the children of her first marriage, for the appeals court considered that without any doubt the first assessment had been set too low.

I suppose it is possible that she believed that this was being done at my instigation and that she and Dinad had worked one another up to find a way of taking revenge. That there was any real thought of the children's good, I cannot begin to believe. They were everything to me, and to them I was the rock on which their little lives were founded. They were wonderfully understanding and intelligent: from the time when it had become an absolute necessity for me to return to work, I had taken them into my confidence as though they had been ten years old instead of three. I explained that we could not afford the things we needed—the nice food, the warm house, the pretty clothes—unless I went to work. Before I ever left them with Raunau, he and his children had become our good and familiar friends, and each day I told them how long I would be away and what we should do together when I got back. No one, absolutely no one, could suddenly take my place without their whole security being undermined. I knew that they would grieve for me as much—and perhaps even more if that were possible—than I would grieve for them. The whole proposition was unthinkable.

The next weeks passed for me in an agony of waiting and indecision. There seemed no way of knowing whether Vrailbran's appeal for custody would be heard before or after my appeal to be granted the same allowances and terms as would be granted to a married woman with dependents. I went to work as usual, but once outside the office I could talk and think of nothing else except

Vrailbran's threat to take away the children. I was sick with anxiety and talked endlessly and feverishly to Tsano and Aniad, and to Raunau, about it, going over and over the same ground as a trapped creature runs round and round its cage, as though it hoped suddenly to find a way out where there had been none before.

The thing that puzzled my friends greatly was why I had been chosen to attend this residential course so many miles away. They all agreed that the normal thing would have been for me to have been given a place at some training center within the city. Raunau even suggested that Vrailbran might have used her influence to bring this about in order to have grounds for launching her appeal for custody, but I could not believe that she would have been guilty of such a piece of Machiavellianism. Raunau was not easily persuaded of this, however, for he himself had suffered a great deal at the hands of his clever and vengeful wife, and he appreciated even more than Tsano did how deeply attached I was to the children and therefore how vulnerable I was through them. We both agreed how strange it was that the one who had inflicted an injury with apparent reluctance at first could then become vengeful, as though she were the injured party instead of the injurer. Here I was, deprived of love, of home, of financial security at one blow, and now Vrailbran, herself secure in all these things, was trying to deprive me of the one thing I had left, my children. Nevertheless, I did not seriously entertain for a moment the idea that Vrailbran had intrigued to have me sent on a distant residential course instead of one in the city.

I did ponder on other possible reasons though, since Tsano and Raunau seemed to find it so surprising. They were vaguely aware of the existence of the residential center, but had believed it to be reserved for high–level conferences or for more advanced training projects than I could conceivably qualify for as far as they were aware. Slowly, a new idea began to form in my mind. Aniad had often been present at the conversations I had had with Tsano where I went wearily round and round over the same ground, seeking some new factor, some way out, and finding none, but she had never joined much in the speculations as to why I had been allotted that particular training course. Now I began to wonder if she, too, had been struck by the idea which had come to me, and I determined to ask her if ever I managed to get her on her own. If she had the same thought as I did, then she must have a reason, at which I could guess, for not expressing it in front of Tsano.

One evening when the two of them had come to see me and Tsano had begged to be allowed to tell the children a bedtime story he had made up for them, I took advantage of his momentary absence to say to Aniad, "I've been wanting to ask you something for some time. Do you think that the decision to send me on that particular course was taken at a pretty high level and for a specific reason?"

"What makes you ask that, Klemo?"

"The idea has occurred to me for reasons that I have never discussed with Tsano, but I have noticed that you have never joined in either the surprise or the speculation about it that the others have, and I thought maybe you knew something they didn't."

"Why do you yourself think that there was any special reason for your allocation to that course?"

"At first it did not occur to me, but gradually I have begun to wonder if that place has some connection with national security." And then I gave her a guarded summary of my interview shortly after I had joined Tsano's department—with what I suppose I should call the security chiefs.

She listened carefully and then said, "That does seem to explain things, at least partially. I am bound by the oath of secrecy which is taken by all who work in such sensitive areas for the state, so I cannot discuss it with you, but I think your conjecture is probably right. You have been most sensible and discreet to say nothing before the others, and I can only recommend you most strongly to continue to act as though you were in complete ignorance of the significance of the facts."

Remain silent though I might, my mind continued to grapple with the implications of this. Perhaps there had been, after all, some liaison between my first interviewers from the security department and those who had accorded me the more recent hearing? But then I remembered how the interview had begun: surely they would have been more interested in me from the first if they had been aware of my previous interrogation? Still, I could not yet make the facts fit any coherent supposition. For the most part, in any case, speculation of this kind was immediately superseded by worry about the two impending appeals.

In the end, Vrailbran's claim for custody was the first to come before the appeals section. We were all called to attend at the appeal room for all the relevant evidence to be recorded and for our own submissions to be made. The senior appeals arbiter would be there to preside and to monitor the proceedings.

I was as full of dread as if this had been some kind of medieval trial by ordeal. And trial by ordeal it certainly was in one sense. The sight of Vrailbran, as beautiful as ever, but icily cold in her stiff acknowledgment of my presence, tenderly escorting or being escorted by—it was difficult to tell which—Dinad–Vlebig sent such a pang through my breast that I could hardly breathe for a moment. How I longed for the sustaining presence of some friend, but all these appeals were held *in camera,* and only the parties concerned and their legal representatives were allowed to be present. So I stood alone on one side of the room, and on the other side, across the wasteland of our ruined marriage, stood Bran with Dinad.

Bran's lawyer was invited by the arbiter to put the case for her client. This she did in the terms which we all expected. Originally her client had had no alternative but to leave the children with their father for she had no immediate home to take them to, and at that time the father was in fact giving them full–time care. Since then, however, a change had taken place in the circumstances of both parties. The mother was now in a position to offer them a stable home with a partner who would provide permanent care for the children. The other party in the case had no further reasonable claim since he had given up full–time care of the children and resumed his previous occupation. Moreover he was known to be applying for a transfer which would effectively disrupt such a poor level of care and responsibility as he was now supplying; if he succeeded in his application he would be moving to a situation where it would be impossible either to provide adequate care or to maintain the children properly. That was Vrailbran's claim.

Asked by the arbiter to clarify her last rather mystifying statement, the lawyer said that there were reasons why this could not be
altogether satisfactorily done, but in effect the father was applying
for a training course which was residential but without facilities for
children, that he would therefore be receiving no emoluments, and
was consequently pressing her client for an exorbitant degree of
maintenance for the children. Clearly it was in the interests of all
parties, and especially of the children, that they should be given into
the care of the mother. Moreover they were both girls—twins, at
that—and everyone knew how important a mother's influence was
in the rearing of children.

I writhed with impotent anger at this submission. There was only
one item in it that was actually false, but the omissions and the whole
emphasis made a fair and reasonable–sounding case out of what had
previously seemed to me only an empty threat.

Bran was then asked if she had anything to add in support of her
case. With all her most persuasive charm she said wistfully that she
found it a great deprivation not to have been able to see her children
during the whole course of the separation and she thought they
would indeed benefit greatly from the kind of care and influence that
a mother could supply. Clearly, however well motivated the father
was, he could never satisfy the special need that girls had for a
mother's influence.

Did I say that I thought she could never have been so Machiavellian as to intrigue against me? Great Mother, Machiavelli himself
could have taken lessons from this one.

My lawyer was now asked to put forward her reply. She put my
case very clearly and fairly, but without the passionate conviction I
should have liked to hear in her voice. The children, she said, had
been excellently cared for, in spite of the fact that, partly due to a
very low maintenance contribution from the mother (and here she
looked hard and sharply at Bran) the unfortunate father had been
forced out to work. He was a devoted father, and the bond between
him and the children, already very close, had been strengthened and
fortified during the period of abandonment by the mother. The
father's application for the training course had been made in the

hope of bettering the position of the deserted family and ensuring a more stable future for the children. The father at the time of his application had not been aware that the course would be a residential one in the country; he had expected it to be held in the city as such courses commonly were. Moreover he had, in his inexperience both as a foreigner and a man, assumed that the provisions made for special allowances to young married women with families would also apply in his exactly parallel case. He had given his assurance that if these objections were not met—that is, that if no allowances for the children were forthcoming and if no provision could be made for accommodating them as well as himself at the residential center—he would have no hesitation in withdrawing and continuing with his present employment, so being able to give the children exactly the same excellent degree of care and supervision which they had enjoyed since their mother's desertion over a year ago.

The arbiter now turned to me and asked me if I had anything to add.

"Madam," I said, "I should like to add that the application for extra maintenance made against Vrailbran–Zenhild was submitted without my prior knowledge or acquiescence by the appeals section of the ministry itself. In considering my application for special family allowances in connection with the training course, they went into the question of the maintenance contribution already being made by the mother, and it was they, not I, who judged it inadequate and put in a claim against her for a higher assessment."

The arbiter looked rather surprised and asked if there were any corroborative evidence of this from the appeals section. A cylinder was immediately produced and played which gave absolute endorsement of what I had said. She then asked if that was all, and I said I should like to make another couple of points.

"First, Madam," I said, "I wish to make it clear that the children's mother has never asked to see them since the day of her desertion. Her claim that she has been deprived of the sight of the children might lead you to think that she has desired it and been denied it by me. That is not so. She has never approached me to suggest it from that day to this. Moreover, as will be well known to

all, she leads a busy and demanding professional life, and for that
and other reasons even before her desertion, her contact with the
children was of the slightest. I do not think they would now
recognize her as anyone with whom they had ever been familiar, let
alone as a parent. My further point is to emphasize what my learned
counsel has already put forward on my behalf. It has been suggested
by counsel for the children's mother that by returning to work I have
been guilty of neglecting my children. You must be aware, Madam,
that in this country a deserted husband cannot provide adequately
for his children without working outside the home. Yet if he does so,
he is regarded as not providing adequate care. Is not this a paradox
in the organization of Capovoltan society that it is customary to
award the custody of the children to the father who has been caring
for them, because it is understood that the mother as the wage earner
of the family cannot provide such close and constant care, but from
the moment this decision is made, the father in almost all cases is
forced out to work and therefore ceases to provide this care also?
Should there not be adequate provision for the deserted family to
enable the father to continue to bestow full–time care upon his
children? I have found much misery from financial deprivation
among deserted families."

"Young man," said the arbiter acidly, "are you presuming to
advise me upon how the laws of Capovolta should work?"

"No, Madam," I said. "I was concerned rather with formulating
what I take to be the laws of a natural universal justice, which clearly
few countries have yet enshrined in their legal code. Since in many
ways Capovolta comes nearer to this than many other countries I
have encountered, I am the more sad that it does not live up to its
high intent."

I suppose this was a foolish speech. I was swept forward on the
tide of my own indignation and found myself saying far more than I
had originally intended. I could see that my lawyer was embarrassed, and I tried to make amends by adding quickly in a more
humble tone, while the arbiter, I think, was trying to master her
indignation, "Madam, pray forgive what may have seemed to you a
presumptuous observation. I apologize unreservedly if this is so. I

only wish to say as some excuse for myself that I have had a long time to reflect upon this matter and much personal experience of it. My concern for the happiness of my children has led me to speak from the heart with too much heat and involvement, instead of from the head. I am sorry.''

The arbiter now rejoined quite mildly, ''Your apology is accepted. I understand that you have been living under some strain.'' She turned a cool, appraising gaze upon Vrailbran and Dinad. After a long moment, she turned back again and spoke to the two lawyers. Finally she addressed us all, saying, ''I have considered the claims made by both sides in this case. While it is true that now the mother's circumstances offer the possibility of a stable home for the children, I find no evidence that the father has in any way been negligent. Independent witnesses have sent in testimony on his behalf, not only to substantiate what he himself has said, but also to emphasize the close bond that exists between himself and his children. Therefore I consider that the best interests of the children would be served by leaving them in their father's care for the time being, the mother to have access by application and arrangement through the appeals section if she so wishes. I reserve to the mother, also, the right to appeal against this judgment in a period of not less than six moons from this date, when the present indecision about the father's future has been settled. By then it should be clear what provision he has been able to make for his children, whether his circumstances have changed or not.''

I could have kissed her for it. Behind the legal jargon and the severe presence beat a real human heart after all. I was weak with relief and, I will confess it, not far from tears. I could only stammer, ''Ah, Madam, I am so grateful. Thank you, thank you,'' as, obeying her slight gesture of dismissal, my lawyer came up and led me out. By a singularly sympathetic and understanding arrangement, plaintiff and defendant entered and left by separate doors on opposite sides of the room, so I had no need to steel myself to face Vrailbran and Dinad. My lawyer, who, as I have said, was a friend of Aniad's, was jubilant at our success, for she now told me that she had not thought it very likely that the judgment would be favorable to us, since Vrailbran had a far more telling case from a purely legal point of view. She said that she thought my unwise outburst would have thoroughly cooked my goose but for the rapid recovery of my temper, and my apology.

I had been surprised to hear the arbiter say that independent witnesses had testified for me, and asked Aniad's friend how this had come about. She smiled a little mysteriously and said that I had more friends in high places than I was aware of, perhaps, and that the testimony had been played over to the arbiter before the case was heard, as the testifiers concerned did not wish their support to be bruited about. She would not reveal the identity of my unknown supporter or supporters even to me now, and this greatly puzzled me, for I could not think who could possibly have given on my behalf evidence which carried such weight and who yet did not want her identity revealed. I say "her" identity, for I think only a woman's evidence would have had such an effect. I could only think of Avgard, but she had no firsthand knowledge of the bond between me and the children, nor could I see why she would not wish me to know that she had intervened on my behalf, if, in fact, she had done so. I did not spend too much time speculating about this, however; it was of small consequence now beside the fact of my reprieve.

CHAPTER
18

All my good, steadfast friends, Tsano and Aniad, Raunau and Zruchi and their children, rejoiced with me at the outcome of the case, and the strength of their regard for me and my little ones was like a warm cloak about me against the cold reality of the outside world. For a few days, this, added to the sheer bliss of waking each morning to the realization that the case was over, was enough to fend off my worries for the future. It was not long, however, before I saw that I must force myself to take stock of my situation afresh. I must face the fact that it was a reprieve only, and that I had only six moons in which to settle myself and the children in whatever future we were to have together before Vrailbran could make a fresh appeal. Somehow I must sort out our affairs in a way that would make her next attempt a more certain failure than this one had been.

I set myself to thinking soberly not only about the immediate future, but also the long–term future of myself and my children. The day–to–day problems of my life had been such that I had been content to solve them as they occurred and not to anticipate too far beyond. Now I could not shirk the more difficult decisions that I must eventually make.

For the greater part of my life in Capovolta, I had, as I have said previously, taken for granted that somehow, some day, I should return to my own country. I had never bothered to think deeply about either the means, or the occasion, or indeed the probability of it. I had an unquestioning confidence that I should find a way once I made up my mind to it, but in the meantime I had been making interesting discoveries about a hitherto wholly unknown civilization—and I had been in love with Bran. The first real doubts and uncertainties began during the dark period after Bran's desertion. Then, had it not been for the children, I should have made some attempt to return to my own people. The almost intolerable irony of my situation was that back in my own country I could have resumed a way of life and a position which would have ensured the children's material welfare as well as given scope to my own ambitions and abilities, but the very existence of the children made it impossible to contemplate any such course without official backing, which my subordinate and disadvantaged position here would certainly have precluded. Yet while we remained in Capovolta, would I ever be free from Vrailbran's claim to custody of the children? What totally satisfactory arrangements could I ever make here that would convince any arbiter, whether kindly disposed to me personally or not, that on purely factual and legal grounds the children should continue to be entrusted to my care?

If I withdrew my application and gave up all idea of the course, there was nothing to prevent Bran bringing a fresh case on exactly the same grounds as before—that is, that I was out at work all day and could not therefore be said to be looking after my children in that sense, while Dinad was permanently at home. The next time, the scales would come down on Bran's side just as this time they had come down on mine.

If my application went forward, but I was refused any allowance for the children, then I should have to withdraw in any case and my situation would be the same. If on the other hand I was awarded an allowance for the children, how could I hope to find anyone as kind and trustworthy as Raunau and Zruchi living handily near the residential center, stuck out in the depths of the country?

I began to speculate once again on the reason for my posting to that distant and somewhat mysterious spot, and to recapitulate to myself some of the disparate facts and happenings which had no visible surface link or explanation, but which some intuition told me should fit into a coherent pattern if I could but find the connection.

The strange circumstances of my arrival in Capovolta had certainly been the reason for the interest the security chiefs had shown in me during my first interrogation. I did not really think that those conducting the second interview were under instruction from the security chiefs, but it occurred to me that their report on me, which must have been a favorable one, might have found its way to the security department. It was possible, for example, that they always scrutinized people selected for such courses. That could explain the decision to send me to that particular course center, if Aniad's veiled confirmation of my own hypothesis were correct. It could be, I thought with a degree of mounting excitement, it just could be that they had taken me sufficiently seriously to believe that I might be worth training, or that I might be able and willing to reveal more about the mission than I had hitherto done.

Was it possible, too, perhaps, that the unknown testifiers who had vouched for me at the hearing were people belonging to the security department who had kept me under surveillance all this time without my knowledge? That thought gave me a little shiver of distaste, but the more I considered it, the more likely it seemed. Certainly I could think of no other equally plausible explanation.

If I were right in this supposition, then for some reason certain people in positions of influence regarded me as of sufficient interest or importance to intervene on my behalf from time to time. On the other hand, why should they not make some much more direct approach, instead of, as it were, taking an almost invisible step every couple of years or so? Again I had the disquieting impression of being slowly and stealthily surrounded. But why? I was absolutely at their mercy. I could have been disposed of quietly and with no questions asked at almost any time. The more I thought about it, the more absurd it seemed to suppose that anyone with hostile intentions toward me should stay her hand for several years. Perhaps, then, the invisible presence, if there was such a thing, was a protective rather than a hostile one? Certainly such interventions in my affairs as I was aware of had been friendly rather than inimical. But, again, why? Once more I could only suppose that someone somewhere thought I might be of service to the state.

It was all very baffling, but it did turn my thoughts on to a new tack. If my final hypothesis was correct, then perhaps I was in a slightly stronger bargaining position than I had thought. If they wanted me badly enough, then perhaps I could make conditions. For example, if they wanted me to attend this course for their own reasons, could I put pressure on them to help me in this question of accommodation for the children, and of making general provision for them? If, on the other hand, someone were working unseen to ensure my attendance at the course, would they not have intervened on the other side—that is, to ensure the return of the children to Bran—so that I no longer had anything to hold me in the city of Capovolta itself? The more I thought about it, the more contradictory the whole thing became.

Begin again. Whatever the reasons, I had been offered a place in the course, and someone had intervened on my behalf against Bran. The logic of this was that they did want me in the course, but did not want to separate me from the children. Why? With a sudden flash of illumination, the answer came to me. For the same reason that Bran and I had been granted permission for a family marriage. Now it was my family, my two beloved girls, no longer my wife, who bound me to this country and all but guaranteed my loyalty. Why did they want such a guarantee of loyalty? Presumably because they believed I had some knowledge which might prove to be a potential danger to the state if it got into enemy hands. And I suppose to some extent this was true.

Stating now the progression of thought which brought me to this position, it would appear that I had arrived there quickly and in a straight line from my starting point. This is not so. I had veered and tacked and made off in the wrong direction many times, and it had taken me many late–night sessions with myself before I had it all as clear in my head as I have made it sound here. Having come to conclusions, I had now to decide what to do about them. Should I wait patiently for the outcome of my application for special allowances for the children, or should I go straight onto the attack and say that I should be unable to attend the course unless I was granted not only the allowances but also accommodation for them as well and help in finding trustworthy day care.

Although I was anxious and impatient because of the possibility of a new appeal by Bran once the six moons were up, I had nevertheless decided to await the outcome of my application to the appeals section when a fresh and yet more devastating attack was launched upon my peace of mind. Even now, I find it difficult to recount this with calm, but I wish to record the truth, however hurtful it may be.

An "Urgent" cylinder was delivered at the house one evening shortly after I had put the children to bed. Tsano's friend Kloni, who was my landlord, as we say, received it and brought it to me, so I do not know who actually delivered it. I put the cylinder into my little machine and played it. It left me sick and trembling, for it was a most scurrilous attack on me by Dinad, in which he maintained that he was the true father of my beloved Sora and Tara, that therefore I had no claim on the children, and that he and Bran proposed to bring a new appeal for custody without waiting for the six moons to pass on the grounds that there were new factors and new evidence to be presented—viz., that I was in no way related to the children! After my first furious repudiation of this vile lie, a horrible, creeping doubt began to invade my mind. I made a quick mental calculation and realized that what he said could be true. It was physically possible that Bran's pregnancy could have dated from that evening after the body competition at the Games. But I could not believe that these dear creatures whom I had tended with such love and for whom I felt as though they had been truly a part of myself—I could not believe that they were another man's children. I stole into the room where they were sleeping and raked their little faces with my gaze, searching for some, any resemblance to myself, however slight, or any evidence of their foreign blood. I found no comfort there. Then I looked for resemblances to Dinad, but their exquisite little countenances even in sleep had the mark of a lively intelligence that, to me, denied his paternity. Both bore the unmistakable inheritance they had from Bran; for the rest, each was her own, delightful self. Here was neither confirmation nor denial. I gazed and gazed—and in the end I knew that whether Dinad was their father or not it did not make one jot of difference to my absolute commitment to them. I could not believe that they were not my children, but even if there had been unimpeachable proof to the contrary, I do not think it would have changed my feelings for them. My love for the twins was compounded by the care I had given them, their utter dependence on me, their quickening response to me as they grew, the way they flung themselves upon me with shrieks of delight when I came home, and the intuitive apprehension we each had of one another. I knew their needs before they expressed them, and they divined my sadness and comforted me with their kisses, or divined my momentary lightheartedness and laughed with pleasure, before I did. They were mine, mine, mine: nothing and no one would take them from me. A hunted vixen with her cubs could not have had a more vivid sense of danger and of fear than I did then.

I began immediately to pack our belongings, first theirs and then my own, with a desperate speed as though I must be gone before morning. That done, I paced about the little apartment trying to decide on exactly what to do. I was in no doubt about my general plan: I had suddenly found myself absolutely clear about that. This new threat had merely precipitated events. I had always had stored away somewhere at the back of my mind, in case of need, the words of the top security chief at my first interrogation: "If at any time you feel that there is more you can tell us without dishonor, please come straight to me and tell me." Honor or dishonor in that context now seemed to me to count for nothing when weighed in the balance against my children's safety, but by now the statutory five years had passed since the launching of the mission and thus I was at liberty to reveal not everything, but more than I had been able in honor to do before. I was therefore determined to go to the top security chief and request asylum for myself and my children in return for the further information I was prepared to give.

It was only the intermediate steps I should take which caused me doubt and concern. I felt the danger to the children so close and so threatening that I feared leaving them in order to seek an audience with the chief. In fact, I was considering actually taking them with me. It was highly likely that Bran and Dinad knew that Raunau looked after them for me during the day; should they present themselves in my absence and demand the children, Raunau would be in a very weak position either to refuse or to prevent Bran from taking the law into her own hands and seizing them by force. Legally they were in my custody, but once they were physically in her possession, I should have no redress except through the slow, grinding process of the law, and this I could not bear to contemplate. I felt that I should know not an instant's tranquillity if I let them out of my sight. There was no time to make an application to see the chief and await the outcome. I had to act immediately, but I did not know how.

Once again, I felt that I must go to Tsano and Aniad for counsel, possibly even for temporary refuge. As soon as it was light, long before the rest of the world was astir, I would take the children with me and present myself at their house. Once there, I would let myself be guided by Aniad as to the best means of getting an interview with the security chief as quickly as possible.

This decision made, I had to wait for morning. I set myself to try to imagine the interview I hoped to have with the chief, and to anticipate the shape it would take. It was hard to discipline the chaos of my mind and force it to think clearly and logically about the issues involved in this, for I was so full of incoherent anxieties and fears that any train of thought was constantly interrupted by some new dread that darted in among my ordered thoughts and brought me to an unthinking panic once again. Although I could not foresee the line my interviewer might take, I forced myself to try to marshal the facts of my case, and to decide on what terms exactly I would trade my information if my presupposition that they would think it valuable proved correct. At first with a great leap of the heart I thought I would ask for safe transport for myself and my girls back to my own country, for after all I had seen and heard in Capovolta, I did not doubt their ability to provide this if they chose. How wonderful it would be to return home to my own people, to find again my true self, to show off my adorable children and bring them up with the freedom and privilege I had enjoyed in my old life. But all too soon I saw the almost insuperable difficulties of this course. To begin with, it was highly unlikely that the Capovoltans—desiring as they did to remain unknown to the rest of the world—would allow me to depart freely, taking with me not only my knowledge of their land and people but also evidence of its existence in the persons of my two children. But even if, for some unfathomable reason of their own, the Guardians were to accept these terms, how could I, loving my children as I did and desiring for them the best that life could give, take them with me to a land where their dark skins would carry a stigma greater than my own fairer one did in this country, and where their sex would be almost as much a disadvantage to them as mine was to me here? In Capovolta my girls would occupy a position of privilege ensured by the simple fact of their feminine sex, and much as I might criticize the system, I could not but be glad for their sakes that they would not meet the frustrations and prejudice that I had. I would try to bring them up with more understanding and a more open mind than their mother had, and perhaps one day they might be instrumental in helping to change the system.

So leaving Capovolta was never really an option at all. To recognize this hope as nothing more than a mirage was bitterly hard. Again, only by the depression of my spirits and the depth of my disappointment did I realize how much I had subconsciously cherished some such dream. What was my future then to be? Forever bound to this land, forever denied my own? I could not, would not accept it. Yes, I must stay while my children needed me, until they were properly launched on lives of their own, but surely the bonds that held me to them must become weaker as they grew—and then, at last, should I not be able to take my discharge?

But that was very much in the future. Now there were immediate and pressing decisions to be made, and by the time first light was breaking I knew that I must return to the plan which I had begun to formulate before Dinad's latest attack had made it urgent for me to act. I would trade my information for permission to have the children with me while at the course, with adequate provision for all our needs. I could not yet envisage quite what this would entail or how it would be achieved, but those were my terms and that was that.

In a frenzy of activity, I roused the children and dressed them. We did not even stop to breakfast properly, for I had already packed some food to take with us, and it was only a matter of minutes before we were ready to leave. I left a recorded message for Kloni, simply saying that the children and I would be away for a few days; if there should be any need to get into touch with me, I could be contacted through the office. I left most of our luggage to be picked up later, once we had reached safety, and taking only our most immediate necessities in the baby carriage with the children, I set off for Tsano's apartment.

There were few people about at that hour, but I scrutinized every fellow passenger and every passerby as though I feared that Bran and Dinad might suddenly materialize and wrest the children from me. Irrational as it may seem, I felt as though the very air around me was inimical, and it was with deep thankfulness that I eventually arrived at Tsano's place. He had given me a key to the outer gate some time before so that if I arrived on a visit with the children before he and Aniad had managed to get home, I could take them in and wait in the vestibule. Never was anyone more thankful to put a locked gate between himself and the outside world than I as I relocked the gate behind us and took the children in to wait. They were still only half awake, and cuddled down willingly in the carriage for a further sleep.

The moment I heard sounds of life in the apartment, I knocked on the door. Poor Tsano, tousled and alarmed, opened it, but when he saw who it was he swept us in with the warmest of welcomes despite his surprise. I poured out my story and all my dreads and fears to him and Aniad, conveying to them the desperate urgency I felt, and why it was that I found myself obliged once again to involve them in my troubles. To Aniad especially I apologized, saying, "I am so sorry, Aniad. I hope you will not think that I am abusing our friendship and that I have acted too precipitately in coming to you like this. But I have no one else to turn to for help and advice."

"Please don't apologize, Klemo. You have done the right thing in coming to us. I do not imagine that your former wife and her husband would really try to kidnap the children, but certainly if they were to do so, with Dinad's new claim to be their true father, you would stand little chance of an immediate injunction to restore custody to you."

You may think that this almost casual reference to Dinad's hurtful claim was unfeeling, but it was not. I was deeply grateful to her for accepting so simply and calmly a new factor in the case, expressing her sympathy only in the warmth and kindness of her tone, but saying and doing nothing to unman me.

The first thing to be done was to inform Raunau that I should not be bringing Tara and Sora to him that day. The quickest way would have been to use the audio communicator (a device that was a cross between a telephone and a radio transmitter), but I fought shy of this instrument, as messages could be easily intercepted by any house equipped for reception, as Bran's undoubtedly would be. I had always found it difficult to accept the underlying assumption that all lives were open to scrutiny and had no secrets to hide. Whatever the truth of that might be, I intended to take no risks. So it was decided that Tsano should leave my message in the receiving box at Raunau's house, so that he would not know how it had reached him. It was not that I did not trust Raunau absolutely, but it would be much easier for him, should my fears be justified and he were questioned by Bran, if he were kept ignorant.

Tsano went off immediately to ensure, as far as was possible, that he would be unobserved. While he was gone, Aniad and I discussed what was to be done next. She did not seriously think that the danger from Bran and Dinad was as great as I feared, but seeing how anxious I was at the very possibility of it, she granted it as a factor in our deliberations. She pointed out that whatever precautions we might take, once they discovered that the children were neither at home nor at Raunau's, the next place they would think of would be her apartment, because of my close friendship with Tsano—but while she or I were there, they could do nothing, for I was the children's legal guardian and they would not dare to browbeat her as they might have done Raunau. Nevertheless, the quicker we took action the better it would be.

We both realized that if I were to present myself at Block C unannounced, demanding an interview with the chief security officer, who had interrogated me originally, I should never even get past the security guards. Aniad had several acquaintances, how-

ever, among the officials of that department from the time when,
before Bran supplanted her, her work at the ministry of justice
overlapped areas under the control of the security department. She
proposed, therefore, to go forthwith to someone there whom she
thought could secure her direct access to the chief. She would then
explain the situation and try to secure for me an immediate
interview. If successful, she would return home and remain with the
children while I was away, for she thought it best that Tsano turn up
for work in the usual way.

"I shall quite certainly have an attack of migraine this morning—
not quite yet, but a little later on. I feel *all* the symptoms." She said
this with the most delightful deadpan seriousness. Dear Aniad—I
could have hugged her.

When Tsano returned, we decided on the line he was to take at the
office to explain my absence, whether the inquiry came from within
or without: he would say that my usual arrangements for the
children had fallen through that day, which was the literal truth, but
was also open to whatever interpretation the inquirer chose to put
upon it.

Left alone with the children, I secured all entrances, even closing
and locking the trap that led to the solar heating on the roof—though
how anyone could get up there from the outside I do not know. My
panic may seem exaggerated and absurd, but something stronger
than reason drove me, and not without cause, for I discovered later
than Bran herself had been both to Raunau's house and to mine. She
had simply told Raunau that she had come to take the children out
for the day, and I think there is no doubt that Raunau would have felt
himself without authority to defy her had they been there. As it was,
he knew nothing and simply repeated the message delivered by
Tsano.

Never had time passed so slowly. My earlier apprehension had
been eased a little by my contriving with Tsano and Aniad and, I
suppose, by the mere fact that I had taken some action. Now the
forced inaction was almost unbearable, and my fears mounted as I
wondered what could have happened to delay Aniad for so long. I
tried to convince myself that the whole business of telling my story

and seeking an interview was likely to be a much longer process than I had calculated, but as the hours passed and still she did not return, I became certain that something unforeseen had occurred.

At last, she appeared. The chief was not available, Aniad explained, and no one seemed to know anything at all about my case. She had had to use great pressure to persuade one of the officials to consult the Confidential Memory Bank for any record of my interrogation, so that at least we would know who else had been present. Even then it was far from plain sailing, for no one there knew the code under which it would have been indexed (remember that all this had transpired some four or more years past). It seemed an impasse until one of the senior security officers happened to come in to consult the Confidential Memory Bank, and inquired, with a natural suspicion, just what was going on. She listened attentively first to the security officer and then to Aniad, who explained her previous connection with the department and that I had urgent reasons for requesting the further interview with the chief, which she herself had originally suggested. Naturally, nothing was said of my personal difficulties.

The senior officer thought for a while, according to Aniad, as though she were undecided about what to do. Finally she said, "As it happens, I have some knowledge of this case. Isn't this the young man who has been granted a place at the up–country training course and is in some difficulty about maintaining his children?"

As Aniad agreed, this really was an incredible piece of good luck. The senior officer seemed well disposed toward me, as far as she could judge, and took Aniad up to her office to discuss matters. There Aniad had been a little more communicative, had discreetly emphasized the pressing nature of my business and had begged her to do whatever she could. Eventually they decided that since the chief could not be reached right away, it would be better for me to have an interview with this lady, who though young was in a position of some responsibility. My appointment with her had been fixed for that evening, after the department was officially closed.

I was relieved, elated, alarmed in rapid succession. Neither Aniad nor I could decide what might ensue from this forced modification of my original plan, and when Tsano came in after work, the three of us fell into a fever of conjecture. Shortly, I set off for my interview with exhortations to have courage from Tsano, with a few pieces of sensible advice from Aniad, and a multitude of good wishes from both. The little girls sensed the tension and were upset and fretful because I was leaving them, but I knew that once I was out of sight and Tsano set about entertaining them with songs and stories, they would soon settle down again, for they were very fond of him and he was one of those people who are "wonderful with children," as we say.

I was less intimidated this time by the interrogatory procedure, which in any case seemed to me less rigorous than on the occasion of my previous visit to the security offices. I was admitted to the interviewing room with a minimum of fuss or delay. It was unoccupied when I entered, its sparse furnishings rearranged so that the dais was more centrally placed. This area was strongly lit, while the far end of the room was in shadow. The effect was to make the room seem smaller and to diminish the space between interviewer and interviewee. As I stood facing the door where the security escort had left me, I heard a faint, muffled sound behind me from beyond the dais. I spun round, the hair prickling at the back of my neck with alarm. In the shadow at the far end of the room, carefully rearranging the wall hanging behind her through which doubtless she had come, I could perceive the figure of the interviewing officer. She spoke as she came forward toward the dais.

"I understand, Klemo–Vrailbran, that you have some business to discuss with the top security chief." The beautiful purring voice was as familiar to me as though I had heard it only yesterday: there before me, without any doubt, in spite of the concealing tubular dress, stood the Cat.

I stared at her stupidly, as bereft of speech as if she had been a ghost, as, in a way, she was—the ghost of my young, carefree past. It seemed a cruel and terrible thing for anyone to confront me at this moment of despair and anguished concern for my children's future, with the embodied reminder of that night of Bran's first infidelity, whence all my present woes had sprung.

I think I must have recoiled, or maybe simply registered shock on my face, for she added in a mollifying tone, "Because she is away and your friend said the matter was both serious and urgent, I thought it best you see me, as I am acting as her deputy during her absence. I can assure you it was chance and not contrivance that brought this about."

"Madam, I am obliged to you," I stammered miserably, "but I do not think the matter is one which I can discuss with you."

"You are mistaken, Klemo, if you think that our past brief acquaintance will prejudice me in any way; perhaps, indeed, because of it I have taken a slightly warmer interest in your case than I might otherwise have done."

"Interest in my case? Then you . . ." It must, I realized, have been the Cat who had intervened when Aniad had been trying to arrange things on my behalf.

"Yes. I know about your application for the up–country course and the difficulties you are having about it. It so happens that the officer dealing with your application came to me for a decision, as she was unsure how the regulations should be applied; we have never had a case exactly like yours, you see. I am glad to have this chance to talk to you directly about it, although I would not normally have done so, of course."

As I still stood mute and uncertain in front of her, she motioned me to sit and sat down herself, not on the dais but on a seat beside me.

"Now, Klemo," she said in a voice of great sweetness and gentleness, "believe me, I do very much want to help you. Unless you tell me everything, it is difficult for me to know how to do that. I will tell you the truth. I have been feeling very guilty since I heard about the breakup of your marriage, in case my thoughtless behavior might have made trouble for you. It was wrong of me to take advantage of you, and I am sorry. I can only say that I found you extraordinarily attractive and that I, too, was a little intoxicated— not with Acumba, but with you. That is my only excuse, though a very inadequate one."

Naturally I practically fell over myself in denying that any blame attached to her, assuring her that the breakdown of my marriage had absolutely nothing to do with her, and in no time all my reserve had gone, and I found myself pouring out the whole story. I held nothing back except my bargaining power, as I saw it, with the top security chief. When at last I had finished, she said, "I did not know about this latest attempt to take the children. It does seem particularly despicable of your former wife and her husband to persecute you in this way. I suppose it must be because of the claim the department put in against her for a higher maintenance contribution for the children. That silly young man she has married is a millstone around her neck with his extravagance, but she has only herself to blame."

"I do wish I were able to manage without her money. I know the children should be just as much her responsibility as mine, but I hate taking it all the same. If I'm ever in a position to do without it, I certainly will."

"Mm. . . That's all very well, but at the moment you really are in a very awkward situation. The rules are pretty strict on this subject of maintenance: the Guardians do not want people to get the idea that they can unload responsibility for their children onto the state, for it might encourage thoughtless and irresponsible parenthood. Legally Vrailbran–Zenhild is obliged to contribute to the maintenance of her children, and while you are looking after them, to yours if you have no other means of support. This means that the authorities would be technically in the right if they demanded full maintenance from her for you and your children during the time you are on the course. Since your attendance there is completely voluntary, however, she could not be forced to provide this, and consequently you would not be able to go."

What cruel, crazy logic blocked me at every turn in this wretched country! It was a black, black day that landed me here to be discriminated against so subtly that both sexes accepted it as some immutable law of nature instead of the result of human error. Unable to restrain myself, I burst into some such bitter speech, reviling my host country for its prejudice and injustice.

When I paused, the Cat let out a long breath and leaned back in her seat, surveying me with deep disapprobation. When she spoke, her voice was sharper and more peremptory: "So I was not altogether mistaken that day on the sledging course at the Games. You did mean to create a disturbance quite deliberately after all."

This extraordinary remark was so utterly irrelevant to our present conversation that for a moment I could not even take in what she had said and simply sat staring at her in bewilderment. Finally I said, "I'm sorry . . . I don't understand. What do you mean?"

"Exactly what I say. Don't play the innocent," she said, more sharply than ever. "You deliberately set out to wreck the sledging contest. What made you change your mind? Courage failed you at the last moment, I suppose?"—and there was something as close to a sneer in that rich and beautiful voice as I had ever heard.

"What on earth had the sledging contest to do with it? Yes, of course I was frightened. Wouldn't you be if you suddenly saw those vicious–looking runners coming straight at you out of the blue when you thought you were on an empty hillside? All right, it was stupid of us, perhaps, not to have realized sooner, but frankly, if the course had been properly marked out it wouldn't have happened. How was poor old Tsano to know they'd gone and changed it since he was there last, I'd like to know? Personally I think the course officials were more to blame than we were." Stung by her tone, I had poured out this indignant tirade without giving her a chance to interrupt, and then another thought crossed my mind, and I added more mildly, "Still, I'm very sorry if you got into trouble about it or something. But you didn't seem to hold it against me that evening. Why are you so cross about it now?"

She was dubious, I could see. "Are you really trying to tell me that it was a genuine mistake and not part of a plan to make trouble?"

"A plan to make trouble?" I repeated blankly. "Who on earth would want to do anything so stupid, and whatever for?"

"Well," she said uncertainly, "there *are* people who want to draw attention to themselves for political reasons."

"Great Mother! Draw attention to themselves indeed! Getting oneself slashed to bits by sledge runners wouldn't be my idea of drawing attention to myself, I do assure you. But anyway, why on earth should I want to? I've never had anything to do with politics.

I'm an absolutely apolitical animal. I'm a scientist, you see, and I believe that each chap should stick to his own and not put his finger into other people's pies."

She looked rather startled, as well she might, with all these metaphors which probably meant other things in Capovoltan. However, she caught the drift of my remarks even if she did not understand my wording. And now her reply was much milder.

"But that was a very political speech you made just now."

"A political speech? When? I've never made a political speech in my whole life. What do you mean?"

"Well—you were being very critical just now about the institutions of a country to which you have reason to be very grateful, accusing us of prejudice and so on. I don't know what that sort of talk is if it's not political."

This almost made me blaze up again. "Grateful" to the wretched place indeed! I knew, though, that from her point of view she had some reason on her side, and I had the sense to see that I should do my cause no good by continuing to rail at a system whose inequalities were invisible to those who had been conditioned to accept them.

"Oh, that?" I said. "I'm sorry if I was a bit vehement about it, but these regulations you talk of are about to mess up my whole life once again—and, you know, oddly enough, I do mind. I don't regard myself as just one more expendable element in any system. I suppose that's why I'm *not* political. I'm an egotist, I suppose, and I'm concerned about my own individual life and the lives of those dear to me. And I don't give a damn for the system."

"If you can talk like that, I agree that you can't be a 'political animal,' as you say. You criticize the 'crazy logic,' of other people, but what you've just said is wildly illogical, you know." She was relaxed and smiling again.

"Illogical?" I said. "What's illogical about it?"

"Ah, I won't go into it, for it might set you off altogether on the wrong tack. It's just the muddled, illogical reasoning typical of your sex, my dear," she said, "but I don't think any the worse of you for it."

I longed to make some crushing retort, but common sense told me to hold my tongue and take advantage of her new conciliatory mood. A short time before I had almost resolved to tell her of the information which I hoped to barter for my children's safety, but now I changed my mind. Thoroughly satisfactory though the Cat might be as a lover, she was as prejudiced as anyone I had met in Capovolta, probably a typical product of her specialized training.

I returned to my fear that Bran and Dinad might after all succeed in taking Tara and Sora from me. I think I made her understand how desperate I felt, and how much my life here was centered on my children. I tried to hint that if they were taken from me, I should have nothing to compel my loyalty to the state any longer. Of course, I dared not say this openly, but if she took the tenor of my emotional outpouring to its logical conclusion, she would see the implications. I wanted to press for an interview with the top chief when she returned, but did not know how to do so without offending. I felt she would not appreciate being told that I knew something so important that it could only be communicated to the top chief herself.

Fortunately for me, her own cogitations brought her to this end, though by a different route. "One way of relieving your mind about this for the time being," she said, "would be for the chief to give your wife a strong hint that her behavior in this affair is causing adverse comment in high places. You know, she's a very ambitious woman, your wife, and I think that would be enough to make her behave more circumspectly. It would also force her to discipline that silly young husband of hers."

This seemed a splendid idea. Even in anticipation, I felt as though some enormous burden had been lifted from me. It also enabled me to say, as though quite casually, "Perhaps you'd be kind enough to tell the chief that I came to see her, as she had asked me to do at my previous interrogation if I had anything to tell her. I have thought of one or two things which might be of some importance to an expert, though, of course, I personally cannot judge."

"What sort of things?"

"Well, one or two observations about upper-air patterns that I remember hearing about," I said as though I were the kind of frivolous half–wit she seemed to think me.

"I'm afraid it's no use talking to me about that. It's not my specialty at all. But I'll tell the chief, and if she wants to see you, I'm sure she'll send for you.''

Although the interview had not been altogether satisfactory, at least I felt fairly sure that the Cat would be as good as her word and would persuade the top chief to intervene on my behalf against Bran and Dinad. Although they might not call off the new appeal for custody, they would be unlikely to try to abduct the children before the case came up. What had not been made clear was how long the chief was to be away. Everyone was very guarded about her movements, but perhaps that is the normal approach in any security organization. The Cat had implied that it would not be very long, but later, as I gave an account of the interview to Aniad and Tsano, I realized that nothing had been said about when I might expect to have this vendetta called off; until that time I must continue to take precautions. It was decided, therefore, that we had better remain with Aniad and Tsano for the time being. Where once I should have feared that this would be an unwelcome imposition, I saw now how genuine was their affection not only toward me, but even more toward the children. To watch the two of them with Tara and Sora made me feel immeasurably sad that they had no children of their own, for they would have made ideal parents.

Now the three of us sat round hashing and rehashing the day's events and speculating on the likely outcome. At first I had not intended to tell them about the Cat, but then I realized that neither of them knew the full extent of my involvement with her. Tsano only knew that she had reprimanded us for that incident on the sledging course and had later taken charge of me as if I were a carelessly misplaced parcel for delivery to Bran. Aniad thought this slight personal acquaintance might be helpful, especially as there must be some flexibility in the regulations or she would not have been consulted on my case. Surely, said Aniad, the Cat would give a favorable ruling if she possibly could.

I was less hopeful, since it seemed to me that her understanding of the regulations would close the door pretty firmly in my face. Tsano, too, felt it was unfortunate that it had been the Cat whom I had consulted, for he thought she would be prejudiced against me as an irresponsible and rather scatterbrained person after the contretemps at the Games, utterly unfair though such an attitude might be. Neither of them thought it likely that the chief would send for me now, but of course neither of them knew how much useful information I might have to barter. I could only hope that if the Cat faithfully repeated my message, the chief would understand the significance of the information I was prepared to give.

A more immediate problem was how to explain my continued absence from work, as I dared not leave the children with Raunau again until the chief had had a chance to warn off Bran. So once again Tsano conveyed a rather vague message to the effect that I was unable to leave the children for the next few days, but would return to work as soon as I could. I did not like doing this, for it would only lend color to the idea that men were unreliable creatures who took leave of absence on the slightest of pretexts, but I could see no other way while the threat of possible abduction remained.

I was busy preparing the children's midday meal—today a thick porridge of grains and nuts flavored with herbs—when the audio communicator began to signal. I went to answer it, expecting to hear the voice of either Tsano or Aniad, but instead some unknown person demanded if Klemo–Vrailbran–Zenhild was there. Immediately I was full of alarm. Who could know of my presence in Aniad's house except someone working on Bran's behalf? I pulled my wits together and inquired who wished to know. The voice said it was speaking for—pause—the Transport Company and wished to know if I would be there to acknowledge receipt of a "Confidential" cylinder which was awaiting dispatch to me.

It was with some foreboding that I awaited this mysterious message. Could it be some even more unscrupulous trick of Dinad's or Bran's to gain access to the children? Once more the audio communicator began to squeak and gibber. This time it was Tsano's voice that spoke, in such a low, hurried mutter that I could hardly catch what he said. Eventually I understood that an inquiry for me had come from Block C—security. When my absence was explained, Tsano had been summoned and asked where I was to be found as the matter was urgent. There was no time for thought or consultation: he had to decide immediately whether to disclose my whereabouts or not. Since the message was undoubtedly genuine, he had acknowledged that I was at his home. He had been unable to use the audio communicator to speak to me privately until all the others had gone off for their short midday break. Even now he was afraid of being overheard.

This brief communication at least put my mind at rest as to whether it would be safe to open the door to the expected messenger, who arrived shortly after. The cylinder was received and acknowledged by me on his recorder, and as soon as I was alone again, I played it over.

I listened with growing excitement. That it was a summons from the top security chief, who had previously interviewed me there was no doubt, although the thing was couched in such a way as to make that clear only to one who had been at the first interview. Presumably this was an additional safeguard in case by mishap the cylinder fell into the wrong hands. It did seem to be carrying security to ludicrous extremes, since I could see no particular reason myself why the fact of my visit there deserved to be a closely guarded secret. The only possible motive I could think of was that someone might be able to gather from it the whereabouts of the chief at a particular time. Anyway, the summons was for the following day, and there followed a strangely worded message to the effect that the sender was pleased to know that my difficulties with custody were over since I was now able to resume the normal arrangements and return to work. At first I did not understand this, and thought that there had been some misinterpretation of my request for leave of absence which I had sent through Tsano. I played it over again in growing puzzlement, and only then, slow–witted creature that I was, did it dawn on me that this was the chief's indirect way of telling me that Bran and Dinad had been warned off.

I felt such an upsurge of jubilation and hope that I swept the astonished children into my arms, laughing out loud and assuring them that our troubles were over. Naturally they did not know what I was talking about, but as children do they caught the spirit of my mood and began to laugh and dance about in an excess of high spirits, so that it was with the greatest difficulty that I got them calmed down enough to eat their nut porridge. (Here I may remark in passing that the Capovoltan diet is almost entirely vegetarian; at least, they eat no meat, although they permit themselves animal products such as milk and cheese. A healthy, well–balanced diet of foods as natural and fresh as possible is almost an article of faith with them.)

When at last Tara and Sora had settled to their after–lunch rest, I began to speculate once again on the precise significance this summons might have for me. As I assessed my chances more soberly, I could see that the outcome might not be wholly favorable for me. All depended on the value the chief would put on my information, and more than that, perhaps, on her understanding and humanity. For the next few hours, as I waited for Aniad and Tsano to come home, my spirits soared and sank, soared and sank according to whether I had momentarily convinced myself of impending success or failure.

Since there was no longer any need to keep the children's whereabouts secret, I spoke to Raunau on the audio communicator and told him that I should be bringing the children over the next day, if that was all right, and that I would explain what had happened when I saw him. I sensed that he was rather upset and reluctant, but in the end he agreed to have them. When I took them to his house the next morning, he met me with the story of how Bran had been to ask for the children and how worried he was lest she should come again. I told him about Dinad's threatening message and explained why I had taken the steps I had. Somehow I had to reassure him without divulging the degree of my involvement with the security department. I told him a part of the truth, that I had appealed to my superiors at the Transport Company for help and protection and that they had intervened with Bran on my behalf; consequently there was nothing to fear for the moment. Raunau was a good friend to me, and I think his relief on my account was not far short of my own.

CHAPTER
19

For the third time I presented myself at Block C. I felt that for the rest of my life the mere sight of that discreet and unassuming entrance would bring butterflies to my stomach. Once again all the security checks were set in motion, and this time you may be sure that I had brought the cylinder which had summoned me.

At last I was conducted to the interrogation room. The top security chief was already there, but alone, and for this I was grateful. She beckoned me to come forward, and although she did not smile as she gave me a formal greeting, her voice and her clever, dignified features seemed to express a benevolent interest.

"So you have something to tell me," she said after a moment's pause. "I should be interested to know what has made you decide to do this. Take your time about it and tell me everything as fully as you can."

I had anticipated several different opening questions and had planned my replies, but now all went out of my head. Given this carte blanche to tell my story in my own way, I was momentarily at a loss. At length I said, "Madam, I hardly know where to begin. First of all I should perhaps explain that five years have gone by since the launching of the unfortunate expedition which brought me to Capovolta. Therefore the secrecy ban is no longer operative for most of the information which I have. In my country, you see, it is recognized that technology makes such rapid advances these days that knowledge five years old is already likely to be out of date and will almost certainly have been arrived at elsewhere as well. Nevertheless I think there may well be material of interest to you. I own I should probably not have come to you for that reason alone, but I will tell you frankly I have urgent personal reasons for hoping that you might be willing to help me in return for such information as I possess. The idea of trying to bargain in this way is not an agreeable one, and it is a mark of my desperation that I should feel impelled to do so. I see, too, that because of this very lapse of time, what I have to offer may be of less value than I had thought."

This last idea momentarily cast me down so much that I paused, and the chief cut in before I resumed.

"Suppose you tell me first then, Klemo, what help you would like from me and why you need it."

To this open–ended invitation I replied by plunging into as clear and unemotional an account as I could give of all the personal difficulties which I have already recounted here, and of the hope which I had begun to entertain that the security department might use its influence to secure my future here and that of my children.

But the further I went in this involved and wretched affair the more hopeless my case suddenly seemed to me to be, and the more wildly improbable it appeared that anyone would care enough about me or my precious information to intervene in any way. My impetuous flow of speech began to falter, and slowly I came to a halt. It was all more than I could bear, and I covered my face with my hands as I sought to regain my composure. The chief said nothing, and at length, without looking up, I said, "I am sorry to have wasted your time, Madam. I see that I have been foolishly deluding myself in thinking that I might find a way out of my difficulties here."

"I should nevertheless like to hear the reasoning which led you to think otherwise originally." She said this in a cool, even voice, and yet for some reason it gave me fresh courage. Looking up, I met her calm, wise gaze, and I determined to hold nothing back. I told her of my conclusion that I had been under a benevolent surveillance during my stay in Capovolta, and of how I thought my loyalty had been ensured, first through my marriage and then through my children. I had thought this must have been because it was assumed that I might have knowledge which could have been a possible danger to the state in the wrong hands. It had therefore seemed to me that there were two factors in my favor: the putative knowledge I might have, and the bonds with which my children tied me to the country while they were still in my care.

When I had finished, there was for the first time a hint of a smile in her glance, and I sensed approval behind her dry rejoinder: "Your logic was not so far wrong. I see no reason for you to lose faith in it now."

"Madam!" I exclaimed. "Do you mean that . . . ?"

"I mean that we *should* like you to attend the course and we *should* like you to have your children with you; regulations can usually bear various interpretations, and we can usually choose one to suit us when we wish!" She raised an eyebrow as she said this, and again I thought I saw the merest flicker of a smile.

"Madam, I don't know what to say," I stammered.

"I will tell you what to say," she cut in quickly. "You may tell me whatever new facts you can about your expedition. My deputy informs me that you were probably investigating problems of upper–air movement. Now that is of great interest to us."

"Well, Madam, I think I am now at liberty to tell you that at intervals over the years before I came to Capovolta, there were a number of accidents to our surveillance aircraft while they were flying at very high altitudes in the stratosphere. From such debris and wreckage as was ever found, it appears that they must have disintegrated in the air, as though they had been torn apart by some explosion. The conjecture is that they were caught by particularly violent electrical storms in the upper air. Again, such evidence as there is seems to point this way, as on most occasions there were corroborative reports of exceptional storms along the routes in-volved. However, the number of these accidents was steadily increasing, and it was felt that some kind of enemy agency could not be ruled out. Our physicists had begun to suspect that it might be possible to tamper with the upper–air patterns by triggering some kind of chain reaction to cause a steeply progressive loss of heat in the upper air. The effect of this would presumably be to increase the prevailing lapse rate beyond the dry adiabatic lapse rate, and so provoke storms artificially. If this were proved possible, it was felt that it might not only explain the fate of our aircraft, but might prove useful as a part of our defense system."

"That is very interesting, but surely it presupposes that your aircraft cannot have been flying at such high altitudes as you suggest. The kind of storm you postulate would be highly unlikely outside the troposphere."

"That is just the point that had puzzled our experts and caused them to make these startling conjectures. The incidence of the accidents was well beyond what could be attributed to chance, considering that they occurred at heights above those usual for such violent turbulence. It is very doubtful whether the atmospheric disturbances which occur naturally in the stratosphere could be an adequate explanation. One possibility which we wished to investigate was whether the electrical current generated by particularly violent storms in the troposphere could, on its way through the lower layers of the stratosphere, damage aircraft flying there. My particular assignment was to process the data which we hoped to record on our expedition, but we had barely begun on our observations when we suffered the same fate as the others."

"Your condition when we first found you puzzled us a great deal. The team of doctors who tended you at that time believed at first that you were suffering from an extreme form of radiation sickness. One of them even suggested that she thought you might have been exposed to ultraviolet radiation of wave lengths below 0.3μ" (I translate into our symbols here, of course).

I stared at her aghast, for had it been so, I doubt if I should have been there at that moment. She smiled and said, "No, I agree it seems unlikely now. At the time we thought you had somehow broken through the ozone layer, so you see we were extremely interested in you. But that was before you became conscious again. You probably do not know even now how many months you lay there, an unconscious object of the most excited speculation. Of course, it was never publicly divulged, and by the time my good friend Zenhild, who by the way is a much finer person than her daughter will ever be, had taken you into her home, the medical team was satisfied that it had been mistaken and that, after all, you would recover."

I realized that I was immensely glad to be alive, and that whatever disadvantages I had suffered in Capovolta counted as nothing beside the one great benefaction they had bestowed on me, the yet unlived part of my life. I was moved to tell her this. She looked at me very keenly and then smiled again as she replied, "Mm . . . yes. I think you do truly mean that in spite of the unhappy setbacks you have had recently. I hope the future will prove rosier for you."

I thanked her and we returned to less personal subjects. There was little more I could tell her, however, for all we had done was to create a hypothesis to fit the facts; we had not had time to put it to the proof. Of course, I in my turn would have been greatly interested to know the details of their own highly sophisticated defense system and whether, as Vrailbran and I had originally suspected, this had been the true cause of the disaster which overtook our expedition. But she blocked my tentative inquiries politely yet firmly, and I went away knowing little more than when I went in. As I was about to leave, she said, "I will see to it that the details of our offer to you come through as quickly as possible. In the meantime, I assure you that you have no further cause to worry."

And with that, I was content.

CHAPTER
20

The chief was as good as her word, and it was only a matter of days before the terms I was being offered to attend the course came through. I was to be allotted a "family living unit," whatever that might be, and the full family allowance that a married woman with a family would have been granted. This was the most wonderful news. It solved most of my problems at one stroke, and it meant that I should be able to do without the maintenance payments made by Vrailbran and to be entirely independent of her. As soon as I was able I went to consult my lawyer, for although I now had protection of some kind from the security department, there was no reason why Dinad's claim to paternity, and therefore to custody, should not result in a court hearing. When my lawyer heard of these new factors, however, and especially of my determination to forgo Vrailbran's maintenance contributions, she decided to try to arrive at an accommodation with Vrailbran's lawyer, and in the end, this is what was done. An out–of–court settlement was reached between the two lawyers under the terms of which Vrailbran and Dinad dropped their claim for custody in return for my promise to make no further claim for maintenance. At last I had complete peace of mind.

The only difficulty that now remained was that of finding someone to look after the children during the day while I was attending the course, for not unnaturally this had been left to me. The one sad thing was to have to take the children away from Raunau, who had been such a wonderful substitute father to them during the working day. He was selflessly pleased for me at my good fortune when I first told him about it, but gradually he became quieter and quieter as the implications sank in, and I went away with the guilty feeling that I had left him sad and depressed. It was no use reflecting that it was not really my fault or my responsibility: I simply felt that it was both. I could see no way out, for I could hardly expect Raunau to uproot himself to come with me, splendid solution though this would have been for me. But the next day, when I went to fetch the children, he looked so very sad as he said; "I shall miss you all terribly when you go. You don't know how much it has meant to me to share things with you," that I said impulsively, "You wouldn't consider coming up there with us, I suppose, Raunau?"

"Of course, I'd come with you like a shot, if you really meant it," he said. "But I suppose it isn't . . . well, practical, is it?"

The poor fellow obviously thought that I should no longer be able to pay him, but I reasoned that if a young married woman was expected to keep her husband and family on the allowances I was getting, I could certainly keep Raunau and his family if we practiced strict economy. We thrashed out the practical details there and then, and we reckoned that it could certainly be done, especially as the little house in which Raunau lived was his own, given to him by his parents. This meant that he could raise a small income for himself by letting it while he was away.

My problems solved, my future as bright and secure as it ever could be in Capovolta, my children and a good friend to share it with me, I had at last come into port.

Aniad and Tsano were greatly relieved when I told them about this, for they had feared that the problem of finding adequate care up there in the country, miles from everyone we knew, might have proved insuperable. They in their turn said they had something to tell me: Aniad was going to have a baby! She was older than Tsano and had begun to feel that if she put off beginning her family any longer, they would never have one. Whereas at one time they had agreed together that because of Aniad's indifferent health, it would probably be best for them not to have children—even though they had been given permission for a family marriage—now they had made up their minds that they wanted a family. I was really extremely surprised and not altogether glad for them, because I could see that it would create all kinds of problems for them both, but especially for my good, kind Tsano. Hesitantly, I voiced some of these doubts. They glanced at one another, each with such a warm, trusting look that I felt a pang of sharp regret that I no longer had anyone with whom I could make such an exchange. It was Tsano who answered: "We haven't exactly rushed into it, Klemo lad, you know that. We've talked it over a great deal, and we both know without any doubt that we do want children. You may not know it, but you have been a most liberating influence on us both. For one thing, I suppose Tara and Sora have been to us the living proof of what having a family means. Yes, yes, all right, I know there are two sides to it, but we have seen both sides, and we think it's worth the risk. I suppose we don't really think there is all that risk for us. Please don't be hurt, but Aniad is a very different sort of person from Vrailbran. I think that Vrailbran ought not to have had children at all."

"That's true," I agreed grimly.

Perhaps I should have added some bitter criticism to this, but Tsano with an apologetic wave of the hand went on, "But you have made us both see that people do not *have* to be typecast, as it were, by the mere fact of their sex. Aniad and I want to share the care of our children much more than most married couples do here, and you have shown us that it can be done. We've thought it out very carefully. I shall take only the minimum leave, just at the time the baby is born. Otherwise I shall work both before and after and Aniad will care for the child as soon as she is able to. So you see there will be quite a long period when we shall be receiving a big income, while Aniad is getting special maternity pay and I am working at the same time. If we are careful, this should tide us over the time when we have to live on my earnings. But you see we mean to have at least two children, so Aniad will qualify for maternity pay again quite quickly, we hope, and then after the second baby is born it will be my turn to stay at home with the children. Of course, it does mean that Aniad will never get to the top of the tree, but she has already had various setbacks in her career, and she has decided it is less important to her than other things."

"The best of Capovoltan luck to you both," I said warmly. "If ever two people deserved to be happy, you two do. I hope so much that it works out for you. You never know. When I have finished the course I may have a chance to help you in some way, as you have helped me. Wouldn't it be splendid if Raunau and you two and I could somehow manage to bring our children up together? I can't really believe that it's a good thing for people to shut themselves off from one another the way most people do now."

"That's all very well, Klemo, and I do think we three might manage it," said Aniad, "but imagine how much one would hate living at close quarters with people one didn't like. That would be worse than being alone."

"Yes, of course. I'd hate it, too—but don't you think that perhaps we'll all have to relearn some kind of cooperative living? Perhaps it's a question of how we are brought up now. We should have to bring our children up learning to live together and being more tolerant of other people's foibles."

"That sounds like a dreamworld, Klemo. Human nature is what it is, and I doubt if you can change it much."

"I'm not suggesting that you can change human nature, Tsano, you old skeptic. I'm simply saying that I don't think any of us really know what human nature, as you call it, really is. I've told you enough about my country for you to realize that what is often taken to be a law of nature is not so at all, but only a pattern which the cultural environment has dictated. I should see no hope for the future at all if I didn't believe that the social forms in which human nature expresses itself can and do change."

It was this conversation as much as anything which decided me to complete this record of my sojourn in Capovolta and of the speculations and conclusions to which I found myself drawn. I had begun this account in the early days of my marriage to Vrailbran, but had abandoned it during the period of my deep personal unhappiness. Now it seemed to me that there was something to be learned from a comparison of the two cultures. My knowledge of each had caused me to see faults in the other which I should otherwise have been less conscious of. Each had something to offer, but neither had solved the problem of making a highly sophisticated technological society into an equitable and cooperative one where no one was discriminated against by virtue of race or sex or class. Each was inclined to regard its own status quo as the manifestation of an inflexible law of nature. I was a living proof in my own person of the fallacy of this axiom, and of just how "flexible" such "laws of nature" really are. It seemed to me that I had a positive duty to bear witness to this for all the rest of my life. Here for the time being I would do it in person by example as well as precept. Perhaps there would come a time in the future when somehow I might return to my own country and give testimony there, too. On one thing I was determined—that whatever happened to me personally, this record should survive to give an account of the civilization of Capovolta and of my adventures there.

·